A LETTER FROM  P9-CJF-500

Hannah Swensen was a senior at Jordan High in Lake Eden, Minnesota, when I agreed to write a suspense novel called *The Other Child*. While Hannah baked cookies for her sister Andrea's cheerleading squad and took care of baby Michelle, while her mother, Delores, went antiquing at estate sales, I racked my brain, trying to think of a scary plot for the book.

That was when the apartment I rented was flooded by a broken pipe and I had to move to a neighboring rental everyone called "The Castle." It was a huge old yellow brick house, and rumor had it that a series of tragic deaths had occurred within its walls. People claimed that a young woman had given birth in the turret on the fourth floor and died in the process, along with her baby boy. The second and third floors of the castle had been converted into rental apartments. Although the turret apartment had been remodeled, and the asking rental had been reduced several times, it was still unoccupied. Of course I rented it.

I met my fellow neighbors, mostly college students, but there was a young mother with a preschool daughter and we got together for coffee in the mornings. She was looking for another apartment. She said her daughter had heard the stories about the baby who'd died and she had nightmares about it. They moved less than a month later.

I liked my new apartment, the view from the fourth-floor turret was spectacular; but every time I climbed the steps, I thought about that young mother and her baby. And since I couldn't seem to stop thinking about them, I decided to use the tragedy as a platform for my suspense novel.

I hope you enjoy reading *The Other Child*. It's set in a mansion on the outskirts of a small Minnesota town. A family from Minneapolis moves in, eager to experience a quieter, friendlier, rural life. They have a child, a girl who is very impressionable and begins to believe that the ghost of a boy who never had a chance to live is whispering to her. . . .

Books by Joanne Fluke

Hannah Swensen Mysteries
CHOCOLATE CHIP COOKIE MURDER
STRAWBERRY SHORTCAKE MURDER
BLUEBERRY MUFFIN MURDER
LEMON MERINGUE PIE MURDER
FUDGE CUPCAKE MURDER
SUGAR COOKIE MURDER
PEACH COBBLER MURDER
CHERRY CHEESECAKE MURDER
KEY LIME PIE MURDER
CANDY CANE MURDER
CARROT CAKE MURDER
CREAM PUFF MURDER
PLUM PUDDING MURDER
APPLE TURNOVER MURDER
DEVIL'S FOOD CAKE MURDER
GINGERBREAD COOKIE MURDER
CINNAMON ROLL MURDER
RED VELVET CUPCAKE MURDER
BLACKBERRY PIE MURDER
JOANNE FLUKE'S LAKE EDEN COOKBOOK

Suspense Novels
VIDEO KILL
WINTER CHILL
DEAD GIVEAWAY
THE OTHER CHILD
COLD JUDGMENT

Published by Kensington Publishing Corporation

THE OTHER CHILD

JOANNE
FLUKE

KENSINGTON BOOKS
http://www.kensingtonbooks.com

KENSINGTON BOOKS are published by

Kensington Publishing Corp.
119 West 40th Street
New York, NY 10018

All Kensington titles, imprints and distributed lines are avail-
able at special quantity discounts for bulk purchases for sales
promotion, premiums, fund-raising, educational or institu-
tional use. Special book excerpts or customized printings can also
be created to fit specific needs. For details, write or phone the
office of the Kensington Special Sales Manager: Kensington
Publishing Corp., 119 West 40th Street, New York, NY, 10018.
Attn. Special Sales Department. Phone: 1-800-221-2647.

Kensington and the K logo Reg. U.S. Pat. & TM Off.

ISBN-13: 978-0-7582-8979-7
ISBN-10: 0-7582-8979-0
First Kensington Mass Market Edition: August 2014

eISBN-13: 978-0-7582-8980-3
eISBN-10: 0-7582-8980-4
First Kensington Electronic Edition: August 2014

10 9 8 7 6 5 4 3 2 1

Printed in the United States of America

PROLOGUE

1892—On a Train Headed West

The train was rolling across the Arizona desert when it started, a pain so intense it made her double over in the dusty red velvet seat. Dorthea gasped aloud as the spasm tore through her, and several passengers leaned close.

"Just a touch of indigestion." She smiled apologetically. "Really, I'm fine now."

Drawing a deep, steadying breath, she folded her hands protectively over her rounded stomach and turned to stare out at the unbroken miles of sand and cactus. The pain would disappear if she just sat quietly and thought pleasant thoughts. She had been on the train for days now and the constant swaying motion was making her ill.

Thank goodness she was almost to California. Dorthea sighed gratefully. The moment she arrived she would get her old job back, and then she would send for Christopher.

She never should have gone back. Dorthea pressed

her forehead against the cool glass of the window and blinked back bitter tears. The people in Cold Spring were hateful. They had called Christopher a bastard. They had ridiculed her when Mother's will was made public. They knew that her mother had never forgiven her and they were glad. The righteous, upstanding citizens of her old hometown were the same cruel gossips they'd been ten years ago.

If only she had gotten there before Mother died! Dorthea was certain that those horrid people in Cold Spring had poisoned her mother's mind against her and she hated them for it. Her dream of being welcomed home to her beautiful house was shattered. Now she was completely alone in the world. Poor Christopher was abandoned back there until she could afford to send him the money for a train ticket.

Dorthea moaned as the pain tore through her again. She braced her body against the lurching of the train and clumsily made her way up the aisle, carefully avoiding the stares of the other passengers. There it started and she slumped to the floor. A pool of blood was gathering beneath her and she pressed her hand tightly against the pain.

Numbness crept up her legs and she was cold, as cold as she'd been in the winter in Cold Spring. Her eyelids fluttered and her lips moved in silent protest. Christopher! He was alone in Cold Spring, in a town full of spiteful, meddling strangers.

Dear God, what would they do to Christopher?

"No! She's not dead!" He stood facing them, one small boy against the circle of adults. "It's a lie! You're telling lies about her, just like you did before!"

His voice broke in a sob and he whirled to run out the door of the parsonage. His mother wasn't dead. She couldn't be dead! She had promised to come back for him just as soon as she made some money.

"Lies. Dirty lies." The wind whipped away his words as he raced through the vacant lot and around the corner. The neighbors had told lies before about his mother, lies his grandmother had believed. They were all liars in Cold Spring, just as his mother had said.

There it was in front of him now, huge and solid against the gray sky. Christopher stopped at the gate, panting heavily. Appleton Mansion, the home that should have been his. Their lies had cost him his family, his inheritance, and he'd get even with all of them somehow.

They were shouting his name now, calling for him to come back. Christopher slipped between the posts of the wrought-iron fence and ran into the overgrown yard. They wanted to tell him more lies, to confuse him the way they had confused Grandmother Appleton, but he wouldn't listen. He'd hide until it was dark and then he'd run away to California, where his mother was waiting for him.

The small boy gave a sob of relief when he saw an open doorway. It was perfect. He'd hide in his grandmother's root cellar and they'd never find him. Then, when it was dark, he'd run away.

Without a backward glance Christopher hurtled through the opening, seeking the safety of the darkness below. He gave a shrill cry as his foot missed the steeply slanted step and then he was falling, arms flailing helplessly at the air as he pitched forward into the deep, damp blackness.

*   *   *

Wade Comstock stood still, letting the leaves skitter and pile in colored mounds around his feet, smiling as he looked up at the shuttered house. His wife, Verna, had been right, the Appleton Mansion had gone dirt cheap. He still couldn't understand how modern people at the turn of the century could take stock in silly ghost stories. He certainly didn't believe for one minute that Amelia Appleton was back from the dead, haunting the Appleton house. But then again, he had been the only one ever to venture a bid on the old place. Amelia's daughter, Dorthea, had left town right after her mother's will was read, cut off without a dime. And it served her right. Now the estate was his, the first acquisition of the Comstock Realty Company.

His thin lips tightened into a straight line as he thought of Dorthea. The good people of Cold Spring hadn't been fooled one bit by her tears at her mother's funeral. She was after the property, pure and simple. Bringing her bastard son here was bad enough, but you'd think a woman in her condition would have sense enough to stay away. And then she had run off, leaving the boy behind. He could make a bet that Dorthea was never planning to send for Christopher. Women like her didn't want kids in the way.

Wade kicked out at the piles of leaves and walked around his new property. As he turned the corner of the house, the open root cellar caught his eye and he reached in his pocket for the padlock and key he'd found hanging in the toolshed. That old cellar should be locked up before somebody got hurt down there. He'd tell the gardener to leave the bushes in that area and it would be overgrown in no time at all.

For a moment Wade stood and stared at the opening. He supposed he should go down there, but it was already too dark to be able to see his way around. Something about the place made him uneasy. There was no real reason to be afraid, but his heart beat faster and an icy sweat broke out on his forehead as he thought about climbing down into that small dark hole.

The day was turning to night as he hurriedly hefted the weather-beaten door and slammed it shut. The door was warped, but it still fit. The hasp was in workable order and with a little effort he lined up the two pieces and secured them with the padlock. Then he jammed the key into his pocket and took a shortcut through the rose garden to the front yard.

Wade didn't notice the key was missing from his pocket until he was out on the sidewalk. He looked back at the overcast sky. There was no point in going back to try to find it in the dark. Actually, he could do without the key. No one needed a root cellar anymore. It could stay locked up till kingdom come.

As he stood watching, shadows played over the windows of the stately house and crept up the crushed-granite driveway. The air was still now, so humid it almost choked him. He could hear thunder rumbling in the distance. Then there was another noise—a thin, hollow cry that set the hair on the back of his arms prickling. He listened intently, bent forward slightly, and balanced on the balls of his feet, but there was only the thunder. It was going to rain again and Wade felt a strange uneasiness. Once more he looked back, drawn to the house . . . as though something had been left unfinished. He had a vague sense of foreboding. The house looked almost menacing.

"Poppycock!" he muttered, and turned away, pulling out his watch. He'd have to hurry to get home in time for supper. Verna liked her meals punctual.

He started to walk, turning back every now and then to glance at the shadow of the house looming between the tall trees. Even though he knew those stories were a whole lot of foolishness, he felt a little spooked himself. The brick mansion did look eerie against the blackening sky.

"Mama!" He awoke with a scream on his lips, a half-choked cry of pure terror. It was dark and cold and inky black. Where was he? The air was damp, like a grave. He squeezed his eyes shut tightly and screamed again.

"Mama!" He would hear her footsteps coming any minute to wake him from this awful nightmare. She'd turn on the light and hug him and tell him not to be afraid. If he just waited, she'd come. She always came when he had nightmares.

No footsteps, no light, no sound, except his own hoarse breathing. Christopher reached out cautiously and felt damp earth around him. This was no dream. Where was he?

There was a big lump on his head and it hurt. He must have fallen. . . . Yes, that was it.

He let his breath out in a shuddering sigh as he

remembered. He was in Grandmother Appleton's root cellar. He'd fallen down the steps trying to hide from the people who told him lies about his mama. And tonight he was going to run away and find her in California. She'd be so proud of him when he told her he hadn't believed their lies. She'd hug him and kiss him and promise she'd never have to go away again.

Perhaps it was night now. Christopher forced himself to open his eyes. He opened them wide, but he couldn't see anything, not even the white shirt he was wearing. It must be night and that meant it was time for him to go.

Christopher sat up with a groan. It was so dark he couldn't see the staircase. He knew he'd have to crawl around and feel for the steps, but it took a real effort to reach out into the blackness. He wasn't usually afraid of the dark. At least he wasn't afraid of the dark when there was a lamppost or a moon or something. This kind of darkness was different. It made his mouth dry and he held his breath as he forced himself to reach out into the inky depths.

There. He gave a grateful sigh as he crawled up the first step of the stairs. He didn't want to lose his balance and fall back down again.

Four . . . five . . . six . . . he was partway up when he heard a stealthy rustling noise from below. Fear pushed him forward in a rush, his knees scraping against the old, slivery wood in a scramble to get to the top.

He let out a terrified yell as his head hit something hard. The cover—somebody had closed up the root cellar!

He couldn't think; he was too scared. Blind panic made him scream and pound, beating his fists against the wooden door until his knuckles were swollen and raw. Somehow he had to lift the door.

With a mighty effort Christopher heaved his body upward, straining against the solid piece of wood. The door gave a slight, sickening lurch, creaking and lifting just enough for him to hear the sound of metal grating against metal.

At first the sound lay at the back of his mind like a giant pendulum of horror, surging slowly forward until it reached the active part of his brain. The Cold Spring people had locked him in.

The thought was so terrifying he lost his breath and slumped into a huddled ball on the step. In the darkness he could see flashes of red and bright gold beneath his eyelids. He had to get out somehow! *He had to!*

"Help!" The sound tore through his lips and bounced off the earthen walls, giving a hollow, muted echo. He screamed until his voice was a weak whisper, but no one came. Then his voice was gone and he could hear it again, the ominous rustling from the depths of the cellar, growing louder with each passing heartbeat.

God, no! This nightmare was really happening! He recognized the scuffling noise now and shivered with terror. Rats. They were sniffing at the air, searching for him, and there was nowhere to hide. They'd find him even here at the top of the stairs and they would come in a rush—darting, hurtling balls of fur and needle teeth . . . the pain of flesh being torn from his body . . . the agony of being eaten alive!

He opened his throat in a tortured scream, a shrill hoarse cry that circled the earthen room, then faded to a deadly silence. There was a roaring in his ears and terror rose to choke him, squeezing and strangling him with clutching fingers.

"Mama! Please, Mama!" he cried again, and then suddenly he was pitching forward, rolling and bumping to the black pit below. He gasped as an old shovel bit deeply into his neck and a warm stickiness gushed out to cover his face. There was a moment of vivid consciousness before death claimed him. And in that final moment, one emotion blazed its way through his whole being. Hatred. He hated all of them. They had driven his mother away. They had stolen his inheritance. They had locked him in here and left him to die. He would punish them . . . make them suffer as his mother had suffered . . . as he was suffering.

ONE

1972—Cold Spring, Minnesota

The interior of the truck was dusty and Mike opened the wing window all the way, shifting on the slick plastic-covered seat. Karen had wanted to take an afternoon drive through the country and here they were over fifty miles from Minneapolis, on a bumpy country road. It wasn't Mike's idea of a great way to spend a Sunday. He'd rather be home watching the Cubs and the Phillies from the couch in their air-conditioned Lake Street apartment.

Mike glanced uneasily at Karen as he thought about today's game. He had a bundle riding on this one and it was a damn good thing Karen didn't know about it. She'd been curious about his interest in baseball lately, but he'd told her he got a kick out of watching the teams knock themselves out for the pennant. The explanation seemed to satisfy her.

Karen was death on two of his pet vices, drinking and gambling, and he'd agreed to reform three years ago when they were married. Way back then he'd made all the required promises. Lay off the booze. No more Saturday-night poker games. No betting on the horses. No quick trips to Vegas. No office pools, even. The idea of a sportsbook hadn't occurred to her yet and he was hoping it wouldn't now. Naturally, Mike didn't make a habit of keeping secrets from his wife, but in this case he'd chosen the lesser of two evils. He knew Karen would hit the roof if he told her he hadn't gotten that hundred-dollar-a-month bonus after all, that the extra money came from his gambling winnings on the games. It was just lucky that he took care of all the finances. What Karen didn't know wouldn't hurt her.

"'Cold Spring, one mile.'" Leslie was reading the road signs again in her clear, high voice. "Oh, look, Mike! A church with a white steeple and all those trees. Can't we just drive past before we go home?"

Mike had been up most of the night developing prints for his spread in *Homes* magazine and he wasn't in the mood for extensive sightseeing. He was going to refuse, but then he caught sight of his stepdaughter's pleading face in the rearview mirror. Another little side trip wouldn't kill him. He'd been too busy lately to spend much time at home and these Sunday drives were a family tradition.

"Oh, let's, Mike." Karen's voice was wistful. Mike could tell by her tone that she'd been feeling a little neglected lately, too. Maybe it had been a mistake insisting she quit her job at the interior-decorating firm. Mike was old-fashioned sometimes, and he maintained that a mother's place was at home with her children. When he had discovered that Karen was pregnant, he'd put his foot down, insisting she stay home. Karen had agreed, but still she missed her job. He told himself that she'd be busy enough when the baby was born, but that didn't solve the problem right now.

Mike slowed the truck, looking for a turnoff. A little sightseeing might be fun. Karen and Leslie would certainly enjoy it and his being home to watch the game wouldn't change the outcome any.

"All right, you two win." Mike smiled at his wife and turned left at the arrowed sign. "Just a quick run through town and then we have to get back. I still have to finish the penthouse prints and start work on that feature."

Leslie gave Mike a quick kiss and settled down again in the backseat of their Land Rover. When she was sitting down on the seat, Mike could barely see the top of her blond head over the stacks of film boxes and camera cases. She was a small child for nine, fair-haired and delicate like the little porcelain shepherdesses his mother used to collect. She was an exquisite child, a classic Scandinavian beauty. Mike was accustomed to being approached by people who wanted to use Leslie as a model. Karen claimed she didn't want Leslie to become self-conscious, but Mike noticed how she enjoyed dressing Leslie in the height of fashion. Much of Karen's salary had gone into designer jeans, Gucci loafers, and Pierre Cardin sweaters for her daughter. Leslie always had the best in clothes and she wore them beautifully, taking meticulous care of her wardrobe. Even in play clothes she always looked every inch a lady.

Karen possessed a different kind of beauty. Hers was the active tennis-pro look. She had long, dark hair and a lithe, athletic body. People had trouble believing that she and Leslie were mother and daughter. They looked and acted completely different. Leslie preferred to curl up in a fluffy blanket and read, while Karen was relentlessly active. She was a fresh-air-and-exercise fanatic. For the last six years Karen had jogged around Lake Harriet every morning, dragging Leslie with her. That was how they'd met, the three of them.

Mike had been coming home from an all-night party, camera slung over his shoulder, when he spotted them. He was always on the lookout for a photogenic subject and he'd stopped to take a few pictures of the lovely black-haired runner and her towheaded child. It had seemed only natural to ask for Karen's address and a day later he was knocking at her door with some sample prints in one hand and a stuffed toy for Leslie in the other. The three of them had formed an instant bond.

Leslie had been fascinated by the man in her mother's life. She was five then, and fatherless. Karen always said Leslie was the image of her father—a handsome Swedish exchange student with whom Karen had enjoyed a brief affair before he'd gone back to his native country.

They made an unlikely trio, and Mike grinned a little at the thought. He had shaggy brown hair and a lined face. He needed a shave at least twice a day. Karen claimed he could walk out of Saks Fifth Avenue, dressed in the best from the skin out, and still look like an unemployed rock musician. The three of them made a striking contrast in their red

Land Rover, with MIKE HOUSTON, PHOTOGRAPHER painted on both doors.

Mike was so busy thinking about the picture they made that he almost missed the house. Karen's voice, breathless in his ear, jogged him back to reality.

"Oh, Mike! Stop, please! Just look at that beautiful old house!"

The house was a classic, built before the turn of the century. It sprawled over half of the large, tree-shaded lot, yellow brick gleaming in the late afternoon sun. There was a veranda that ran the length of the front and around both sides, three stories high with a balcony on the second story. A cupola graced the slanted roof like the decoration on a fancy cake. It struck Mike right away: here was the perfect subject for a special old-fashioned feature in *Homes* magazine.

"That's it, isn't it, Mike?" Leslie's voice was hushed and expectant as if she sensed the creative magic of this moment. "You're going to use this house for a special feature, aren't you?"

It was more a statement than a question and Mike nodded. Leslie had a real eye for a good photograph. "You bet I am!" he responded enthusiastically. "Hand me the Luna-Pro, honey, and push the big black case with the Linhof to the back door. Grab your Leica if you want and let's go. The sun's just right if we hurry."

Karen grinned as her husband and daughter made a hasty exit from the truck, cameras in tow. She'd

voiced her objections when Mike gave Leslie the
Leica for her ninth birthday. "Such an expensive
camera for a nine-year-old?" she'd asked. "She'll
probably lose it, Mike. And it's much too complicated
for a child her age to operate."

But Mike had been right this time around. Leslie
loved her Leica. She slept with it close by the side of
her bed, along with her fuzzy stuffed bear and her
ballet slippers. And she'd learned how to use it, too,
listening attentively when Mike gave her instructions,
asking questions that even Karen admitted were
advanced for her age. Leslie seemed destined to
follow in her stepfather's footsteps. She showed real
talent in framing scenes and instinctively knew what
made up a good photograph.

Her long hair was heavy and hot on the back of her
neck and Karen pulled it up and secured it with a
rubber band. She felt a bit queasy, but she knew that
was natural. It had been a long drive and she remembered getting carsick during the time she'd been carrying Leslie. Just a few more months and she would
begin to show. Then she'd have to drag out all her
old maternity clothes and see what could be salvaged.

Karen sighed, remembering. Ten years ago she was
completely on her own, pregnant and unmarried,
struggling to finish school. But once Leslie was
born, it was better. It had been exhausting, attend-
ing decorating classes in the morning, working all
afternoon at the firm, then coming home to care for
the baby, but well worth any trouble. Looking back,
she could honestly say that she was happy she hadn't
listened to all the well-meaning advice from other

women about adoption or abortion. They were a family now, she and Mike and Leslie. She hadn't planned on getting pregnant again so soon after she met Mike, but it would all work out. This time it was going to be different. She wasn't alone. This time she had Mike to help her.

Karen's eyes widened as she slid out of the truck and gazed up at the huge house. It was a decorator's paradise, exactly the sort of house she'd dreamed of tackling when she was a naïve, first-year art student.

She found Leslie around the side of the house, snapping a picture of the exterior. As soon as Leslie spotted her mother, she pointed excitedly toward the old greenhouse.

"Oh, Mom! Look at this! You could grow your own flowers in here! Isn't it super?"

"It certainly is!" Karen gave her daughter a quick hug. Leslie's excitement was contagious and Karen's smile widened as she let her eyes wander to take it all in. There was plenty of space for a children's wing on the second floor and somewhere in that vast expanse of rooms was the perfect place for Mike's studio and darkroom. The sign outside said FOR SALE. The thought of owning this house kindled Karen's artistic imagination. They *had* mentioned looking for a house only this week and here it was. Of course it would take real backbreaking effort to fix it up, but she felt sure it could be done. It would be the project she'd been looking for, to keep her occupied the next six months. With a little time, patience, and help from Mike with the heavy stuff, she could turn the mansion into a showplace.

They were peeking in through the glass windows of the greenhouse when they heard voices. Mike was talking to someone in the front yard. They heard his laugh and another, deeper voice. Karen grabbed Leslie's hand and they hurried around the side of the house in time to see Mike talking to a gray-haired man in a sport jacket. There was a white Lincoln, with a magnetic sign reading COMSTOCK REALTY, parked in the driveway.

Rob Comstock had been driving by on his way home from the office when he saw the Land Rover parked outside the old Appleton Mansion. He noticed the painted signs on the vehicle's door and began to scheme. Out-of-towners, by the look of it. Making a sharp turn at the corner, he drove around to pull up behind the truck, shutting off the motor of his new Continental. He'd just sit here and let them get a nice, long look.

This might be it, he thought as he drew a Camel from the crumpled pack in his shirt pocket. He'd wanted to be rid of this white elephant for years. It had been on the books since his grandfather bought it eighty years ago. Rob leased it out whenever he could, but that wasn't often enough to make a profit. Tenants never stayed for more than a couple of months. It was too large, they said, or it was too far from the Cities. Even though the rent was reasonable, they still made their excuses and left. He'd been trying to sell it for the past ten years with no success. Houses like this one had gone out of style in his grandfather's day. It was huge and inconvenient, and keeping it up was a financial disaster. It seemed nobody wanted to be stuck with an eight-bedroom house . . . especially a house with a reputation like this one.

Rob finished his cigarette and opened the car door. Maybe, just maybe, today would be his lucky day. He put on his sincerest, most helpful smile and cut across the lawn to greet the owner of the Land Rover. He was ready for a real challenge.

Leslie and Karen came around the corner of the house in time to catch the tail end of the sales pitch. Mike was nodding as the older man spoke.

"It's been vacant for five years now, but we check it every week to make sure there's no damage. It's a real buy, Mr. Houston. They don't build them like this anymore. Of course it would take a real professional to fix it up and decorate it, but the price is right. Only twenty-five even, for the right buyer. It's going on the block next week and that'll drive the price up higher, sure as you're standing here. These old estate auctions bring people in from all over. You'd be smart to put in a bid right now. Get it before someone buys the land and decides to tear it down and put in a trailer court."

"That'd be a real shame." Mike was shaking his head and Karen instantly recognized the thoughtful expression on his face. She'd seen it enough times when he was in the market for a new camera. He really was interested. Of course she was, too, she thought, giving the house another look. They'd already decided to get out of the Twin Cities and Mike could work anywhere as long as he had a studio and darkroom. The price was fantastically low and there was the new baby on the way. They couldn't stay in their two-bedroom apartment much longer. Out here she could raise flowers and enjoy working on the house. They might even be able to swing a tennis court in a couple of years and Leslie would have lots of room to play.

"I'd really have to think about it for a while," Mike said, shrugging his shoulders. "And I'd have to see the inside, of course. If it needs a lot of work, the price would have to come down."

"No problem, Mr. Houston." The real estate agent turned to smile at Karen and Leslie. "Glad to meet you, ladies. I'm Rob Comstock from Comstock Realty and I've got the keys with me, if you folks would like to take a look. We've got at least an hour of daylight left."

Karen had a sense of inevitability as she followed Leslie and Mike inside. She'd been dying to see the interior and here she was. One look at the huge high-ceilinged living room made her gasp. This room alone was bigger than their whole apartment! Stained-glass panes graced the upper sections of the floor-length windows and the hardwood floors were virtually unblemished.

"Oh . . . lovely," Karen murmured softly. Her voice was hushed as if she were in a museum. She began to smile as she followed Rob Comstock up the circular staircase and viewed the second floor. Huge, airy bedrooms, with polished oak moldings; a separate dressing room in the master suite, with an ancient claw-footed dresser dominating the space—the interior was just as she had imagined. If only they could afford it.

"The furniture on the third floor is included." He was speaking to her now and Karen smiled. Rob Comstock could see she was interested. There was no denying Karen's excitement as she stepped up on the third-floor landing and saw what must have been the original ballroom, filled with old furniture covered by drop cloths. What she wouldn't give to poke under the shrouded shapes and see the intriguing pieces that were stored and forgotten in this enormous, shadowed space.

A small staircase, with a door at the top, led to the cupola and Leslie was scrambling up before Karen could caution her to be careful. The steps were safe enough. The whole house seemed untouched by time, waiting for some new owners to love and nourish it, to bring it back to life again. Karen could imagine it was almost the same as it had been when the original occupants left, with only a bit of dust and cobwebs covering its intrinsic beauty.

"Plenty of real antiques up here, I'll bet!" Rob Comstock was speaking to her, but Karen only half heard him. She anticipated squeals of delight from Leslie over the view that stretched in all directions from the windowed cupola. Strange that there was only silence overhead.

Karen excused herself reluctantly. "I'd better go up and check on Leslie." A prickle of anxiety invaded her mind as she started up the narrow staircase into the dusty silence.

Karen was convinced there was something wrong when she reached the landing and pushed open the door to the cupola. Leslie was standing at one of the twelve narrow windows, staring out blankly. She looked preoccupied and started as Karen spoke her name.

"Kitten? What's the matter?" The still, stiff way Leslie was standing made Karen terribly nervous. She rushed to put her arms around her daughter.

"Huh? Oh . . . nothing, Mom." Leslie gave her a funny, lopsided smile. She looked miserable. "I'm afraid Mike won't buy it!" There was a quaver in her voice. "This house is perfect for us, Mom. We just have to live here!"

"Now, don't be silly, darling." Karen gave her a quick squeeze. "This is the first house we've seen and it really is awfully large for us. We'll probably see other houses you like just as much."

"No! We have to live here in this house!" Leslie's voice was stronger now and pleading. "You know it's the right house, Mom. We can't live anywhere else. This house was built just for us!"

"I think you should have Mr. Comstock's job," Karen said, smiling down indulgently. "You're an even better salesman than he is. But really, kitten, we have to be sensible. I know you love this old house and I do, too, but the final decision is Mike's."

Karen was firm as she turned Leslie around and guided her toward the stairs. "Come on now, honey.

We have to get back downstairs before it gets dark.
The power's not turned on, you know."

"But you'll help me convince Mike to buy it, won't
you, Mom?" Leslie asked insistently, stopping at the
top step. "You know it would be perfect for us."

"Yes, I'll help you, silly," Karen promised, brushing
a wisp of silvery-blond hair out of Leslie's eyes. She
breathed a sigh of relief as her daughter smiled fully
and hurried down the stairs in front of her. Leslie
would be persistent and she might just manage to
convince Mike. Leslie was right. It was almost as if
the house had been waiting all this time just for
them.

TWO

Karen bit her lips nervously as they took the turnoff into Cold Spring. Mike was humming a tune, keeping time by tapping his fingers against the steering wheel and Leslie was chattering away a mile a minute. The rental trailer rumbled and squeaked with every bump and Karen felt a headache coming on. Worry and lack of sleep always gave her headaches and this time she had no one to blame but herself.

She had assumed that the moving would be easy. They had sold their large furniture and Karen had been sure the packing would take only a few hours. Mike took care of his photographic equipment and Leslie boxed and labeled everything in her room, but Karen was dismayed to find how many odds and ends had accumulated over the past three years. She had been up until midnight packing the kitchen things and this morning she was exhausted.

"Never again!" Karen muttered under her breath. "We're going to stay right here in Cold Spring until we die!"

Just then the house came into view and Karen stifled a morose sigh. Why hadn't she noticed before how huge this house was? It stared at her, imposing and sedate, filling her with a sense of dread. What on earth had possessed her to agree with this move? Getting the house in livable shape would take months, perhaps years. She might never be finished. All those rooms to clean and wallpaper and paint; the measurements to be taken for drapes and curtains; the floors to be resurfaced or carpeted. It was a gigantic project and now Karen was sure that she simply couldn't do it. It was too much for an army of decorators and she was only one woman, one pregnant woman at that. What colossal lapse of reason had convinced her she could do it alone?

"It's ours, Mom," Leslie breathed in her ear. "Isn't it beautiful? I can hardly wait to pick out my room and start putting everything away!"

Something in her daughter's voice made Karen smile in spite of her ill humor. Leslie was so eager to get started. She wasn't a bit worried about all the work that had to be done. They had a house. That was all Leslie cared about.

Karen's smile grew wider. Leslie had a point. They did have a house and it was beautiful. It wouldn't be that difficult to get settled if they all pitched in. Leslie would be a big help and she could count on Mike to lend a hand, because he'd be working at home. And think of what they'd have when they finished! Leslie was absolutely right—the house was a dream, and it was all theirs. They had signed the papers for $23,500, and it was on a Contract for Deed. All their friends told them they had made a really good deal.

"It really *is* beautiful." Karen grinned at her daughter. The house was lovely . . . just waiting for her to restore it to its full beauty, inside and out. She'd take it room by room, and before she knew it, everything would be just fine.

Two hours later Karen still hadn't found the aspirin. She knew it was in a box somewhere, but they all looked the same. If she had to look through one more box, she'd scream. Her headache was pounding and her stomach rumbled uneasily.

"Is there anything to eat, Mom?" Leslie stepped over cartons of cooking utensils to peer anxiously at her mother. "I'm starving and Mike says he is, too."

Karen pressed the heel of her hand against her forehead and sighed. The last thing she wanted to do right now was tackle the stack of boxes containing the foodstuffs. How on earth was she supposed to unpack everything and get lunch together on top of it?

"I guess I'll have to go to the store and pick up some sandwich fixings." Karen gave Leslie a wan smile. "I think I need a little break anyway. I swear these boxes are multiplying faster than rabbits."

"I'll drive you there," Mike offered, appearing in the doorway. "Come on. Leslie can hold down the fort while we're gone."

"I'll pick out my room, Mom," Leslie volunteered. "I'm through helping Mike unload the truck. Can I have any room I want?"

Karen nodded. "Any one on the second floor, except the master bedroom. We'll be back in a couple of minutes, kitten. Then we'll both help you with your room."

Karen pushed the cart down the narrow aisles and picked items off the shelves at random, two bottles of aspirin to be on the safe side, a can of sardines for Mike, some peanut butter and grape jelly for Leslie, tuna packed in water and alfalfa sprouts for her. Now all she had to do was find the aisle with the bread and she'd be through.

There were two women standing at the meat counter and Karen smiled in her friendliest manner. She could feel their eyes on her back as she passed by and snatches of their whispered conversation reached her ears.

"Just bought the Appleton place . . . from Minneapolis. . . ."

"Imagine appearing in public dressed like that! I don't think they're the kind of people . . ."

Karen's face felt prickly and hot as she hurriedly ducked down another aisle. She looked down at herself, perplexed. Her brief sundress was fashionable and her sandals were comfortable. The two women were wearing stockings and heels, but that was no reason to criticize her. There was nothing wrong with the way she was dressed. In the Cities a sundress on a hot day was standard attire.

The woman at the checkout stand was friendlier. "You must be Mrs. Houston," she said, smiling as she started to ring up the items in Karen's basket. "I'm Janet Wilson and we own this supermarket. I hear from Rob Comstock that you folks are moving in today."

Karen smiled back. "That's right, we are. And please call me Karen." She felt a little better now. At least Janet Wilson didn't seem to be staring at her outfit.

"Rob says your husband's a photographer. Isn't that nice! Is he planning on setting up a business here in town?"

"No, Mike works for *Homes* magazine," Karen replied, opening her purse to find her wallet. "We're remodeling the house so he can have a darkroom and work right here."

"You have a little girl, isn't that right?" Janet shook open a brown grocery bag as she talked. Everyone who came in this afternoon would ask about the new family, and she meant to find out as much as she could.

"Leslie's nine. Do you have children, Janet?" Karen was doing her best to be casual, but she'd never been asked so many questions in a grocery store before.

"I have just the one—my boy, Gary. He's going on twelve. And do you model for your husband?"

"I used to model, just for fun, when Mike was getting started," Karen answered. "Then I worked for an interior-decorating firm in the Cities until we found out I was—" Karen stopped and blushed a little. "We're expecting our first child in December," she confessed.

As Janet's eyebrows rose, Karen almost groaned aloud. She wished she hadn't phrased things quite that way.

"I—I was married before," she hesitated to say.

She could feel the heat rise to her face in a wave, but the little white lie was easier than trying to explain the truth. It wasn't Janet Wilson's business anyway, and she didn't want to start small-town gossip.

"I just love our new house," Karen hurried on, flustered. "It's a good thing I'm an interior decorator, though. Fixing up the inside would cost a fortune if I couldn't do it myself."

"An interior decorator . . . my, my!" Janet shook her head. "Nobody here could afford to hire a decorator to do their houses—except for the Comstocks, of course. The people here aren't fancy—just plain, honest folks who believe in saving their money."

Karen smiled self-consciously. "We can't afford to hire anyone, either. I'll do most of the interior work myself."

"You're going to have a real job on your hands with that old Appleton house." Janet shook her head. "I wouldn't tackle it for love or money! Now listen, Karen"—Janet reached out to grasp her wrist—"don't let anybody scare you with those old, tired ghost stories. I've always said they were a lot of nonsense anyway. You know how it is, a big old house is empty for a while and people start talking about how it's haunted. I don't believe a word of it, personally. Stories have been going around for years and no one's actually seen anything, so just don't pay any attention to the things you might hear. People here just like a little excitement and the Appleton place gives them something to talk about."

Janet released Karen's wrist and smiled. "Cold Spring's a nice town and you folks are going to love it here. We've got the finest dude ranch in the state right outside of town. They call it El Rancho Mañana, and it put us on the map. City people come for miles to ride the horses and camp out by the lake. And there's snowmobile trails for the winter. Then there's our school; it's the absolute best. My husband's on the board. Progressive and growing . . . that's what Cold Spring is. That'll be fourteen dollars and fifty-three cents."

Karen handed over the money and took her change. She hurried out of the store, feeling as though she'd just gone through an inquisition. As she looked back through the plate glass window, she saw the two women shoppers hurry to the checkout stand. Janet Wilson gestured widely and the women bent closer to hear. Karen sighed and shook her head. By the end of the day everyone in town would know exactly what she'd said.

"Looks like a nice store," Mike said conversationally as she got into the passenger side of the truck. "Did you get everything you needed?"

"Yes. And those women in the store got everything they needed, too."

"Huh?" Mike turned to look at her quizzically.

"Oh . . . nothing." Karen gave him a small grin. "I'm just not used to small towns, that's all. But I'll learn soon enough."

"This one?" Leslie was talking to herself as she stuck her head into one of the bedrooms and made a face. It was much too big and boxlike to suit her. She had planned to pick a room close to her mother and

Mike, but they just weren't right. Now she was at the end of the hallway and there was only one room left.

Leslie's face lit up as she opened the door. Perfect! There were two windows, one facing the rear, overlooking the greenhouse, and the other directly over the rose garden. The room was sunny and not too big, with a nice-sized closet on an inside wall. It was the room she had always wanted and it was hers.

Leslie stood in the center of the room and listened. She could hear the wind blowing outside the window, but that was the only sound in this whole huge house. She knew she could be happy here in this room, even though she'd be alone at this end of the hallway. She was a big girl now and she didn't have to sleep right next to her mom and Mike. This room was tailor-made for her.

A soft rustling sound made Leslie stop and hold her breath. It sounded like someone walking right below her in the rose garden. She tiptoed to the window and looked out. Maybe Mom and Mike were home already.

"No one," she whispered, frowning slightly. The rose garden was a wild tangle of green below her, weeds and roses intertwined from years of untended growth. She must have imagined the noise.

Leslie shivered and hugged her arms around her body. She was beginning to feel a little strange now, all alone in the house. They ought to be back from the store pretty soon. She hoped so.

She turned from the window and sighed. Somehow she didn't want to put her things away right this minute. She wanted to do something else, but she

wasn't quite sure what it was. The tower room? Yes—
that's what she wanted to do. She would go up in
the cupola and look out over their new town. It
would be all right to go up there if she was careful.
Mom hadn't told her not to. That was almost as good
as permission.

The sunlight streamed through the high windows
and dust particles hung in the golden light as Leslie
crossed the wooden floor of the third story. The
draped furniture was kind of scary in a way. She was
glad it was daylight. The shrouded shapes might look
frightening in the dark. The thought made her hurry
a little faster up the steep stairs and she was panting
as she opened the door to the cupola.

"I'm here!" Leslie announced, feeling silly at the
thought of her own, make-believe fright. She stood in
the very center of the small, square room and looked
around her, thinking there was something about the
size of this room that pleased her. It was almost like a
dollhouse, perfect for her but really too small for her
mother or Mike. It was a personal place, her own little
corner in this mammoth house.

A smile came to her face as she drank it all in. The
view was a complete circle, she could see the white
church steeple she had noticed on the first day and
the streets crossed in perfect squares of dark asphalt
below. From her high vantage point she could see
every roof in town: red, blue, yellow, and brown lids
on tiny toy houses. The river sparkled to the east and
the highway outside of town was a thin gray ribbon in
the distance. Here she was above the trees and they
looked like puffy green clouds below her.

A flash of light caught her eye and Leslie looked down into the rose garden. She had seen something sparkle there, but now it was gone. In its place was a shadow.

Leslie's heart began to race and she blinked hard. The shadow looked almost like a boy standing small and dark beneath her. She heard the leaves rustle and the wind whispered past the windowpanes of the cupola.

Hurry, Leslie . . . find me.

It was just like the first day, when she had come up here alone. The wind had whispered then, too, and told her to come and live here. She'd been convinced that this house and no other house would do.

Her feet moved closer to the window until her face was pressed against the pane. The shadow seemed to wave in a greeting and then vanished like a cloud of smoke, dissipating in the air.

Leslie squinted, but she could see nothing now. The flash and the shadow were there no longer, but she stood watching until her eyes hurt from the bright sun. It was hushed and golden here and time seemed to stand still, waiting for something to happen.

"Leslie? Leslie . . . where are you?"

Their voices were faint, coming from downstairs. They were home! Mom and Mike were home and Leslie was suddenly eager to escape the small, windowed room. Something about the shadow had been vaguely unsettling and she shivered as she fled quickly down the steep steps. She wasn't going to tell anyone about the shadow and the wind whispering to her. If she told, Mom would say she was being silly and Mike would laugh and explain it all somehow, but they wouldn't really understand. No, she wouldn't tell anyone that her imagination had run away with her again.

THREE

"Mike, this is simply decadent!" Karen grinned as she rolled over and stretched, her long, graceful body hugging the sheets. "I feel like I'm playing hookey. You know we've got a million things to do today."

"This is more important." Mike put on a serious face. "It's an old family custom. When you get a new bed, you have to break it in right."

"This bed isn't exactly new, but you do have a point." Karen smiled, reaching out to cover his hand with her own. "Just look at this wonderful canopy. Do you realize what we'd have to pay for an antique like this? Rob told me it probably belonged to the Appletons, the family who built this place."

"Not now, Karen." Mike put a finger to her lips. "Antiques are the last thing on my mind. Let's forget all about the house for today. Is it a deal?"

"But—" Karen felt a shiver that ran the length of her body as Mike's lips touched hers. She supposed he was right. They both needed to forget about the house and the restoration for a while. They'd talked of nothing else since they moved in, three weeks ago.

Mike's fingers caressed her lightly and Karen sighed with pleasure. Lying in this beautiful bed in the middle of a warm summer afternoon was wonderful. Lugging it down from the third floor this morning had been worth all the effort. It made the whole room into something special, into something out of another time. The four cherubs on the carved mahogany newel posts were a work of art, and the original canopy overhead made it a truly authentic piece of period furniture.

Mike's fingertips were stroking now, smoothing her hair and then the satiny skin of her shoulders. She tried to concentrate on him and forget about all the work that needed to be done.

"Honey?" Mike nibbled at her ear. His lips traced a path to her neck and desire filled her mind. Then her arms were reaching out for him eagerly and she was lost in the joy of pure sensation.

"Mmmm . . . that's better." Mike smiled as he felt her response. At least her mind wasn't on antiques now! It was almost like old times, when swift passion came upon them at delightfully unexpected moments. He remembered having her in his first dark-room at the studio, on the couch in the living room, and once in the kitchen when Leslie had been tucked into bed. Just as soon as the house was finished, it would be like that again. He'd have his darkroom right here and she'd be at home, precisely where he wanted her. Now that she didn't have to work, he'd have a full-time wife and mother for his child. It would be a peaceful time for both of them; finally they were a real family.

"I love you, Mike," Karen murmured, minutes

later. She brushed her tangled hair back from her face and sighed with contentment. It was warm and secure under the lovely canopy and she closed her eyes against the hot, bright sunlight streaming in through the undraped windows.

"The drapes!" Karen's eyes snapped open and she slid out from under Mike's arm. "I'm supposed to call in the measurements for the drapes this afternoon!"

"Hey, I thought we were going to take the afternoon off." Mike sat up and reached for her, but she eluded his grasp. She was already stepping into her terry cloth shorts as she answered him.

"It's not really working," Karen tried to explain. "If I don't call in those measurements, they won't deliver on time. I promised myself I'd have the second-floor windows done by the first of next month."

Mike groaned and sat up. He'd counted on spending the entire afternoon in bed. Still, there was no sense staying here by himself. He might as well get up and help her.

"Damn!" He scowled as he gathered up his clothes. Karen had set some imaginary deadline for the restoration and she was bound and determined to meet it. He just didn't understand why she was in such a hurry. She had the rest of her life to work on this house.

It wasn't her idea of a fun afternoon, but Leslie trudged along after the girls on their way to the vacant lot. If she had her way, she wouldn't be here at all, but Taffy Comstock had called and here she was, tagging along after a bunch of girls she barely knew.

Leslie sighed loudly as she lagged behind. These kids were a lot different from her friends in Minneapolis. In the Cities there were lots of things to do. The girls from her ballet class used to practice together and put on programs for the parents. They all went to rehearsals of plays at the Guthrie and spent afternoons at the Walker Art Museum. They had the photography club and the craft lessons at the youth center. The kids in Cold Spring weren't interested in anything like that. These girls were only interested in boys, especially Bud Allen and Gary Wilson. It was stupid! Gary and Bud were just ordinary boys who bragged a lot and had loud voices. There must be something wrong with Taffy and the girls if they thought these two boys were so special.

"Come on, Leslie. You can be on my side." Taffy sighed impatiently as she ran back and dragged Leslie into the group of giggling girls. "You know how to play kickball, don't you?"

Leslie nodded quickly. There was no way she was going to admit that she'd never played before. Taffy might tell her to go home and then Mom would be disappointed. Her mother really wanted her to be friends with Taffy.

"You'll have to leave that camera somewhere," Taffy instructed. "Here—take it off and put it under this tree."

Leslie swallowed hard, but she complied. It made her uneasy leaving her Leica unattended, but she wanted to please Taffy and she could keep an eye on it during the game.

"You can be up first because you're new," Taffy decided, nodding at the rest of the girls. "Give her a nice, easy grounder, Susie. My dad said to make sure she had a good time."

The ball came toward her before she was ready and Leslie kicked too late, missing it entirely. A couple of the girls tittered and Leslie blushed painfully. This was harder than it looked. Next time she'd make sure to get it right.

Leslie missed the second pitch, too, catching it with her knee for a foul ball. Taffy groaned and rolled her eyes heavenward in exasperation. The redhead's petulant sigh made Leslie even more determined. She had one pitch left and she was going to kick that red rubber ball all the way out of the vacant lot. They'd never let her play again if she kept on missing.

Leslie's toe hit the third pitch hard and the ball soared over Susie's head. It bounced crazily on a rock and two girls chased after it as Leslie streaked toward first base. She was just rounding second when she saw Bud Allen heading toward the tree where her camera was stashed. She stopped midway between second and third, not sure what to do. He wouldn't take it, would he? Should she run over to make sure?

"Go, Leslie, *go!*" Taffy shouted, spurring her into action. She had to run around the bases if she wanted to score, and Leslie really wanted to show these girls that she could play their silly game right.

Another squeal from Taffy made Leslie run as if demons were chasing her, past third and straight toward home base. As she crossed the square drawn in the dirt for home, she heard Taffy's happy shouts.

"A home run! Didn't I tell you? Leslie's a natural. That's beginner's luck if I ever saw it. Good for you, Leslie!"

Leslie laughed and panted as Taffy pounded her on the back. The girls on Taffy's side jumped up and down and cheered. This wasn't a silly game after all. It was fun and she'd scored. Now these girls were bound to like her.

Leslie remembered her camera and she stood on tiptoe to look over Taffy's shoulder. In a split second her exaltation turned to alarm as she discovered Bud had her Leica.

"Hey! Look what I found!" Bud grabbed the camera and hung it around his neck. It swung wildly as he yelled at them. "Finders, keepers! Right, guys?"

"He's got my camera!" Leslie gasped. "Oh, help me get it back, Taffy! He'll break it!"

Taffy shrugged. "Don't worry about it. He's just teasing us. He does things like this all the time. When he's through clowning around, he'll give it back."

"But . . ." Leslie struggled to explain. "You don't understand, Taffy. Mike made me promise I wouldn't let anyone touch it. It's really expensive. Please help me get it back!"

"We'll have to stop the game." Taffy sighed in irritation. "Don't make such a fuss, Leslie. I'll call time-out."

Taffy shouted at the girls and they came in from the field. She stared at Leslie's worried face for a moment and then she sighed again. She'd have to get that stupid camera back somehow. If her dad heard about this, he'd have a fit. He'd given her strict orders to take care of Leslie.

"Come on, Bud—the fun's over!" Taffy called out in a loud voice. "Bring that camera over here and give it back to Leslie."

Bud made a face. "I found it and I'm going to keep it!" he hollered back. "I'll take a nice picture of you girls if you hold still."

"He's taking pictures!" Leslie's voice was shocked. "He's going to ruin my film, Taffy!"

"Oh, all right." Taffy was resigned. "I'll get your camera back for you if you're that freaked."

Taffy took off running while Bud was squinting through the viewfinder. He didn't realize she was there until she jumped on him, knocking him to the ground. They rolled over and over as Leslie watched, horrified. Her Leica was going to get broken it they kept on wrestling in the dirt.

"*Ouch!* All right . . . *All right!* Take the stupid camera!"

Bud pulled away from Taffy and she grabbed at the camera. There was an audible snap as the strap broke. Bud stood glaring at Taffy, with his hands on his hips. He was breathing hard through his mouth. His face was red and he looked mad enough to grab Taffy and break her in little pieces. There was a long bleeding scratch on the inside of his arm and he winced as he touched it.

"Somebody ought to lock you up in a cage or something!" he shouted, waving his fist in the air as Taffy backed off a couple of steps. "Come on, guys. Let's go somewhere more peaceful, and play by ourselves, away from these dumb girls."

Taffy picked up the Leica and dusted it off as best she could. Her face was bitter with disappointment as she carried it back to Leslie. She handed it over, grimacing.

"Now look what you did!" she hissed. "If you'd just

waited until he had his fun, everything would be fine. Now all the boys are leaving!"

The girls stood like wooden statues, watching the boys swagger from the vacant lot. Then a heavy silence followed and they turned to stare at Leslie resentfully.

Leslie drew her breath in sharply. For some reason they were all mad at her! She hadn't done anything wrong. They were all mad at her because the boys had left.

Taffy shifted and sighed morosely. "I've had it," she declared. "I'm going home to take a bath. Wrestling Bud for that stupid camera got me all dirty."

In groups of twos and threes the girls walked off, leaving Leslie standing alone at home plate. Even though she didn't understand how she was at fault, they were all mad at her. Not one girl stopped to say good-bye.

Leslie looked down at her camera and blinked hard. The case was scratched and the leather strap dangled uselessly from one ring. She had taken such good care of it and now it was all dirty and scratched. It might even be broken. What was Mike going to say?

She cradled the Leica protectively against her chest and walked slowly to the street. It was a mistake, trying to be friends with these kids. They were mean, blaming her for something that wasn't her fault, and she wouldn't play with them again, even if her mother insisted. She'd be better off staying home, with no friends at all.

* * *

They were sitting at the kitchen table when she got home. Leslie came in haltingly, carrying her wounded camera.

"I think my Leica's broken," she admitted in a small voice. "Bud Allen had it and he and Taffy were wrestling. I think they broke it, Mike."

Mike groaned as he saw the scratched case. "What was Bud Allen doing with your camera? I told you not to let anyone else use it."

"I didn't!" Leslie protested. "I was playing kickball and Taffy said to leave it by the tree. Bud stole it and Taffy had to fight him to get it back. Then Bud got mad because Taffy scratched him and all the boys left. Now the girls are mad at me and I didn't do anything!"

"Of course you didn't," Karen said soothingly, pulling Leslie close. "They won't stay mad for long, honey, you just wait and see. They'll forget all about it by tomorrow."

Mike shook his head and sighed deeply as he turned the Leica over in his hands. "If you'd left it at home, this never would have happened. Do you realize this is a five-hundred-dollar camera, Leslie? Let's just hope I can fix it and that the lens is intact. If I have to send it out for repairs, it won't be back for months."

"I'm sorry, Mike." Leslie's face clouded over and tears rose in her eyes. "I guess it was stupid, taking it along. I just thought I might come across a one-of-a-kind picture, something special."

One look at Leslie and Mike relented. The broken camera was clearly an accident and he could tell she was miserable about it.

"Hey. I broke a couple of cameras that way myself when I was a kid," Mike admitted. "Come on, now, cheer up, honey. I'll take it up to the darkroom tonight and see what I can do. Maybe it's not as bad as it looks."

"I'm glad you're home early anyway, kitten." Karen put on a wide smile for her daughter's benefit. "I need a nice big bouquet for the table. Do you think you could wade through that tangled garden out there and cut some roses for me?"

"Sure, Mom." Leslie's face cleared immediately. She gave both of them a relieved look and hurried out the kitchen door. Mike wasn't mad after all. And he said he'd fix her camera if he could. Everything was going to be all right, but she still wouldn't play with these Cold Spring kids ever again. They were too mean.

Karen waited until the door closed before she spoke. "Taffy's friends don't sound very nice. I don't understand why they were all so upset with Leslie. It certainly wasn't her fault the boys left."

Mike shrugged. "I remember when I was the new kid in town." He pulled up a chair and sat down next to Karen. "The new kid's always the outsider for a little while, honey. Just don't get too worried about it. If Leslie keeps trying, they'll accept her eventually."

"But it's not fair!" Karen's voice rose with emotion. "Leslie's always made friends so easily. Why is it so different here?"

"It's a small town—the kids have been together since they were born. And maybe it's not as bad as Leslie's making out. The girls'll come around soon enough. I'm sure it'll all work out if we give it some time. A year from now when kids are swarming all over this place, you'll wish Leslie had fewer friends hanging around."

Karen sighed. She supposed Mike was right and she should give Leslie time to adjust on her own. These children were bound to like her if they gave her half a chance. She'd encourage Leslie to go right out again tomorrow and try to make friends.

Later on Leslie was in the cupola, snuggled down in the pillows that lined the small, windowed room. She had asked to come up here and read, but all she really wanted to do was rest, safe in her own little room, for the remainder of the afternoon. Her eyes were heavy and she let them close for just a minute.

It was twilight and she was floating down a huge tunnel, suspended in a fog. Spinning around and upside down, she bumped against the walls of the tunnel, but she wasn't hurt. At the end of the passage, she saw a bright light and tried to navigate toward it. She moved her arms and legs desperately, making swimming motions through the grayness, but instead of going forward toward the cheerful light, she was being pulled back into the deepest, darkest part of the tunnel. Someone was gripping her arm, pulling her deeper and deeper into the frightening blackness.

She wanted to scream, but she couldn't. Now she was hurtling backward, her hair streaming out in front of her, whipping against her face. She opened her mouth and tried to cry out, but her voice didn't work. She struggled and kicked, but that made her fly backward into the black part of the tunnel, faster and faster. She came to a halt, and suddenly she saw him, a small dim shape in the darkness. She blinked, but he was still not clear, not in focus.

Leslie. She sensed he was smiling. *I knew you'd come if I waited long enough.*

Now the grasping hands were gone and she settled down to rest against a cold, damp wall. She seemed to be in a small earthen box. For one heart-stopping moment Leslie thought she was in a grave; but as she opened her mouth to scream, she realized the space was lined with jars and shelves. It was a small cellar of some sort, under the ground. The cold chilled her skin.

You're doing fine, Leslie, the boy said. *Don't let them fool you. They're wicked, just like they were before. I'm your only real friend.*

Somehow, Leslie knew he spoke the truth. She tried to find her voice to ask his name, but the boy seemed to hear her without asking.

I'm Christopher, he said, holding out his hand. *Come closer, Leslie. You don't have to be afraid.*

She held out her hand to him. As his fingers touched hers, she felt warmth and a pleasant tingle, but it was different from shaking hands with anyone else. She couldn't feel his fingers at all. It was like trying to shake hands with the sun or a warm breeze.

Now we're friends, he said, dropping her hand. *Friends help each other, Leslie. I'll help you if you help me.*

He smiled as she nodded and again he answered her unspoken question. *You can help me by finding the key. It's outside in the yard. If you look carefully, you'll find it.*

She dipped her head in a nod. She would find it. She wanted to help her new friend, Christopher.

He was smiling and speaking her name and his voice was soft. Now she could feel his fingers on her arm. *Leslie,* he said, his voice as soft as a kiss. *Leslie . . . Leslie . . . Leslie?*

She blinked and the bright sunlight startled her. The tunnel was gone and the dark chamber with it. She was in the cupola, with the sun streaming in the west windows, but his voice was still calling her name. The fog of sleep lifted from her mind. It was her mother's voice.

"Leslie? Wake up, kitten. Wash your hands and face, honey. It's almost time for dinner."

"Oh!" Leslie sighed, blinking and stretching. "Hi, Mom! I must have fallen asleep up here. I had a funny dream . . . all about a boy named Christopher."

"Christopher?" Karen smiled. "Is there a Christopher here in town?"

"No, I don't think so." Leslie thought for a moment. "I haven't met anybody named Christopher . . . yet. Maybe I had one of those dreams people are always talking about. A dream that tells the future."

"A prophetic dream?" Karen's smile widened. "Well . . . you'll just have to wait and see. You can tell me all about it later. Right now I have to hurry and get dinner on the table. Mike wants to do some more work on the darkroom tonight."

"I'll be right down, Mom." Leslie stood up, yawning. She hadn't had a chance to tell her too much about the dream. Actually, her mom was very sensible, as most moms are. Leslie would bet she didn't believe in voices in the wind, or boys calling out to her in dreams. Leslie was sure she wouldn't really understand. But the first thing tomorrow, she was going out in the yard to look for that key. If she found it, then she'd know the dream had been real. That boy Christopher would be grateful to her for helping him, and then he'd be her friend. He'd be a much better friend than any of the kids in Cold Spring, and she wouldn't be alone any longer.

But as Leslie wiped the sleep from her eyes, she began to doubt that there was a dark, earthen room, and a boy waiting there for her. How silly the whole thing was. Of course there wasn't really a boy named Christopher, waiting somewhere for her to find the key. She didn't seriously believe that dreams come true exactly the way you dreamed them. There *might* be a key in the yard, though, and it was possible that there was a boy named Christopher in Cold Spring somewhere. Anything was possible. In any event it wouldn't hurt to look around for an old key. It would give her something to look forward to, something fun to do tomorrow. She'd be so busy looking for the key that she'd forget all about the kickball game, and the dumb kids that lived in Cold Spring.

FOUR

"Engraved invitations for a birthday party?" Marilyn Comstock passed the pale pink envelope to her husband and frowned, shaking her head. "I've never heard of such a thing. They're strange people, Rob. Can you imagine spending all that money on engraved invitations? Are they trying to prove they're better than everyone else in Cold Spring?"

"I'm sure that wasn't their intention at all," Rob explained patiently. "You just have to bear with them, Marilyn. Remember, folks do things different in the Cities. They haven't gotten the hang of small-town living yet. You have to give them a chance. I'm sure you'll like them if you keep an open mind."

Marilyn shrugged and pressed her lips together. She supposed she should be a little tolerant. After all, the Houstons had bought her house. Rob had deeded the house over to her years ago for tax purposes and every cent of the house payment was deposited automatically to her account. She was earning more money every month they stayed. Still, she had her doubts about the new owners. If the Houstons wanted to be accepted in Cold Spring, they were going about it all the wrong way.

"From what Mike says, it's going to be a great party," Rob went on, even though Marilyn was still frowning. "Taffy's going to love it. They're bringing in a clown from the Cities and a professional magician. It's even being catered. I think it's going to be the biggest birthday party Cold Spring ever had."

"Well . . . to each his own." Marilyn sighed, wrinkling her nose slightly. "I don't know what's wrong with a small old-fashioned party, though. No one else in Cold Spring puts on such airs. I can't see why the Houstons have to be so fancy with a simple thing like a child's birthday party."

Rob cleared his throat and folded the paper over to look at the sports section. He wasn't inclined to argue with Marilyn this morning, and he certainly wasn't going to tell her that Mike had gotten the birthday money from the gambling he'd been doing lately. Rob had raked in a little extra cash, too, thanks to Mike's tip on the Astros. Marilyn might not realize it, but Mike Houston's heart was in the right place, using his winnings to throw a big birthday party for Leslie.

"Well, Taffy will probably be excited." Marilyn put the invitation back in the envelope and placed it in the exact center of the table, where Taffy would be bound to see it. Then she turned in her chair and faced Rob directly.

"Why do you like them so much?" she asked. "You're always over there, helping them with things."

Rob shrugged. It would be impossible to explain to Marilyn. He couldn't tell her that at the oddest moments, sometimes in the middle of the night, he imagined himself doing something completely out of the ordinary—escaping the web of small-town life, drawing all his careful savings out of the bank and sinking every penny into something creative and daring. Marilyn assumed he was perfectly content here in Cold Spring, running his father's real estate business, and he guessed he was, usually. Still, it cost nothing to dream. Mike Houston was an individual, one of those rare people with talent, personality, and the balls to do something with them.

"I guess he kind of reminds me of my lost youth," Rob replied finally, folding his paper and placing it neatly in the magazine stand.

"Did you get one?" It was midafternoon and Taffy was down by the river with Mary Ellen and Susie. "Mine came this morning."

"Sure, I got one." Mary Ellen flopped down on her stomach to stare at the glistening water. "Every kid in town got one, I bet. I can go, too. My mother says it would be impolite to refuse."

"My dad said the same thing," Susie offered, tossing a pebble halfheartedly at the shallow water. "Do you know if Gary and Bud got them?"

"Everybody did," Taffy answered importantly. "My dad helped them make out the guest list. Every single kid in town is invited. All the boys are coming and Dad says they're bringing in all kinds of entertainment for us from the Cities."

"I don't care!" Susie retorted, tossing her dark

blond braids. "They can bring in a whole circus and it won't change anything. I still think Leslie is stuck-up."

"I do, too." Mary Ellen raised her eyebrows. "You can tell by those designer jeans she wears. My mom says Sears is good enough for anybody."

"She's got a new outfit every time I see her." Susie rolled her eyes and sighed. "And all she can ever talk about is her ballet lessons and how she went to the theater every day when she was living in Minneapolis. My mother says those Gucci shoes she wears cost over a hundred dollars!"

"Who cares what they cost!" Taffy shrugged and stood up to go. "Let's face it. Leslie's just a weird kid. All she ever wants to do is talk about her important friends back in the Cities or take pictures with that dumb camera of hers. I wouldn't play with her at all if my dad didn't make me."

They had been working on the house for a solid month now and the restoration was coming along at a slow, steady pace. The kitchen was finished, dishwasher and modern conveniences hidden by clever rustic covers. The old pump was still in the corner and a pail hung on the handle, just as it had a hundred years ago. The modern sink was concealed by sliding panels, which doubled as counter space. When it was completed, it was an authentic old-fashioned kitchen, right down to the cast-iron "spiders" hanging on the wall.

"Well, it's a perfect day for it." Karen flipped two eggs on a plate and handed them to Leslie. The stove looked old-fashioned, but it was a modern gas range.

Karen loved cooking on it. "We ordered good weather for your birthday, kitten, and it looks like we got it."

Mike grinned. This year the third of July was clear and sunny, perfect for an outdoor party. "And just wait until you open our present." He reached over to ruffle Leslie's straight blond hair. "Remember now, honey—you can't go near the cupola until after the party. That's where we hid your present."

"This is going to be the best birthday party ever." Karen dropped a quick kiss on Leslie's head as she took her place at the kitchen table. "You just wait and see. Everything's going to be absolutely perfect!"

Leslie smiled, but the smile never quite reached her eyes. She was a little worried about her elaborately planned birthday party. She'd heard about the birthday parties they usually had here; lemonade and homemade cake in the backyard. Her birthday party was going to be much bigger and fancier than that. Would the other kids think she was trying to show off?

"Hey—nothing but smiles on your birthday," Mike chided her gently. "Come on, Leslie. Eat your breakfast and then you can help us get ready. We've got a lot of work to do before the party people get here."

By midmorning everything was ready. The trees in the yard were hung with banners and bunting in bright colors; balloons on strings bobbed above the spikes on the wrought-iron fence; and a huge soda-pop fountain was in readiness for the first arrivals. When it was switched on, the strawberry soda would bubble up in a spray to be caught in the guests' cups. The ice cream cake waited in the freezer for the right moment, and gay party favors nestled in striped hats at the gate.

The caterers were in the kitchen, preparing miniature hamburgers and tiny hot dogs on decorative platters. Leslie rushed past them and ran around the corner of the house to the rose garden. She wanted to pick one perfect rose for her mom. It would be a thoughtful way to say thank you for all the work she had done to get this party ready.

She pushed her way carefully through the tangled vines. There was one red rose just opening on a tall bush in the middle of the garden.

She snipped it off with the gardening shears and smiled happily. It was the prettiest rose she'd ever seen. The petals were still covered with morning dew and its fragrance made her feel dizzy with pleasure. She looked up and saw the cupola directly above her and her heart beat faster. This was the exact spot she'd seen the shadow. It was quiet and bright, the sunniest spot in the whole garden. Perhaps the perfect rose was a clue, a sort of signpost leading her to something.

The key! Leslie drew her breath in sharply as she thought of it. She had looked for a week now with no success. Could it be here?

Leslie pulled aside the tangled vines, carefully avoiding the sharp thorns. She gasped as she saw a flash of light near the stem of the rosebush.

A gum wrapper. It was only an old gum wrapper. Leslie picked it up and stuffed it into her pocket. She was so bitterly disappointed that tears came to her eyes. She dug the toe of her Nikes into the dirt and kicked hard. Then she stopped, not quite believing what she had accidentally uncovered.

It was still partially buried and Leslie pushed aside the dry leaves and raked mulch with her fingers. A moment later she had the key in her hand—the key from her dream!

"I found it!" Leslie's voice was almost a sob, she was so happy. "There really was a key and I found it!"

Carefully she polished the key with her handkerchief. As she gazed down at it, her mind whirled in excited circles. It was her birthday present . . . from Christopher. Did that mean her dream was coming true? Would she meet him, now that she'd found the key? It could happen today. She could meet Christopher right here, at her own birthday party!

Her excitement grew and Leslie laughed right out loud. Anything was possible. She'd found the key, hadn't she? She had promised to look and she'd found it, right where he'd said.

"Mom?" Leslie rushed through the doorway, banging the screen behind her. "Look what I found! It's an old key! Can you help me find the lock it fits?"

Karen took the key from Leslie's hand and looked at it. "I think it belongs to a padlock," she said, examining it closely. "I don't believe we have anything padlocked, honey. Perhaps someone walking in the yard lost it."

"Maybe it's a padlock we haven't found yet." Leslie's voice was high and eager. "That could be it, couldn't it, Mom?"

"Well . . . it could be, I suppose." Karen smiled a little. Leslie certainly was ecstatic over finding an old key. She couldn't imagine why it was so important to her.

"I can keep it, can't I, Mom? Even if it doesn't fit anything, I need to keep it. Please?"

"Goodness, kitten! Of course you can keep it. I don't need an old key for anything and neither does Mike. It's all yours, honey."

"Thank you, Mom!" Leslie flung her arms around Karen's neck and hugged hard. "I'm going to find a string and wear it around my neck. Then I'm going to check every lock around here and see if it fits something."

"First you're going to bathe and get dressed." Karen was firm. "Go get a piece of string from that drawer next to the sink and I'll help you tie it around your neck if you must. But no looking for any old locks until after the birthday party."

Leslie looked pained, but she didn't argue. At least her mom had said she could keep the key. That was something. And tomorrow she'd have all day to look for the lock. There was a smile on her face as she ran up the stairs to get ready for her party.

When she was bathed and ready, Leslie slipped her birthday dress over her head. It was a special present from her mother and it made her happy just to look at the white dainty voile with hand-embroidered pink roses. There was an underskirt of pink, a deeper rose velvet ribbon for her hair, and a pair of matching pink satin shoes.

The shoes were as soft as ballet slippers and Leslie smiled as she put them on. She wished she could take ballet lessons again, but there were no classes here. The kids in Cold Spring didn't seem interested in ballet at all.

Leslie did a pirouette around the room, humming a few bars from *Swan Lake*. She felt wonderful in her new dress and shoes. Perhaps this was going to be a good party after all.

"Oh, kitten! You look lovely!" Karen stepped into her daughter's room. Leslie was growing more beautiful every year.

"I love this dress, Mom!" Leslie lifted her arms gracefully and grinned at her mother. "And these shoes! I just wish I could take ballet again."

"We'll talk about that later, darling." Karen frowned and a tiny worry line appeared on her forehead. She really wished that Leslie could continue with her dance lessons, but the round trip to the Cities five days a week would be impossible.

"Sit down now, honey, and let me fix your hair," Karen urged. "Only half an hour and your first guests will arrive."

At last her mother was finished and Leslie stood up, twirling in front of the mirror so her dainty white skirt swirled out in a bell. Maybe her mother was right and this was going to be the best birthday party ever. The Cold Spring kids might be pleased that Mike was spending all this money so everyone could have a good time. She pushed aside her nagging doubts and fixed a smile on her face. Of course all the kids would come, and they'd have a wonderful time. Then all the children in Cold Spring would change their minds about her and really like her, all because of this wonderful birthday party.

"Wow! He's good, isn't he?" Mary Ellen stood in the front row, between Taffy and Susie. "I never saw a real live magician before!"

"He's got stuff up his sleeves," Bud hissed in Mary Ellen's ear. "Watch him. You can tell he's a fake."

"I've seen better on TV," Gary joined in. "And he's doing tricks I must have seen a hundred times."

"Shut up, both of you!" Taffy turned around and glared at the two boys. "I'm trying to enjoy the show!"

"Ahhhhhh!" There was a hushed cry from the audience as the magician drew a rabbit out of his tall silk hat. Scarves changed to fluttering doves and flowers sprouted from the tips of his fingers. Leslie glanced around happily. The kids seemed to be enjoying the magic show. The clown act and the magician had been big hits with almost everyone here. So far it was a great birthday party.

"Time for another game!" Karen stepped up on the raised platform in the center of the lawn. "We're going to play musical chairs now. Does everyone know how to play?"

"Musical chairs?" Bud's voice was high and scornful. "That's a babies' game!"

"I haven't played that since the second grade." Gary shook his head. "Well . . . come on, Bud. Maybe we can liven it up a little."

Chairs were set up in rows at the side of the house. Karen took her place at the portable phonograph and blushed uncomfortably. She had heard Bud's rude remark. Perhaps musical chairs was a little childish for this group, but the caterers had provided the chairs and it was an easy game to engineer. Musical chairs was a game she remembered from her own childhood.

She faced the group of assembled children. "There are twenty-six of you and twenty-five chairs. Form a line and parade around the chairs until the music stops. Then grab a chair. If you don't get a chair, you're out. At the end of the game, only one person will be left and there's a special prize. All set? Let's go!"

Leslie marched in a line with the rest of the children. She kept her eye on Bud Allen and Gary Wilson. They were whispering to each other about something and Leslie didn't like the looks of it. She hoped they weren't going to start any trouble. She didn't trust either of them to act nice even at a party.

The music stopped and pandemonium reigned for a moment. There was a burst of laughter as the kids scrambled for seats.

"Ouch! Cut it out, Bud!" Susie gave a squeal as she landed on the grass. "That was my chair, you ape. You can't pick it up when I'm already sitting in it!"

"Let's be careful, boys," Karen cautioned, starting the music again. The strains of a Sousa march floated across the lawn and the children dutifully paraded around the row of chairs again. Susie was glowering on the sidelines and Leslie felt sorry for her. Bud had been playing much too rough.

When the music stopped the second time, there was another scramble for seats, and this time Taffy was the victim.

"You cheated!" She stamped her foot hard on the ground and made a face at Gary Wilson. "You tipped me right out of my chair! Look . . . you got dirt on my best dress!"

"We'll spot-clean it before you go home, honey." Karen drew the angry redhead aside. Then she went over to Bud and Gary and took both smirking boys by the arms.

"Please try to be careful, boys. This is supposed to be a game, not a battle."

"Sure enough, Mrs. Houston," Bud replied, flashing her a grin. "Guess we just don't know our own strength, huh, Gary?"

Karen sighed and walked back to the phonograph. Even though the boys had seemed agreeable enough, she sensed trouble. She'd be sure to keep her eye on them this round.

"Let's get Leslie this time," Bud whispered under his breath. "Don't let anyone see you do it, though. We'll pay her back for siccing Taffy on me that day at the vacant lot."

Another chair was removed and the music started again. Leslie glanced around for Bud and Gary, but she didn't see them in the crowd. Maybe the warning her mother had given them had done some good. At least they wouldn't dare pick on her with Mom and Mike right here.

"Ouch!" Leslie gasped, tears springing quickly to her eyes. Someone had elbowed her in the back. A moment passed and another shove made her stumble. The kids were piling up at the end of the row chairs and she looked back to see Gary grinning at her. She was sure he was the one who had shoved her.

Leslie walked a little faster, attempting to put several other kids between Gary and herself, but he followed just as fast. She was getting a little frightened now. Bud Allen was there, too, right behind Gary.

Karen watched, but it was difficult to pick out Leslie in the crowd of laughing children. Perhaps her little talk with the boys had helped. They were apparently behaving themselves now.

Karen looked away for a moment to switch off the music. That was when it happened. She heard Leslie's sharp cry; and when she looked up, her daughter was facedown on the grass, the sleeve of her birthday dress ripped at the seam.

"He pushed me!" Leslie accused, glaring at Bud. "Both of them did! Make them go home, Mike—they're awful!"

"That's enough, Leslie!" Mike's voice was sharper than he had intended, but he didn't want Leslie to make a scene. There was a sudden stillness as all the children stopped talking and waited to see what would happen.

"I'll take care of it, Karen." Mike helped Leslie to her feet. "You start a different game and I'll see that Leslie gets cleaned up. Just go on playing, kids. Leslie's not hurt."

With a hand on her shoulder, Mike hurried Leslie toward the house. He heard Karen's voice explaining the next game and the children laughed as they started to play. He was embarrassed at the scene Leslie had made. The boys were a little too rough, but that was natural for boys their age. Leslie had acted as if they'd personally attacked her. Taffy and Susie hadn't made that much of a fuss when they were pushed down.

"Come on now, Leslie. It's not that bad." Mike shook his head as he opened the door for his stepdaughter. "Your mother can fix your dress and it was an accident."

"It was on purpose!" Leslie's voice was stubborn. "I'm not going back out there until they leave!"

"They're guests, Leslie." Mike's voice was sharp. "It's not polite to ask an invited guest to leave, you know that. You'll never make any friends here if you do something like that!"

As he spoke, Mike ushered Leslie up the stairs and into her room. He smoothed her hair and wiped a smudge of dirt from her cheek.

"Now, put on another dress, honey." He gave her a quick hug. "I know how you must feel, but you do have to go back to the party. You're the birthday girl and you have an obligation to your guests."

Leslie's mouth dropped open in surprise as Mike spoke. The Cold Spring kids were more important to him than she was. It made her feel as if they were choosing up sides, and Mike was on theirs.

"Hurry up now, Leslie." Mike's voice was firm as he turned to leave. "We're going to have lunch in a couple of minutes. After that you'll cut the cake. Now, be a good sport and let everyone see you know how to act."

As the door closed behind Mike, Leslie drew a deep breath and dried her eyes. There was no use arguing. She'd have to go back to the party, but she didn't have to like it.

Scowling, Leslie dressed quickly in a silk blouse and a skirt. She glanced at her key on the dressing table and on an impulse dropped it into one of the deep pockets of her skirt. Maybe it would bring her luck. Somehow she had to get through the rest of this afternoon. If she didn't go back out there with a smile on her face, Mike would be mad at her.

Several children stared at her when she reappeared, but no one spoke to her. Leslie calmly watched the game, fixing her face into a proper smile. If Mike wanted her to be a good sport, she'd do it, but she'd get even with Bud and Gary somehow. Maybe it wouldn't be today, but she'd never forget how mean they'd been.

Leslie looked over to find that Bud and Gary were talking to Mike now—making up excuses, probably; she could tell from the relieved look on Mike's face. All three of them headed her way. Leslie tried to duck into an opening in the crowd of children, but Mike put his hand on her arm.

"Leslie? Bud and Gary want to apologize for being so rough. They told me how sorry they are that you got hurt."

Mike grinned down at the two boys. Then he tipped Leslie's face up to look at him. "Now, what do you say, Leslie?"

All three of them were looking at her and Leslie felt hot and uncomfortable. Bud and Gary didn't look sorry at all. They were almost smirking as they stared at her.

Mike was waiting. Leslie knew she was supposed to say something nice. The moment stretched, tense and silent, until she couldn't stand it anymore.

"I . . . it's all right," Leslie managed to force out.

"Well, now that that's settled"—Mike gave Leslie an approving nod—"let's go get something to eat, guys. I think they're bringing out the food right now."

Leslie stood still and bit her lip. She was getting

that bad feeling again. Mike was on their side and she just didn't understand it. Somehow these Cold Spring kids had managed to fool Mike, but they didn't fool her for one minute. They were still the meanest kids she'd ever met. It was just hidden underneath their phony party manners. And the girls were just as bad as the boys. She saw the way Taffy and Mary Ellen huddled on the edge of the games, looking at her. They'd poke Susie and whisper and then all three of them would giggle. All conversation stopped when she approached a group, and most of the kids, even the ones she didn't know, looked uncomfortable. That proved they were all talking about her behind her back.

Leslie did her best to keep smiling, but her face felt as if it were cemented into place. Lunch was over quickly and it was time for the cake. Leslie swallowed nervously. She'd be the center of attention again and everyone would stare at her.

"Time for the birthday girl to blow out her candles!" Karen announced brightly, stepping out to the middle of the lawn with the cake. It was enormous, enough for seconds and even thirds, made of frosted ice cream in the shape of a clown.

Karen made her way through the crowd of whispering children and set the cake on the table draped with streamers. She was smiling gaily.

"Make a wish, darling, and blow out your candles. Then we can all have a piece of your yummy strawberry cake!"

Leslie made her way on stiff legs to the table. She felt hot and prickly all over and slightly dizzy. She knew everyone was watching her as she approached the huge cake and there was a smothered giggle from the children as she stumbled slightly on the uneven grass.

"Wish for something wonderful, honey," Karen whispered in Leslie's ear. "Birthday wishes always come true."

The candles on the huge cake were flickering brightly and Leslie squinted as she took her place behind it. Moments before there hadn't been a cloud in the sky, but suddenly the afternoon had turned overcast and gray. The pinpoints of flickering candlelight hurt her eyes and Leslie knew she had never felt so lonely. These kids didn't want to be here at her birthday party. They didn't like her at all. They had only come because their parents had told them to be polite.

"Shut your eyes and make a wish, honey!" Mike called out, his camera ready. "Everyone's waiting."

Leslie shut her eyes to block out the shimmering candles. Her mind was blank and she couldn't think of anything to wish for. Instinctively, her fingers curled around the key in her pocket and she squeezed it tightly. At least one good thing had happened today. She had found the key, even though she hadn't met Christopher yet.

Yes, you have. The voice was faint and crackling, like that of someone talking over a telephone with a very bad connection. *I'm Christopher. Just hold the key and I'm with you.*

Leslie opened her eyes, startled, but she knew that no one at the party had spoken. No one else had heard the voice, either. They were all standing there quietly, waiting for her to blow out the candles. The distant voice was inside her own head. She was imagining the whole thing. It was what her mother called wishful thinking.

"What's taking her so long?" She heard Bud's low voice.

"She's so dumb, she can't think of anything to wish for." Gary laughed out loud as he replied.

It wasn't true! Leslie shut her eyes and squeezed the key hard. Now she knew exactly what to wish. She'd wish that the party would end right now. And she'd wish that these horrid kids would feel just as miserable as she did.

"Blow all the candles out, honey!" Karen said, raising her voice. She couldn't imagine what was the matter with Leslie. She was standing there, staring at the cake, stiff and still.

At last Leslie moved. The small golden-haired girl bent over and gazed at the top of the cake, where ten candles blazed brightly. Her eyes were half closed, as if the light hurt them. She stared for a moment, swaying slightly, and then she pursed her lips and blew a soft stream of air that was more like a sigh.

"Harder, darling!" Karen coached. As she watched, the candles wavered and grew brighter. Then they flickered out as if some unseen hand were snuffing them one by one.

Up here, Leslie . . . in the tree. I'll make your birthday wish come true.

This time the voice didn't startle her. It was as if she had been expecting it to continue. She raised her eyes and saw the old grayish-white hornets' nest Mike had sprayed days ago. He had said it was empty, but he was taking no chances. A hornet's sting was painful and they could sting you over and over again.

It paid to be doubly careful when you were dealing with hornets.

Even though there was no noticeable breeze, the hornets' nest swayed back and forth like a pendulum. As Leslie stared at it, the other children began to look up, too.

"Hey! Look at that!" Bud's voice was a whisper, but everyone heard him in the sudden stillness.

"It's moving! Get back, girls—I think it's going to fall!" Karen pulled Susie and Mary Ellen back a few steps.

"Don't worry about it, kids." Mike's voice was loud and reassuring. "I sprayed it last week and the hornets are dead. There's nothing to worry about at all. It's just the wind. Come on, Leslie—let's cut the cake!"

Mike moved a few steps toward Leslie, but all eyes were on the swaying hornets' nest. Leaves rustled as the branch swung harder and one of the children screamed. Then there was a sharp crack as the branch snapped and the cone fell, landing on the table only inches from the birthday cake.

"Too bad it didn't fall right on the cake!" Gary remarked, laughing loudly. "Or maybe right on top of Leslie's head."

Leslie stood perfectly still, staring at the hornets' nest intently. Her eyes were huge and dark. Through the buzzing in her ears, she heard the children's laughter and she wished harder than ever. There should be hornets in the nest. Then they wouldn't be laughing at her like this.

Her fingers gripped the key tightly; and as she wished, a low whine began to emanate from the nest. The sound rose in volume and pitch and one by one the children began to scream as fat, healthy hornets emerged from the paper cone with an angry buzz.

"Hornets! Let's get out of here!" Bud's voice was high and frightened. "Run, you guys! *Run!*"

They were running even before Bud's urgent warning, pushing and shoving wildly to escape the menacing whine. Leslie watched them all panic, shoving and scrambling to get out of the way as the swarm of hornets descended. The crowd of angry insects was attacking now, chasing the children as they fled from the yard.

Leslie supposed she should run, too, but she couldn't seem to move her feet. Somehow she knew that the hornets weren't after her. They buzzed all around her, but not one of them stung. A small smile of satisfaction crept across her face as her guests fled, screaming from the swarm.

"Leslie, *move!* Run for the house!" her mother was shouting to her, but Leslie knew she was safe. She stood in the cloud of hornets, unharmed, as the other children scattered and raced away. Mom had been right and Leslie shivered slightly. Birthday wishes always came true and her party was definitely, finally, over for good.

FIVE

Leslie stood, transfixed, in front of her melting birthday cake. The frosting ran down in bright rivulets of color and a lake of strawberry ice cream was growing on the silver platter. She lifted blank eyes as the hornets darted down in a straggling line to chase after the screaming children.

They followed only to the perimeter of the yard, humming and whining angrily. Then they turned and formed a dark cloud above Leslie's head as Mike and Karen watched, horrified. The hornets were suspended there for a full minute while Leslie stared up at the ominous black shadow. Then they quivered and were gone, streaking off in a ragged line toward the river.

"Help me, Mike! Get her, quickly!" Karen was almost hysterical as they rushed to Leslie. She was still standing there, shaking, staring blankly at the spot where the hornets had disappeared.

"In the house, Leslie—move!" Mike grabbed his stepdaughter and helped her across the lawn and into the safety of the house.

"He's gone," Leslie said, sighing, the blank look still on her face. "He was here, but now he's gone."

"Are you hurt, honey?" Mike dropped to his knees so that his face was level with hers. "Did you get stung?"

"No." Leslie gave a strange and mirthless smile. "He's my friend. He wouldn't let the hornets sting me."

"What's she talking about?" Mike turned to Karen with alarm. Leslie was smiling a peculiar, lopsided smile and her whole body trembled violently.

"She's in shock!" Karen whispered. "Oh, God, Mike! We'd better check her to make sure she's all right."

Leslie stood woodenly as her mother and Mike made a fuss over her, checking her arms and legs for stings. There weren't any.

"Are you sure you're not hurt, kitten?" Karen asked again, amazement showing in her face. "I've never seen anything like it! They swarmed all around her but none of them stung."

"Maybe the other children didn't get stung, either. I don't know about any species of hornet that doesn't sting, but perhaps this bunch was some kind of weird mutation."

"The others got stung." Leslie's voice was slow and measured. She couldn't seem to think clearly and she felt strange, as if she'd been awakened in the middle of a nightmare. "I know they got stung. I heard them screaming."

"Well . . . I hope not." Karen brushed a strand of hair from Leslie's face. "They might have been screaming because they were frightened."

"Maybe," Leslie admitted, staring up at her mother with wide, unfocused eyes.

Just then the telephone rang. While Mike went to answer it, Karen watched Leslie closely. She was worried. Leslie's eyes were dilated, black and huge in her white face. It had been a nasty shock, and on her birthday, too!

"That was Mrs. Wilson." Mike came back to place his hand on Karen's shoulder. "It looks as though Leslie was right after all. Gary has stings all over him and he thinks most of the other kids were stung, too. Mrs. Wilson said she'd contact the other parents and call us again tonight. She doesn't think there'll be any trouble. After all, it was an accident. Leslie was really lucky she didn't get stung."

"Maybe it was because she was standing so still and not running," Karen suggested. "I bet that was it, Mike. When hornets are angry, they attack any moving object, don't they? I think I remember reading that somewhere."

Mike shrugged. Karen could be right. Now that they were sure Leslie was unharmed, there was a lot of cleaning up to do.

"Leslie? I think you'd better sit right here for a while," Karen guided her daughter to a chair. "Mike and I will clean up the party things and take care of the caterers. You just rest right here at the table. And try not to feel too bad, honey. You were a wonderful hostess today, and nobody can blame you for that awful accident with the hornets."

"Just stay here until we bet back inside," Mike added. "We'll hurry as fast as we can. And if you need anything, just come to the door and holler. We'll be listening for you."

Leslie closed her eyes for a moment. She was still dizzy and confused. She remembered holding the key and wishing the party would be over. That was when she had first heard the voice. Then the hornets' nest had fallen and the rest was a blurry montage of images.

Carefully Leslie drew the key out of her pocket and looked at it. Why had she found it? Had she heard a voice or had she just willed herself to hear it? Could it possibly belong to a boy named Christopher? Had he made the hornets' nest fall, and could he make all her wishes come true?

She dropped it back into her pocket and shuddered. It couldn't have happened that way. She was making up stories again. The key was just any old key and the voice was only her imagination. The hornets had been an awful accident, just as her mother had said.

She sat quietly for a long time and finally raised her head. She felt better now. She blinked and stared out the window. Her eyes hurt a bit, but that was all. Now that her mind was starting to clear she felt silly for having imagined things.

She could see Mike and her mother working in the yard. He was taking down the decorations and Mom was gathering up the plates. The caterers were making trips back and forth to their trucks, and two men were dismantling the soda-pop fountain. Leslie sighed in disappointment. She hadn't even had a cup of strawberry soda and it was her favorite.

At last the job was finished. The caterers drove off

and Karen and Mike came back into the house. Mike flopped into a chair, and Karen sighed as she poured herself a cup of coffee.

"You look much better, honey—I bet you can't wait to open up all those presents. I know it won't be as much fun without the rest of the kids, but the three of us will have our own little party right here."

"Presents!" Mike snapped his fingers. "We forgot all about Leslie's present from us!"

"Let's give her that one first," Karen said, cheerful again. "I think this would be a good time, don't you?"

"Come on, Leslie—up to your tower room." Mike pulled her to her feet. He could hardly wait to see what Leslie would do when she saw the telescope.

They let her open the door and step in alone as they stood on the landing and watched expectantly. Leslie took one look inside the cupola and stopped in the doorway, her eyes wide with surprise. Then she wheeled around and hugged both of them hard.

"Oh, Mom! Mike! What a super present! Is it really mine? Is it really just for me?"

"You bet it is!" Mike nodded. Leslie's reaction was worth every cent he'd spent on the telescope. There was no doubt he'd have to win on Sunday if he wanted to pay it all off, but that shouldn't be a problem. He was on a lucky streak now and it was going to last. He might even bet a little heavier on this Sunday's score and really clean up. In any event, the money he'd spent on Leslie's birthday had been worth it. He could tell she was absolutely delighted.

"And that's just half of it." Mike's smile widened as Leslie caught her breath. "I got your Leica all cleaned up last night. The case has a couple of bad scratches, but otherwise it's in fine shape. You really lucked out, Leslie. You're going to need your camera more than ever now that you have the telescope."

Leslie looked puzzled and Mike chuckled. "I think, if we do a little jury-rigging, we can hook it up to the telescope lens so you can take pictures of the moon and stars."

"Oh, super!" Leslie's smile was rapturous. She'd been completely wrong about Mike before. He really was on her side. The kids from Cold Spring had just gotten her confused, that was all. Mike must be on her side to have bought her such a wonderful birthday present.

Leslie gazed at the new telescope with love in her eyes. Then she turned a pleading expression to her mother.

"Can I come up here during the day, too?" she begged, watching Karen anxiously. "I could learn about the clouds then and I could take pictures of the town from up here. I could see all sorts of interesting things in the daytime. Please?"

Karen hesitated. It was exactly what she had feared. Leslie would be up here every minute and she'd never go out and socialize.

"Mom? I won't come up here very often if you don't want me to." Leslie's voice was small and disappointed.

Karen was caught in a bind. She didn't want to put a damper on Leslie's spirits, and her daughter looked crestfallen.

"Yes, you can use your telescope during the day, too," she conceded. "But you have to promise to tell me first. I don't want to be looking all over the house for you when I need you."

"I promise!" Leslie ran over to her mother and hugged her. "You're wonderful, Mom! And you're wonderful, too, Mike! Will you show me how to use my new telescope now?"

Karen stood in the doorway as Mike and Leslie huddled over the telescope, Leslie's blond hair touching Mike's dark. They were talking about light refraction and powers now. Karen wasn't particularly interested in hearing Mike's instructions, so she slipped out quietly and made her way down the narrow staircase. She had other, more practical matters on her mind; for one thing, there was still cleaning up to be done. Karen stopped for a minute at the third-floor landing and gazed around longingly. She wished that she could start uncovering things right away, but it would have to wait. She'd come up here first thing in the morning, right after her regular housework was done.

The ghostly covered shapes drew Karen like a magnet, and she ran her hand over several of the more intriguing pieces. She had taken a peek at the large items when they first moved in. The lovely spinet piano in the living room was waiting for repairs and she'd found beds for most of the rooms on the second floor. That was as far as she'd gotten. There were still crates and trunks to be explored, and Karen was anxious to begin. Now that the rest of the house was somewhat in order, she could reward herself by spending some time up here, just cataloging the useful items.

It was still and quiet here in the ballroom. Karen

heard Mike's deep laugh and Leslie's excited voice from above. A feeling of peace and the rightness of things came over her. They were at home in this huge old house. Living here made her feel she had roots with the past. Her own parents had died when she was young and she had lived with a succession of aunts and uncles, shipped from one family to the next. There had never been a family home like this. Now, in this lovely house, she felt steeped in tradition. It would be home to her and her children. It was the kind of house that would welcome generations of Houstons.

Karen smiled. She felt better now. While she tried not to make much of it, the hornets had upset her dreadfully. She had thought of them as a bad omen, a warning of worse things to come. Now she could laugh at her foolishness. Perhaps her condition was to blame for these morbid thoughts. Or, more likely, Janet Wilson's harebrained story about this house being haunted. Whatever the cause, she wouldn't mention any of it to Mike. He scoffed at any hint of the supernatural. He'd laugh his head off if she told him Janet's haunted-house story. Karen usually agreed with him, but it was strange that the hornets had only stung the Cold Spring children and not Leslie, who was standing in the middle of them.

"Oh, no, you don't!" He caught her by surprise and Karen whirled around, a guilty expression on her face.

Mike grinned and flipped the dust cover back over the antique trunk she'd been about to open. "You promised there'd be no work on the house today; it's a birthday, and we're supposed to be having a party."

For a moment Karen was irritated. She wasn't working. She had just been amusing herself while he was busy with the telescope.

"Right." She nodded, putting on a smile. "Let's get Leslie and have a piece of the birthday cake. It melted a little, but I stuck it in the freezer."

"Sounds good to me. Then we can watch Leslie open her presents. I'll wait until she goes to bed before I finish up in the darkroom."

Karen's mouth tightened as she went down the stairs. Mike didn't want her to work today, but he'd be stuck in the darkroom for hours again tonight. He really wasn't being fair. Her decorating was just as important as his photography, but she wouldn't get upset about it now. It was an old argument and it shouldn't spoil Leslie's big day. She had to lighten up and make the rest of the day a success for Leslie.

"Mike?" She turned at the bottom of the stairs and looked back. Mike was looking down at her questioningly.

"You want pickles on your ice cream, too?"

SIX

Karen sighed as she approached the green two-story house. She didn't want to be here, but Mike had insisted. Marilyn Comstock had invited her for coffee to meet some of the "girls," and Karen just knew she wouldn't enjoy herself. They probably wanted to talk about Leslie's party the previous weekend and rehash the hornet incident.

She straightened her shoulders and gave a final pat to her hair. She wore it loose, tied back with a beige ribbon that matched her two-piece suit. She'd added a touch of lipstick and faint eye shadow for the occasion. She was a bit nervous as she crossed the open porch and rang the doorbell.

"How's Leslie?" Marilyn asked, just as soon as the introductions were made. "That was a real shame about her birthday party!"

"Leslie's fine." Karen sat down in a rose-colored chair and crossed her legs properly at the ankles. "I hope Taffy's recovered from her stings."

"Her arm's still swollen, but it's healing." Marilyn passed the plate of cookies. "Taffy says Leslie was right in the middle of those awful hornets. Was she stung badly?"

"Well . . . no." Karen drew a deep breath. "Actually, Leslie wasn't stung at all. We think the hornets only attacked the children who were running. Leslie stood still and they left her alone."

"How odd!" Janet Wilson raised her eyebrows. "My Gary had stings all over him. That means all the children were stung, except Leslie."

"It is odd, but odd things always happen at the Appleton Mansion." Sylvia Ness laughed dryly. "I've heard enough stories about that house to write a book!"

Janet cleared her throat. "Let's not get started on that old haunted-house business. I must have heard it all a hundred times. I'd much rather talk about the church bazaar. Has Reverend Mason set a date yet?"

Karen balanced the glass snack tray on her lap and tried to look interested as the women discussed the bazaar. Just sitting in Marilyn's living room gave her a headache. The room was done in lime green and pink, and Karen had a hard time keeping a pleasant smile on her face as she gazed around her. She didn't mean to be snobbish or cruel, but the house really was decorated badly.

"You're going to bring knitted slippers again this year, aren't you, Roberta?"

Karen tuned into the conversation again and shifted her attention to Roberta Allen. She was an overweight brunette, hair done in a fifties upsweep, so heavily sprayed that it resembled a plastic sculpture.

"I made some darling pot holders from an article

in *House and Home* magazine," Sylvia Ness volunteered. "You know those little loops you can buy at Woolworth's? I made one in every color, so they're bound to sell."

Alice Marshal sighed and smiled hesitantly at Karen. "I just don't know what to bring," she confessed. "I've started four or five projects, but I don't seem to have the time to finish anything."

She was older than the other women, and her voice was timid. Alice looked harried and disorganized. Wisps of gray hair escaped from the bun on top of her head and she wore no makeup. She reminded Karen of a small gray dove, quick mannered and easily startled. Karen tried hard to imagine them becoming good friends, but it didn't seem likely.

"We haven't seen you in church, Karen," Marilyn commented. "Are you and your husband Protestant?"

Karen swallowed hard. "Actually, Mike and I aren't big on organized religion. And we haven't had a chance to bring Leslie regularly to any particular church." Karen knew she was hedging. Religion just wasn't an important part in either Mike's or her life.

The women exchanged glances. "We'd love to have you visit our church," Alice said. "Reverend Mason's very progressive and Leslie would love our Sunday school."

"I'll tell Mike." But she thought, *Wait until Mike hears about this!*

"My, that's a pretty outfit." Roberta Allen stared at Karen's raw-silk suit. She took a bite of a cookie and smiled weakly. "You're so lucky you're thin. I could never wear anything that formfitting."

"She won't be thin for too much longer," Janet

observed, laughing gaily. "Karen's pregnant, didn't you know? She's expecting in December. You don't think there'll be a problem with Leslie, do you, Karen? I mean, with the new baby, and you just married to Mike?"

"Oh! No . . . I . . . I don't think so." Karen was furious. Her fingers tightened around her coffee cup. She regretted having slipped up that first day in the grocery store, but she didn't see why everyone in town had to know Mike wasn't Leslie's father. And to hint at "problems" with her Leslie, as if their own children were so well adjusted.

"Remember Mavis Barber?" Roberta chewed and swallowed quickly. "She had the same situation, except she was widowed, not divorced. She married Paul and got p.g. right away. There was all sorts of trouble with the new baby and her other kids. One of them tried to push over the baby's crib. I remember that plain as day."

"Well, I'm sure we won't have *that* problem." Karen was shocked, but she tried to smile. "Leslie's very excited about the new baby."

There was a long silence as the women shifted uncomfortably on Marilyn's slipcovered chairs.

Marilyn started the conversation again. "You're not going back to work once the baby's born, are you, Karen?"

"Well . . . Mike doesn't approve of working mothers," Karen hedged.

"Neither do I!" Janet agreed vehemently. "I didn't go back to the store until Gary was in school. I believe a woman's place is with her child."

"You worked when Leslie was small, though, didn't

you, Karen?" Marilyn waited for Karen's nod. "Do you think it had an effect on Leslie?"

"It might have." Karen tried to be fair as she answered. "I had a very good babysitter, though, and I spent every evening and weekend with Leslie."

"It still makes a difference," Sylvia contended. "You can always tell the child of a working mother. They're moody and they keep to themselves a lot. I never wanted to work when Mary Ellen was small and I wouldn't work now. Careers are for single women. You shouldn't have children if you aren't responsible."

Karen sighed as the other women entered the discussion. She'd have to be careful not to alienate these women completely. Their attitudes could make Leslie's adjustment even harder.

"Are there any dance teachers in town?" Karen asked politely when there was a break in the conversation. "Leslie had two years of ballet in the Cities and I'd like to find another teacher for her here."

"Ballet?" Sylvia laughed. "A ballet teacher wouldn't do much business here. Why, naturally, the boys think ballet's sissy, and our girls are more interested in practical things. I'd get Leslie involved in 4-H, if I were you. Now, that's a worthwhile organization. It teaches skills you can use all your life and prepares the girls to be good wives and mothers."

"You'll never guess what I heard in the store this morning." Janet leaned forward and lowered her voice. "Peggy Miller is leaving Bill. She caught him out at the Dew Drop Inn with Jessie Blair. And they weren't just dancing, either!"

"I knew that one wouldn't last." Marilyn shook her head. "Once a girl-chaser, always a girl-chaser, I say."

"I'm glad I never had a problem like that." Roberta plucked another cookie off the plate and popped it into her mouth. "Delbert has his faults, but he's never cheated on me."

"I don't know what I'd do if Harry ran around." Janet sighed and tightened her lips. "I wouldn't divorce him . . . that's for sure! I think divorce is wrong!"

She looked at Karen and had the grace to blush. "At least it's wrong ninety-nine percent of the time," she amended.

Karen gave her a bewildered look for a moment and then she remembered. She had told Janet that she had been married before. If these women were so shocked at divorce, it was a good thing they didn't know the true circumstances of Leslie's birth. Karen could imagine what they'd say if they knew she had been an unmarried mother.

"Did you hear about the Pfeffers?" Marilyn stepped in to cover the awkward moment. She looked smug as the other women leaned forward eagerly.

"I heard this from Donna Weisner. She just started work in the insurance-claims department at the hospital. Donna told me she came across a claim for George Pfeffer. He had a vasectomy last April. And just yesterday Sharon told me she could hardly wait to have another baby. Doesn't that beat all? George must have had it done without telling her!"

"If Sharon turns up pregnant, we'll know something's rotten in Denmark." Janet giggled.

"George is Catholic." Alice sounded shocked. "I

wonder if he confessed to Father Miller? They can't use any birth control, you know. It's a mortal sin."

"Well . . . if you ask me, birth control is the same as abortion!" Roberta sniffed. "There were times when I wished I didn't have five, but the Good Lord saw fit."

Karen took a gulp of her coffee and coughed. She just couldn't believe the conversation going on around her. These women were so narrow-minded, so provincial—it was almost a crime. They preached morality and God's will, but they weren't exactly practicing brotherly love or Christian forgiveness, either. In fact, it appeared to Karen that engaging in vicious gossip was the most popular pastime among her neighbors in Cold Spring.

She looked up to find all eyes on her as she set down her cup. Karen drew a deep breath and plunged in.

"Actually, I think birth control is an individual decision. And abortion is, too. Surely you have to consider the circumstances."

Karen knew she had said too much as the women fell silent. Marilyn frowned and cleared her throat.

"You have a point, of course." Marilyn didn't sound convinced. "But circumstances change and the easiest way out isn't necessarily the right way." There was another long silence as the women avoided Karen's eyes.

"Well . . . I must be getting on home now." Karen set her snack tray down on the plastic Parsons table and stood up. "Thank you so much for inviting me. I'll return the hospitality just as soon as we get the house organized."

The good-byes were friendly and polite, but Karen

noticed that none of the other women made a move to leave. She was sure they couldn't wait to begin to talk about her the moment she was gone.

What a relief it was to be outside. Karen took a deep breath of the warm summer air and sighed deeply. If the children were anything like their mothers, no wonder Leslie had failed to make friends in Cold Spring.

SEVEN

Two weeks had passed since Leslie's ill-fated birthday party and the July day dawned muggy and sweltering. It was too hot to do anything, Karen decided, as she stirred two teaspoons of sugar into Mike's freshly ground coffee and placed the cup on a tray with a plate of Fig Newtons. She hadn't found time to bake and today wasn't a good day to light the oven. At least Mike had an air conditioner for the darkroom. Without it the third floor would be stifling.

Karen picked up the tray and started up the stairs, groaning a bit. She was so clumsy lately. In the past week her weight had skyrocketed and her ankles were swollen. Her energy had all but disappeared. She didn't remember this kind of thing happening when she was pregnant with Leslie, but she was born before the really hot weather set in. Rob Comstock claimed they'd have a lot more heat before the summer was over. It was only mid-July and he'd predicted August would be a killer.

Karen hesitated at the darkroom door, wondering if she should disturb Mike. He'd worked most of the night, checking for light leaks. She knew he was frustrated, but perhaps a little coffee and something to eat would help. She knocked softly, holding the tray in one hand.

"Yes! Come in if you have to." Mike's voice came through the door, impatient and tired.

"I brought you a little snack." Karen breathed in deeply and smiled. Perhaps they could have their coffee together up here. It was deliciously cool with the air conditioner on high. "Did you find the light leak yet, honey?"

Mike's face was a study in irritation. "No. I haven't found the damn leak. Now I have to reprint every one of these and hope it doesn't happen again."

He forced a smile for her benefit, but she could tell he felt more like scowling. "Thanks for the tray, but I can't take a break now if I want to get done on time. Why don't you just leave it on the table?"

Karen set the tray down and backed out, leaving him to his work. He'd probably forget all about the coffee until it was stone cold. At least she'd made the effort. He was working much too hard lately, but Karen had wisely kept her silence. In a sense his problems with the darkroom were her fault. She and Leslie had talked him into buying this house, and building the darkroom had taken longer than he'd expected. Now he was behind schedule and the pressure was on.

She stopped at the hall window and looked out at the lawn. Leslie was sitting under a tree, paging through a book. It made Karen's heart ache to see her daughter alone in their huge yard. She should be out playing with friends or swimming in the river. She understood Leslie's problem, but that didn't solve it. The Cold Spring children weren't very friendly and they had different interests, but Leslie wasn't even trying. Perhaps she'd send Leslie to the store when the list was finished. She might meet some of the other children on the way and invite them home to play. It wasn't good for her to be so isolated.

Karen was sitting at the kitchen table working on the shopping list when Leslie came racing in. "Can I go up to the tower room for a minute, Mom?" she asked. "I want to check something out."

"Just a minute, kitten." Karen wrote *BROWN RICE* on the growing list. "Then I want you to go to the store for me."

"Okay, Mom." Leslie's voice trailed off as she ran for the stairs. She had a new idea for a picture. She'd focus the telescope on the river and do a series of the kids playing in the water. The telescope was wonderful. She could take pictures without even leaving her favorite room.

Leslie bounded up the stairs, then stopped at the third-floor landing and frowned. She'd forgotten which setting to use on her camera. She'd better check with Mike so she wouldn't make a mistake.

Mike was in the darkroom, his head bent over the enlarger, when Leslie knocked on the door. "Just a sec!" he hollered out, hurrying his print a little. It came up as he'd expected it would, and he swore impatiently.

"Okay—come in! What is this, Grand Central Station?"

Leslie pushed open the door cautiously. Now she wished she hadn't bothered Mike. She could have looked up the setting in one of her photography books.

"I'm sorry, Mike," Leslie said contritely. "I just wanted to take a picture of the river through the telescope and I forgot exactly how to do it."

"Can't you see I'm busy now?" Mike ran his fingers through his shaggy hair. He looked a mess, shirt rumpled and eyes red. "We went over this the other day. I told you to use F eight at a thousandth of a second. You focus the telescope, set the camera on infinity, and clamp it on. That's simple enough, isn't it?"

He noticed her silence, and his voice changed. "Hey . . . it's all right, honey." He was ashamed of himself when he saw her lower lip tremble. "I'm just aggravated, that's all. Nothing's going right in here today. I guess it's time to knock off and get some sleep."

Leslie relaxed a bit at Mike's apology. She walked over to look at the prints in the wash and nodded. She could see that Mike had a problem.

"The highlights are really gray, Mike. That resin-coated paper sure is flat, isn't it?"

"It's not the paper. I've got a fog problem somewhere. I figure it's either a light leak or my safety filter's going. It's the third time I printed these negatives this morning and they're still foggy."

Leslie was wise enough not to comment. She could tell that Mike was frustrated. The prints were definitely not good enough for a feature.

"Maybe this house isn't such a good place for a darkroom, after all," Mike said with a sigh. "First we had the dust problem and now this. I'm beginning to think the whole setup's wrong."

Leslie tried to be helpful. "Do you want me to get you some coffee, Mike?"

"No, thanks anyway, honey." Mike rubbed his chin where the bristle was beginning to itch. He needed a shave and a shower. Then he could think clearly and fix whatever was wrong with the setup in here. Actually, what he wanted right now was a stiff drink, and that was out of the question. He'd been on the wagon for three years now, ever since he married Karen.

"If you have to reshoot, I'll help you," Leslie volunteered. She felt better when Mike smiled at her.

"I appreciate that, but reshooting won't solve the basic problem." He ruffled her hair. "I'll pick up a new safety filter this afternoon and see if that does it. If it doesn't, I'll just have to try something else."

Leslie was really sharp to have noticed what was wrong with the prints. Mike thought she was going to make a first-rate photographer someday. He just wished she wasn't such a loner here in Cold Spring.

"Honey, I've been thinking." Mike's expression sobered. "You've been spending too much time in the house lately. Why don't you go out and play? Call Taffy or one of the other kids and invite yourself over. You haven't seen any of them since your birthday party and I think you should make the first move. They'll probably be glad to see you."

Leslie's lips tightened into a straight, stubborn line. "I don't want to see any of them," she declared. "They don't like me, and I don't like them."

"Come on, Leslie. Be reasonable." He put his hand on her shoulder. "These kids just aren't used to you yet, that's all. It always takes a while when you move into a new neighborhood. They'll never get to like you if you don't make the effort. Your mother would be tickled pink if you made a couple of new friends."

"I'll try, Mike." Leslie's voice was very small and she didn't meet his eyes. Mike was wrong, but it would be impolite to argue with him. She knew the Cold Spring kids would never like her, no matter what she did. Mike just didn't understand.

"Run along now, honey." Mike gave her a smile. "The magazine's in a hurry for these."

Leslie closed the door of the darkroom quietly behind her. She really shouldn't have bothered Mike when he was so busy.

"Can I go up to the cupola when I come back, Mom?" Leslie took the shopping list from Karen and folded it carefully. "I want to take some pictures with my new telescope."

"I guess so." Karen smiled. "If you meet any of the kids, you can invite them, too. Taffy might like to see your telescope."

First Mike and now her mother. Leslie sighed deeply. Why was it so important for her to have the Cold Spring kids for friends? She was perfectly happy all by herself.

"I'll ask Taffy if I see her, Mom," Leslie agreed readily. It was easy to agree because she had no intention of running into Taffy or any of the other kids. Most of them would be at the vacant lot or the swimming hole and she didn't have to go near either place. She should be able to get to the store and back without running into anyone.

* * *

The late-morning sun was warm and the air smelled of freshly cut grass and clover. Leslie stretched her legs a little as she walked up the tree-shaded driveway and turned at the sidewalk. She didn't mind running errands at all as long as she didn't meet any of the kids.

She avoided the vacant lot, where she could hear a softball game in progress. She cut through the alley and ran the rest of the way to the store, her key brushing lightly against her chest. She wore it around her neck constantly now; it was like a good-luck charm to her. Of course she didn't think it was magical anymore. Nothing would happen if she held it and squeezed it. At least she was pretty sure nothing would happen, but she hadn't quite dared to try it, not since that awful accident at her birthday party.

The store was cool and Leslie took her time, going up and down the aisles in order and placing a little checkmark in front of the items on her mother's list as she put them in her cart. She didn't want to miss anything and risk being sent back for a forgotten item.

She was almost through now. The cart was partially filled and she needed only a loaf of rye bread to complete the list. Leslie parked the cart behind a pyramid of cans and ran back to the bakery section. She was about to push the cart back out into the aisle when she heard them talking.

"Every time I see her, she's by herself. I don't understand why the other children don't play with her."

Leslie recognized Mrs. Allen's voice. Mrs. Comstock was with her. Leslie had seen them by the meat case.

"It's just the other way around," Marilyn Comstock retorted. "*She* won't play with *them*. Taffy's made the effort. Rob made her invite Leslie over, but she just doesn't fit in. She thinks she's too good for Cold Spring. Look at those designer clothes she wears. Can you imagine dressing a child like that? Plain old JCPenney is good enough for Taffy, and we're not exactly destitute, either."

"You can't blame the child, Marilyn." Roberta Allen sounded righteous. "You can see where she gets her attitudes. Did you notice the suit Karen wore to your house last week? It was raw silk and must have cost a fortune. She'll probably have her maternity clothes designed in Paris!"

Both women laughed loudly and Leslie caught her breath. She stood glued to the spot as Roberta continued.

"I told Bud he had to be nice to Leslie." Roberta's voice was firm. "It's not fair to judge the child by her mother. That big, splashy birthday party was Karen's doing, I'm sure. She was just showing off. The poor little girl was probably embarrassed to death."

"That could be." Marilyn sounded doubtful. "But I think Leslie's just as bad as her mother. Taffy says she's terribly stuck-up. Her manners are dreadful. Do you know she hasn't called once since the party to see how Taffy's hornet stings are healing? All she did was send a little thank-you note for the handkerchiefs."

Leslie's mouth dropped open. She had called twice! And she'd even invited Taffy over on the last call!

"Wasn't that party strange?" Mrs. Allen had lowered her voice a bit. "It doesn't seem right that every child got stung, except Leslie. Something like that almost makes me believe in those old haunted-house stories."

"Haunted houses in this day and age?" Marilyn laughed sharply. "I don't even consider that kind of nonsense! It's the people inside that makes a house look bad and that place has had its share of strange people . . . crazy, old Mrs. Appleton . . . the man from Omaha who shot his wife . . . the young couple that disappeared in the middle of the night in their night-clothes. . . . It just attracts them, I guess."

"I still feel sorry for that little girl." Mrs. Allen lowered her voice even further, but it was clearly audible. "Having a mother who puts on airs, and who knows what the child's real father was like?"

Leslie's knees began to shake and she reached up to finger the key around her neck nervously. She didn't want to hear any more, but she didn't dare leave. Mrs. Allen and Mrs. Comstock would see her and know she'd been listening if she so much as moved. She was trapped here, forced to listen to their awful gossip. The more she thought about it, the more angry she became. Someone should stop them from saying mean things. Someone should tell them it isn't right to tell lies about people.

Without realizing it, Leslie was gripping the key tightly. She gulped when she heard the familiar buzzing voice in her ear. It was the voice from her birthday party. Somehow she had wished hard enough and Christopher was here!

I'll stop them, Leslie. People said awful things about my mother, too, and it isn't nice.

His voice was strong, and Leslie began to tremble.

Suddenly she understood everything. She was holding the key, and her friend had come to help her. Their house really was haunted and Christopher was the ghost!

She panicked. She wanted to drop the key and run for home, but she was too frightened even to move. She was frozen where she stood, holding the key, listening to a ghost.

You don't have to be afraid of me. His voice was very clear now. *I'm your best friend. I'll take care of those old gossips for you. Just watch those cans.*

Leslie squinted as the fluorescent lights in the store flickered brighter and brighter. Her eyes hurt, but she couldn't shut them. They were dilating, the blue receding until only the pupils remained. There was a throbbing in her head and she felt sick and hot. Her knees shook so hard she thought she'd surely fall down.

As she watched, the pyramid of cans started to move slightly, jiggling and trembling at the bottom. Instinctively, she reached out to try to steady them, but it did no good. The shaking motion spread until the top cans swayed precariously. Then they started to tumble down.

"Marilyn! Watch out!" Mrs. Allen's shrill warning came too late. Both women tried to move out of the way, but the cans were hurtling down, raining on their heads and arms, bruising them as they stared up in horror. The cans weren't just falling; they were diving and plummeting, twirling and crashing to the floor as if some invisible hand was throwing them in gleeful spite.

"Ladies? My God! Are you all right?"

Everyone from the front of the store was there now, helping Mrs. Comstock and Mrs. Allen to their feet. There was an obstacle course of cans, Libby's corn and peas and mixed vegetables scattered the length of the aisle.

Leslie moved slowly, pushing her cart carefully to the front of the store. She felt a little dizzy and she leaned against the shopping cart, waiting patiently for the checker to come back to the register. All she wanted to do was go home. There was a commotion in the back of the store and Leslie turned, puzzled. She remotely remembered some cans falling; she remembered the crash. She supposed she could offer to help pick up the cans, but she was just too tired. The minute she got home she'd go up to the tower room and take a nice, long nap.

EIGHT

The traffic was unusually heavy for a Wednesday afternoon and it was broiling hot, even with the windows open all the way. This last week in July was humid and the inside of the truck felt like a steam room. Mike gripped the steering wheel tightly and swore. He could feel the tension in his arms and shoulders, and his neck was stiff and aching. The drive in hadn't been so bad, but the return trip was taking every bit of patience he had left. He barely controlled the urge to smash into the bumper of the rattling white station wagon poking along ahead of him on the two-lane road into town. Twenty miles of following a bad driver had put him in a vile mood.

The house looked deserted. Mike parked at the end of the driveway and called out, but no one answered. He supposed that Karen was busy with her decorating, and Leslie was holed up in her tower room. It gave him an empty feeling to come home and find no one to meet him. Back in the city they used to greet him with happy smiles and hugs and they'd all tell each other about how they'd spent their day. But that hadn't happened since they'd moved out here. Mike was beginning to think the move had been a mistake. Each of them had different interests now, and in this big house it was easy to go their separate ways.

He let himself into the kitchen and gave a holler, but still there was no answer. The antique kitchen chair creaked as he sat down heavily. He lit a cigarette and stared out the window at the tall, straggling bushes in the yard. The rose garden was a mess and the hedge had grown wild. Things had to be pruned and clipped soon or the townspeople would start to talk. Originally he'd planned to hire a gardener, but they couldn't afford it now, not with the money he'd dropped this week on the sportsbook. He had to make up for it next week for sure.

The kitchen was silent and even the bright sun streaming in the west windows did nothing to lift Mike's spirits. They hadn't been happy with him at the magazine. Of course they'd accepted the condo prints; it was too close to deadline to do anything else. But he'd have to come up with something great for his next feature or he'd be in hot water. Even Rose Avery was upset with him and she had been his staunch supporter in the past. Without her help he never could have gotten the job as feature photographer.

"Damn!" Mike growled as the cigarette burned down to scorch his fingers. Everything was going wrong lately and it was just too much to handle. He felt himself losing control. Small things were beginning to add up, and he wasn't able to stop what was happening to all of them. Leslie didn't have a single

friend here in Cold Spring, Karen was so concerned
with the restoration that she didn't have time for anything else, and he was in trouble at the magazine.
And on top of all that, he was losing on the sportsbook. If only he could come up with a great feature
he'd be back in their good graces at the magazine,
and then he'd have a little more money to bet and
play the odds. If there were winnings, he could afford
to hire someone to help Karen with the house. She'd
feel better and take charge of Leslie. With Karen her
normal, energetic self, Leslie would straighten right
out and make some friends here in town. As usual,
everything boiled down to money. And, one way or
another, he had to get some.

Mike stared absently out the window. The sun was
high and the white crushed-stone driveway gleamed
like bits of glass. This was a beautiful estate. With the
grounds done properly and the exterior painted and
fixed, it could be a real showplace. Everyone he knew
would be envious of a home like this. It could be truly
elegant, but it took money and a lot of hard work.
What he wanted to do most was show all those idiots
out there how beautiful an old house could be if you
fixed it up right.

"That's it!" The idea began to take form. He was
sitting on a gold mine here and he'd been too dumb
to see it. Sure, he'd counted on using a shot or two of
their house in his feature on Victorian estates, but
he'd been thinking too small. The Appleton Mansion
would be the perfect subject for a whole series, a
do-it-yourself, fixer-upper special! He'd show a step-
by-step restoration, starting from scratch with the

pictures he'd shot when they first saw the house: the waist-high lawn with the FOR SALE sign out front, the stately brick structure with paint peeling on the trim, the empty rooms with undraped windows. It would kindle the reader's imagination. Then he'd show them exactly how to restore it.

The first step would be the grounds. They'd hire a gardener and re-landscape the place. For the next installment they'd concentrate on the trim and the new paint job. Another installment could focus on the greenhouse as it was restored and filled with plants. Then the inside, room by room. Gradually everything would be done and each major improvement would be a separate installment. Not only would he have a dynamite series, but all their expenses would be fully tax deductible. The whole renovation would be a complete tax write-off!

"How idiotic! Why didn't I think of it before?" He was amazed. Pushing back his chair, he stood up, beaming. He was going up to the darkroom right now to develop those negatives he'd taken the day Rob showed them the house. And if he didn't have enough, he'd shoot more. Then they'd all pitch in and fix this big monster up. The magazine would love it. Rose Avery would love it. Everything was coming together again and it felt great!

"Hey . . ." Mike stopped halfway up the stairs and grinned again. There was another bonus with this idea. He'd mention Cold Spring in the text and get in a free plug for the town. The people here would like that and their kids might be nicer to Leslie.

* * *

   Mike paced the floor as he waited for the completion of the developing process. He sipped his cold coffee and whistled. He'd call Rose tomorrow and see if they could start the series running in the next issue. That meant they'd have to hustle on the house, but it would be worth it. He was positive Rose would authorize an advance on a project this big. And just as soon as he got a little money ahead, he'd hire a housekeeper so Karen could concentrate on the decorating. It would be a family project, something they could work on together. They hadn't done anything together since they moved here.

   At last the timer rang and Mike breathed a sigh of relief as he lifted the film out of the tank. The negatives seemed clear enough. Now he was glad he'd spent all that time looking for the light leak. He certainly wouldn't want to botch up these prints. They had to be perfect. He wanted to show every paint chip and loose shingle so the reader would realize what a huge project it was. Then, every month, they'd see the results of good planning and hard work. This series could run on for a year or more if he wanted to milk it dry. And he could demand more money from the magazine and get it. All his problems would be solved.

   Today Karen was determined to catalog the furniture in the ballroom. Mike was at the magazine and Leslie was busy with her telescope. That meant she had the entire morning free.

Notebook in hand, Karen climbed the stairs. She held the railing tightly. Yesterday she'd fallen and scraped her knee and today she was taking no chances. Her balance was off, but the doctor said that was normal. He blamed it on her sudden weight gain and told her not to be alarmed. This sort of awkwardness was to be expected in the second trimester of pregnancy.

She stopped for breath on the third-floor landing, unable to understand why this pregnancy was so much harder than the first had been. She was terribly out of condition and each day she felt more bloated and uncoordinated. It was such a contrast to her normal state that Karen sometimes felt her awkward body belonged to someone else. The real Karen Houston was slim and energetic, not at all like the tired, clumsy image she saw in the mirror.

With effort Karen forced her mind to more pleasant channels. It did no good to dwell on her condition. She still had four months to go. Thank goodness she had the redecorating to take her mind off things.

It took only a few minutes to list the large items in her notebook. She'd gotten this far before. Mike would have a fit if he knew what she was doing, but someone had to move this furniture around and crawl behind to see what was hidden in the back. He certainly didn't have time to help her.

Karen moved a chair and squeezed through the space. Then she let out a squeal as she discovered a lovely highboy china cabinet, with rounded glass doors. She could hardly wait to bring it down to the dining room. A huge wooden table was stored against the wall, and Karen managed to find all twelve chairs after a careful search. They needed a bit of work, but they were definitely restorable. The price of this house was worth it for the antiques alone.

Two hours passed quickly and Karen's excitement grew. There were several oaken washstands, an old icebox cabinet, a huge knickknack shelf, and a French love seat. There were also assorted lamps, stools, and objects of art too numerous to list. This ballroom was practically a museum.

She pulled the dust cover from a wooden steamer trunk and sneezed twice in the process. Obviously, none of the previous tenants had cared to poke around up here in the dust and the cobwebs. All this furniture was hers. If she had a guideline, she'd restore the house exactly as it was at the turn of the century.

The trunk stubbornly resisted her efforts to open it. Karen broke a fingernail on the brass fasteners and winced. She pushed up, applying pressure strategically, and finally the lid gave a sharp crack. The varnish had stuck in the airless heat of so many summers. She gave another push and it lifted, revealing fold after fold of lace and ivory satin.

"Oh! How lovely!" She lifted the ornate dress from its bed of yellowed tissue paper. This wedding gown could be Amelia Appleton's! It certainly looked like the style of that period. She would put it away, maybe for Leslie's wedding. It was a gown fit for royalty; and Karen sighed, indulging in romantic daydreams as she placed it over a chair next to the trunk.

More clothes turned up under a wooden divider. They would be wonderful dress-up clothes for Leslie. There were ball gowns and silk dresses, hats and gloves, and even high-button shoes. A whole wardrobe from a bygone age was packed in this trunk.

She found a carved wooden box under some dried flowers and examined it closely. The initials *D.A.* were intertwined with roses on the cover. She tried to open it, but it was locked securely. Her curiosity was aroused, but she was obliged to put it aside to open later.

"Marvelous!" Karen's eyes sparkled as she lifted out a huge oil portrait. The inscription read: *DORTHEA APPLETON, DAUGHTER OF WILLIAM AND AMELIA—1885.*

An attractive young woman in her late teens stared out of the frame, her dark hair arranged in a fashionable bun. This painting was a real find. She could hang it over the fireplace in the living room. It would be a great topic of conversation when they invited their first guests.

Karen's heart beat fast as she caught sight of the treasure in the bottom of the trunk. A glass display case fit tightly into the space. Inside the glass was a complete miniature of the house and grounds, a tiny dollhouse done in breathtaking detail. She gazed with disbelief. What an amazing stroke of luck.

Carefully Karen removed the heavy glass case. She opened the top and gasped in admiration for the workmanship. It was superbly built and the roof was hinged to reveal the whole top floor. Now she could see just how the ballroom had been decorated, including the placement of the furniture.

Karen found two other hinging sides, each lifting to reveal a floor and its furnishings. It was as if Amelia Appleton had crafted this delightful miniature just for her. The tiny furniture was detailed and perfect. Every light, picture, and object of art was in its place. It was an exact replica of the house in Amelia's day, down to the rugs on the floors and the paper on the walls.

"Of course," Karen breathed, peering in at the living room. The room was lit by candelabras with the piano at an angle near the inside wall. It was exactly where she planned to place it. Now she didn't need to worry about where to position the other furniture. It was all right here, in breathtaking miniature.

As she gazed at the miniature, enraptured, Karen was filled with an urgent desire to restore the house accurately. She'd make it the same grand mansion Amelia had created in the eighteen hundreds. Most of the furniture was still here, and she'd have the missing pieces duplicated now that she had the miniature for comparison. She was positive that Mike would agree to a total restoration once he saw this marvelous model. Of course they'd have to scrimp and save, but it would be heaven to live in a genuinely restored Victorian mansion. It was like having a child-hood dream come true.

She sat on the dusty floor and stared at the minia-ture for long moments, imagining what life had been like in Amelia Appleton's day. There would be won-derful parties, the ballroom filled with crowds of styl-ishly dressed men and women. Young Dorthea would wear silks and satins hand stitched by talented dress-makers. It would be almost like living in a fairy tale, in the sort of lifestyle Karen had always secretly fan-cied. She wished she could go back in time for just a moment so she could experience growing up in a lovely setting like this.

Lifting the hinged side again, Karen concentrated on the first floor. She had decorated the kitchen almost perfectly. There were only a few minor changes to make and it would match the model. The dining room wouldn't be difficult now that she'd found the table and chairs. She just hoped that the rug in front of the fireplace was up here somewhere. It was a pattern she'd never seen before, and it would be costly to duplicate.

Slightly puzzled, Karen reached in and removed the miniature painting over the fireplace. The paint on the tiny replica was cracking and she could see another picture under it. She chipped away a small portion of the paint and her curiosity grew.

Yes . . . under the pastoral scene was another painting, and Karen chipped and brushed until she had uncovered the original. It was a miniature of Dorthea's portrait! Obviously, Dorthea's likeness had once hung in the place of honor over the fireplace.

"How strange!" Karen mused aloud, rehanging the tiny replica on the model wall. She couldn't imagine why Amelia had replaced her daughter's portrait with such an ordinary picture. It was a complete mystery, but Karen was determined to solve it. There were still trunks to examine, crates and boxes that might provide the answer. There might even be a clue in the locked box.

Karen picked up the box again and turned it in her hands. Something heavy hit against the sides. She was sure that the initials D.A. stood for Dorthea Appleton. She'd leave the box right here and try to open it when there was more light. Solving the mystery of the portrait would be her secret hobby, something to do when Leslie and Mike were busy with their own projects.

As Karen got stiffly to her feet, she noticed that twilight had settled outside. She'd been up here for hours; an entire day had gone by without her noticing. Mike would be back by now and poor Leslie was probably starving. She hadn't even planned what to fix for dinner.

Karen closed the steamer trunk and dusted herself off. She'd whip up something for dinner and then she'd ask Mike to rig a makeshift light up here. They'd have a little coffee after dinner and then she'd show Leslie and Mike her discoveries. Mike would be fascinated by the miniature model of their house, and Leslie would love the wardrobe she'd found. And tomorrow she could start decorating in earnest.

NINE

It was only after he dried the print that he saw it—a small face in the cupola window. At first he thought it was Leslie, but that was impossible. They hadn't even seen the inside of the house when he took this picture. It certainly looked like someone standing there, staring out into the street. Could it be a flaw in the paper?

Mike made another print with the same result. The hazy face was still there. He supposed the blurry image could be a reflection on the windowpane from the trees. It was interesting, in any event. Reflection or whatever, it looked like a child peering out of the tower-room window.

He scratched his head thoughtfully and frowned. The focus was perfect and he didn't have another shot from this angle. It clearly showed the exterior of the house, with the loose shingles on the roof. In order to duplicate the shot he'd have to take down all the drapes in the living room, and Karen wouldn't appreciate that. She'd just finished hanging them last week. It was too much trouble to reshoot. The hazy face wouldn't hurt anything and it was a really good picture.

Prints in hand, Mike ran two flights down to the kitchen. Karen was taking something from the oven and it smelled fantastic.

"Pork chops and scalloped potatoes!" Mike sniffed the air appreciatively. "What's the special occasion? I didn't forget an anniversary or something, did I?"

"You didn't forget anything." Karen laughed as she set the casserole on a trivet. "I'm just celebrating tonight. You wouldn't believe all the antiques I found in the old ballroom, honey! Almost all the original furniture is there, and after dinner I've got a real surprise for you."

"I've got a surprise for you, too." Mike smiled, reaching out to pat the portion of Karen's anatomy closest to him. "I just came up with a fantastic series for the magazine, and you and Leslie are part of it."

"I'm part of what?" Leslie rushed into the kitchen. She saw the prints in Mike's hand. "Is that the fantastic series?"

"Just sit down for a minute and I'll tell you." Mike put his arm around Leslie and drew Karen closer. "Remember all those pictures I took of our house right before we bought it?"

"Ohhh . . . nice, Mike!" Leslie gasped as Mike spread out the prints. "These are great! Not like those awful condo pictures at all!"

Mike winced. Leslie didn't pull any punches when it came to his work, but she was generous with her praise now. She and Karen examined the prints and exclaimed over them until Mike couldn't wait any longer to spring the rest of his surprise.

"You're looking at the first installment in a series about renovating an old house," he explained, "and the old house is ours. We'll run three or four pages every month until the project's completed. I want to take lots of exterior shots before the grounds are landscaped and after. Then we'll get some mileage out of painting the trim. See those loose shingles up there on the cupola? We'll have those repaired and take another shot of that. Then we'll—"

"Mike!" Leslie interrupted, pointing at the cupola window. "You've got me in this one. Look at that! You can almost see my face!"

"I made the same mistake, kiddo." Mike chuckled. "It's just a reflection, though. It can't be you. I took that one on the first day, before Rob unlocked the house. You were standing right next to me in the yard, remember?"

"It looks like her, Mike." Karen peered closely at the photograph. "Are you sure you didn't take this one after we moved in?"

"I'm positive," Mike assured her. "I used the roll back on the Linhof that day and I haven't used it since. I know these were shot before Rob took us inside."

"It is a strange coincidence." Karen blinked and looked again. "That reflection certainly looks like a child."

Leslie stared down at the photograph and frowned. She remembered exactly when Mike had snapped that picture and he was right. She had been standing right next to him, taking her own pictures with her Leica. It wasn't her face in the tower-room window. It couldn't be.

She gave a small cry. It wasn't her face, but it could be the ghost's. This could be a picture of Christopher.

"What's the matter honey?" Mike turned to look at her. "Is something wrong?"

"I know what it is—it's a picture of that ghost!" Leslie's voice shook. "I heard Mrs. Allen say our house was haunted!"

"That's a good one!" Mike laughed and patted the top of Leslie's head. "I tell you what, Leslie . . . you take this picture and keep an eye out for the ghost. If you find him, we'll sell this series to the *National Enquirer.* Then we'll all be rich."

"Mike!" Karen's voice was sharp. "Don't make fun of her! Now, calm down, honey." Karen could see Leslie was close to tears. "Our house isn't haunted. It's just a reflection, like Mike said. You know how silly it is to believe in haunted houses. They always turn out to be fakes."

"Your mother's right. Mrs. Allen was just teasing. People always make up ghost stories about old houses when they're empty for a long time. There isn't any ghost here. I can promise you that."

"But there might be, Mike." Leslie was insistent. "You don't know for sure. There could be a ghost here and you'd never even know."

Karen could see they were getting nowhere. It was best to change the subject and take Leslie's mind off haunted houses and ghosts.

"You said that Leslie and I were part of the series," she reminded Mike. "Just where do we fit in?"

"I'll take pictures while you two redecorate." Mike patted Leslie awkwardly. He hadn't meant to upset her with his teasing. "We'll make this a family project and your names will be in the article. How does that sound?"

"Wonderful!" Karen looked down at her daughter and gave a sigh of relief as Leslie nodded. Right after dinner she'd show them the miniature. It would take Leslie's mind off her fears.

Leslie was too upset to eat very much, but luckily her parents didn't notice. She forced a smile and pretended to listen to their conversation, but her mind was far away. Mike's picture proved everything. The voice in her head wasn't her imagination. Christopher was a ghost. She'd spoken to a boy who was haunting their house. And she couldn't tell Mike or Mom, no matter how much she wanted to. They'd think she was crazy. Maybe she *was* crazy. This couldn't be happening to her. They'd never believe her, never!

At last the meal was over. Mike found an extension cord and a trouble light and Leslie followed them up to the ballroom.

"It's incredible, honey." Mike hung the light on a nail and stared at the miniature in its glass case. "I'll take some pictures of this and we'll run a full-scale comparison in the magazine. This model's a work of art in its own right."

Leslie hung back, keeping in the shadows. Mike and her mother were so excited about the miniature that they didn't notice her silence.

"That's not all I found," Karen said proudly, pulling the portrait out into the light. "Just look at this! It was in the trunk, too, where it's been for almost a hundred years. It's a portrait of Dorthea Appleton, Amelia's daughter."

Mike nodded as he examined the painting. "Let's hang it downstairs, honey. It'll add an authentic touch."

Karen agreed. "We should hang it over the fireplace just like it is in the model. See, Mike? Even the pictures are duplicated in miniature. Mrs. Appleton had another picture there, but Dorthea was under it. She must have changed it for some reason. If I poke around enough up here, maybe I'll find out why."

Leslie trudged along as they carried the model downstairs and set it on a table in the living room. She stood back, a small figure alone, as Karen and Mike exclaimed over the details, discussing wallpaper patterns and furniture. She wanted to join in the fun they were having, but she was still too upset.

"Leslie? Don't you want to help us plan the wallpaper?" Karen tried to draw her close, but Leslie pulled back.

"I—I'm really tired, Mom. Do you mind if I go up to bed now?"

"Of course not, kitten." Karen smiled warmly. "Don't forget to turn off the light in your room when you go to sleep. You left it on all night last night."

They were silent a moment, listening to Leslie's footsteps on the stairs. Then Mike frowned.

"I turned her light off a couple of times last week, myself," he remarked. "Maybe you should buy her a night-light, Karen. I think she's afraid of the dark."

"But she's never been afraid of the dark before." Karen looked thoughtful. Mike could be right. All children went through stages, and Leslie hadn't been acting herself lately. Perhaps this ghost business was really scaring her.

"I'll buy one tomorrow," she agreed. "Now, honey—what shall we do about fixing the dining-room chairs?"

Leslie looked at the print again when she got to her room. She was positive it was a picture of Christopher. She shivered and switched on her brightest light. It was kind of scary up here all alone.

Unconsciously, she reached up to hold the key for comfort, and then she remembered. Her hand dropped quickly back down to her side. She'd found the key because Christopher helped her. Whenever she touched it, he spoke to her. Maybe she should throw it away or put it back in the rose garden, where she'd found it. She just wasn't sure what to do.

Leslie sighed deeply. Christopher had said he was her friend. Did ghosts lie? He hadn't hurt her. Actually, Christopher had protected her. He had kept the hornets from stinging her at the birthday party. And he had stopped Mrs. Allen and Mrs. Comstock from gossiping. At least she thought he'd done all those things, unless it really was a coincidence, as Mike would say. What should she do?

She stood undecided for a moment and then got quickly into her warmest nightgown. She was very careful not to touch the key. She climbed into bed and pulled the blanket up, almost covering her head. That was better. She didn't feel quite so scared anymore. Was it dangerous, having a ghost for a friend? Would something bad happen to her? Leslie wished she had someone to ask. She closed her eyes, her mind troubled, and slipped into an uneasy sleep.

TEN

It was the first time they'd been out of the house for days. Karen started the truck and backed slowly out of the driveway. Leslie sat next to her on the seat, her face cloudy. Leslie didn't want to go to the bazaar, either, but everyone would say they were being unfriendly if they didn't put in an appearance. And they had to deliver their contribution. It was a matter of courtesy and a way of showing themselves to be part of the community.

When Marilyn Comstock had called and asked for donations, Karen had agreed reluctantly. She was simply too busy with the house to put up homemade preserves or to make craft items. Then, luckily, Mike came up with an answer to the problem. Thank goodness it was possible to buy what she didn't have the time or the inclination to make.

"Here's five dollars, kitten." Karen drew a crumpled bill from her purse and handed it to Leslie. "Make sure you buy something from the ladies . . . anything. It's for charity."

"Okay, Mom." Leslie looked grim. She hoped her

mother wouldn't spend very much time at the bazaar. She didn't want to run into any of the Cold Spring kids.

Karen's headache didn't start until they rounded the corner. It grew steadily worse as they drove down Main Street and up the hill. By the time they found a parking place in front of the church, her face was white with pain.

"What's the matter, Mom?" Leslie looked worried.

"Headache," Karen said through stiff lips. The sound of her own voice made the throbbing worse and she winced as she reached out to shut off the motor. She thought it was strange; with all the fresh country air you'd think her headaches would be less frequent. Since they'd moved to the house, she found once in a while she'd be totally knocked out by them. But she could never predict when they'd come or go. "You take in the jelly and buy something for both of us." She handed Leslie another ten dollars. "Say I have a headache and hurry, honey. I want to get home and take some aspirin."

Karen closed her eyes as Leslie lifted the jelly out of the truck and ran inside. The throbbing tightness at her temples was excruciating.

Leslie was back in less than five minutes and Karen gave a grateful sigh as she set the truck in motion again. She began to feel a little better when she'd made a U-turn and started for home. The pain lessened slightly with every block they drove, fading to a dull ache as she pulled into their driveway.

"Whew!" Karen drew a relieved breath. "Get me some aspirin and a glass of water, will you, honey? I'm going to sit down."

Her headache was almost gone by the time Leslie

brought the aspirin bottle. Karen swallowed three, just to be safe, and smiled. "Now let's see what you bought."

Karen opened the package and glanced inside. Her eyes widened and she made a face. "Oh, great, Leslie—just what we need!"

Leslie giggled as her mother drew out two purple-and-green pot holders. "You said to get anything."

"I think you did it on purpose." Karen laughed. "Now, what's this?"

"It's a doll." Leslie practically doubled over with laughter. "See that tie at the bottom of her skirt? You put a roll of toilet paper inside and it sits on the bathroom shelf so you've always got a spare. Mrs. Ness made it."

"I should have guessed." Karen shook her head.

"There's some strawberry jam and a box of fudge in the bottom of the bag." Leslie looked hopeful. "Would you like to try a piece of candy right now?"

"That's just what I need." Karen pulled Leslie close and gave her a hug. "And because you're such a super shopper, I'll let you have that precious toilet-paper doll for the bathroom . . . on *your* end of the hall!"

"*J-A-L-A-P-E-N-O* jelly." Janet held up a jar and raised her eyebrows. "I wonder what it is! Have you ever heard of it before, Marilyn?"

Marilyn took the jar and read the label. "Jalapenos?" She shuddered. "They're hot peppers! You don't make jelly out of hot peppers! Is this some kind of joke?"

"It's from Karen Houston." Roberta came up to

the table. "Leslie brought it in. There's twenty-four jars of it in that box over there. Leslie said it was her mother's donation to the bazaar."

"That's Karen Houston for you." Marilyn gave an exasperated sigh. "When we ask her for a donation, she brings something nobody in their right mind would eat. It just shows what kind of taste that family has. They're really odd, you know? And downright unfriendly, always keeping to themselves. I haven't been invited over once to see all that fancy redecorating they're doing."

"She didn't even have the nerve to bring it in herself." Roberta sniffed. "She sent Leslie with some excuse about a headache. Now, if that isn't a slap in the face, I don't know what is. Can't see how they expect to make any friends at all in this town. Well, let's toss this out before some poor unsuspecting person buys a jar and tries to make a jelly sandwich."

ELEVEN

"You're sure you can do it?" Karen clutched the phone so tightly her knuckles turned white. Two weeks had passed since they'd photographed the miniature and sent out pictures of the couch. At last someone had responded!

"Cream-colored satin . . . that's right . . . as close as you can come to the material in the photograph. Yes, I realize it'll be expensive . . . eighteen hundred? Oh, dear!"

She bit her lower lip sharply as the furniture maker explained the painstaking skill that was necessary to duplicate the intricate carving on the arms and legs. She didn't have time to shop around for a lower estimate. It was the second week in August and she had promised Mike the parlor would be done by September first.

"All right." Karen sighed in resignation. No one else could do it and she had to pay the price. "And you can deliver by September first? Fine, then. I'll mail the check today so you can start immediately."

"What was that?" Mike appeared in the doorway, unshaven and rumpled. He'd been up in his darkroom all night again and he rubbed his red-rimmed eyes.

"Sebastian Furniture in St. Paul can do the sofa." Karen poured him a cup of coffee and set it on the table. "They promised delivery by September first. The only bad news is the price—eighteen hundred."

"Can they duplicate it exactly?" Mike's mouth tightened as Karen nodded. He didn't want to lay out eighteen hundred dollars for a sofa, but it was the focal point of the room. The pictures of the miniature were due to run in the September issue; and now that they'd committed themselves to the restoration, they had to carry through. Rose wanted the parlor for the October issue and that meant they had less than a month before the deadline.

"We can always make do with something else"— Karen's voice was hesitant—"but that piece is one of a kind. Nothing we can buy in a regular outlet will even come close, Mike."

"Then we'll have to do it, won't we?" Mike shook his head and looked pained. "Just make sure to keep all the receipts. We're going to have one hell of a tax write-off."

"Of course, dear." Karen let her breath out in a relieved sigh. Thank goodness Mike realized that the sofa was necessary to preserve the character of the room.

A tiny worry line appeared on Karen's forehead as she stared up at Mike. He looked terrible. There were dark circles under his eyes and his hands were shaking. He'd never looked this tired before.

"Why don't you try to get some sleep, Mike?" Her

voice was filled with concern. "Don't you think you're overdoing it a bit? Working too hard?"

"I've got to, if we want to meet the deadlines." Mike slurped a mouthful of coffee and grimaced. He was sick to death of coffee. Karen had hooked up an old percolator in the darkroom and he'd been swigging the stuff all night. Everything was going so slowly and he had trouble concentrating. This series had to be his best work, but he wasn't satisfied with anything he'd done so far. What he really wanted was something to take away the taste of stale cigarettes, but he couldn't bear the thought of breakfast. His stomach was churning and he blinked to clear his vision.

"Another hour and I ought to be through. Then I'll sleep for a couple of hours and run in with the prints. Call a gardener, will you? The grounds have to be done and ready to shoot in two weeks—just the area around the house for now. We'll cover the rose garden and the greenhouse later. Maybe Rob can suggest somebody around here who does gardening cheap."

"I'll do it right away, honey . . . but really, Mike, you ought to think about getting a little more rest, or at least some food in your—" Karen stopped in midsentence as she realized she was talking to an empty room. Mike was clumping up the stairs to his darkroom again.

Karen shook two aspirins out of the bottle on the kitchen table and washed them down with her coffee. She could feel another headache coming on. Two weeks ago, when she'd first found the miniature, she'd been so sure everything was looking up. Now she knew better, and her tension headaches were coming back. It seemed as though their lives were in a continual crisis. Leslie was still alone and moody. She spent all her time in the tower room or out in the yard by herself. Karen had taken Mike's advice about buying a night-light, but she still found the overhead fixture burning brightly in the morning. Leslie was having nightmares.

Then there was Mike. Karen sighed and pressed her hand to her head. He was running things around here like a general, giving her orders when she knew perfectly well what had to be done. Every time they talked he gave her another task to add to her list.

She looked down at her notebook, open to the section on the parlor: *Clean fireplace, order new granite slab for mantel, polish gas fixtures, clean and rehang drapes, repair Oriental rug, replaster and hang paper, reposition artwork. Deadline: September 1.*

With a sigh she turned the page to the dining room: *Resurface parquet floor, clean wainscoting, locate china for display, order drapes, repair chairs, fix chandelier. Deadline: September 15.*

Karen shut the book with a snap. The worst of it was that Mike didn't care if things were done well, with complete authenticity. She was sure that he'd approve of stapling the wallpaper to the walls as long as he could save time and paperhanger fees. It was all just another magazine piece to him. All he cared about was his damned darkroom. Once the feature was finished, he might even want to sell the house and buy another place to fix up and photograph for the magazine!

"No!" Karen's voice was anguished. He couldn't do that! Didn't he realize how important this house was to her and Leslie? It was the only house for her, the only house for them. She'd never forgive him if he sold it. The house had given Karen a sense of the past. She felt that she was part of a family—the Appletons. It filled a void, and it gave her a purpose—a reason to wake up every morning.

"I'm just tired." Karen spoke the words aloud and she was surprised at how weary her voice sounded. And she looked every bit as exhausted as she felt. She hadn't been sleeping well, alone in her beautiful antique bed. Mike spent most nights in the darkroom and she awoke at the slightest sound, padding down the hallway on bare feet to check on Leslie at least twice a night. And when she was finally in bed, she tossed and turned all night, planning, going over details in her mind.

Karen pushed back her chair resolutely. Calling Rob about the gardener could wait. The wallpaper selection could wait. The whole house could wait for a couple of hours while she took a much-needed break.

Karen armed herself with tools and climbed the stairs to the ballroom. She deserved a little time to herself, and she was determined to get the cover off the carved wooden box to find out what was inside.

It took a long time, but finally, after careful manipulation of her tools, Karen managed to pry off the lock. She lifted the lid and frowned when she saw what was inside. Old books bound in leather . . . somehow she'd expected something else.

"What on earth?" Karen's voice was a mere whisper as she opened the first book and began to read.

They were Dorthea Appleton's diaries, this volume dated January of 1890.

The Midwest is so barren. How I long for Boston again. I am pining for color and gaiety, longing for romance. I'm only seventeen; naturally, surrounded as I am by granite masons and farmers, I suffer an empty and utterly boring existence!

Karen smiled. Poor Dorthea was obviously experiencing the restlessness of youth. She was sure that life here wasn't that boring. Such a pretty girl must have been very popular.

Karen stopped to smile again as a passage written in mid-June caught her eye.

He has come. I am alive again! Kirby Shaw. He is a portraitiste, having studied in Paris under Duval himself. He brings the news from Boston. Silk is in fashion and running to greens this season. He is doing a portrait of Mary. If I were she, I would be enraptured. Mother has been promising to have my portrait done for well over two years. I shall ask Father to commission Kirby this very afternoon!

Karen laughed aloud. There, that's more like it. Such enthusiasm! The diary was a peek into the past, into the life of young Dorthea, who had actually lived in this lovely mansion. She might have danced right here, on this very spot.

Kirby Shaw . . . Karen wrinkled her forehead in concentration. Yes, his name was on the portrait downstairs. Dorthea had convinced her father. But why had the painting been hidden in the bottom of the trunk? Eagerly Karen read on.

He loves me! He told me so!

The entry was dated early July. It was written in Dorthea's elaborate hand, but the letters were huge, filling the whole page. They were in love!

Karen glanced quickly over the next few entries. Dorthea feared her father's disapproval. Their love must be kept a secret until the time was right. Kirby would be an unsuitable match until he had gained recognition. Poor Dorthea.

Karen stopped at a page that contained several angry ink blots. Catching her breath, she read Dorthea's angry words.

Mary came to call this afternoon. She said that Kirby sought to compromise her one night in the moonlight. She is lying! I am convinced Kirby would not touch the hem of her gown, much less kiss her as brazenly as she claims. Mary is a poor foolish girl. I wanted to shout that Kirby loved me, but I kept our promise. Mary is woefully ignorant.

Karen raised her eyes from the diary with a start as she heard Mike calling her name. He sounded impatient and she got quickly to her feet.

It took her a moment to pull back from the past. She blinked and steadied herself, still caught up in Dorthea's story. It was entrancing, like reading a

Victorian novel—a glimpse into the life of a woman who had lived and died years ago, a woman who had gone to fancy-dress balls wearing lace, a girl who had fallen in love with a handsome artist. She wasn't sure she wanted to come back to reality, to her own not-so-glamorous time and place—coping with housework, Mike's demands, and Leslie's strange moods. She wanted to hide here in the past, where life was romantic, and people so cultured and well mannered.

"Coming, Mike!" Karen shouted, forcing her mind back to the present. This was 1972 and her husband and daughter needed her. She closed the diary quickly, feeling a little guilty about taking so much time for her own private thoughts and pleasure. She'd have plenty of time to read when she had finished the work around here.

Karen carried the carved box down to the bedroom and slipped it into her desk drawer. It was strange how real Dorthea's life seemed to her. Perhaps it was the restoration, working on the house, bringing back the appearance of Dorthea's time period. It made the young girl seem so real. Karen half expected to see Dorthea emerge from the doorway and take her place at the old desk in the corner of the bedroom to write another entry in her diary.

"Hey! How about some breakfast for a starving man?" Mike's voice carried up the stairway. Karen blinked and closed the drawer hastily. She'd make some breakfast for Mike and then she'd get started on the woodwork in the parlor. There were a million things to do and never enough time to do them.

* * *

At the end of the day Mike felt he was finally entitled to a break. The layout was good. He smiled with satisfaction and stubbed out a cigarette in the overflowing ashtray. That about did it for today. Rose would be pleased and he could hardly wait to show her. Now all he had to do was drive into the Cities and he'd be back in time for dinner with Karen and Leslie.

"Where did I put them, damn it?" Mike grumbled impatiently as he rummaged through the antique storage chest. He was sure he remembered putting some print folders in here somewhere. Perhaps they had fallen down in the bottom of this huge old wooden cupboard.

He reached in as far as he could and felt around in the back. The shelf tipped and his finger scraped against some sort of catch.

Curious, Mike knelt down and examined the space carefully. What he had taken for a solid piece of wood was a false bottom. As he released the catch and raised it, his eyes widened in astonishment.

"Well, I'll be!" Mike drew out a dusty bottle and pursed his lips as he read the label. Napoleon brandy bottled in 1897! This was a real find and there appeared to be a full case here. Twelve bottles of valuable, aged brandy. What an incredible discovery!

Mike ran the tip of his tongue over his lips. He'd never tasted brandy this fine, but he could imagine the smooth, rich gold ambrosia, created to be sipped and savored. For superior brandy of this vintage he could get two, maybe three hundred dollars a bottle at a collector's auction.

"I suppose I should sell it. . . ." His voice trailed off in a sigh. Of course it would bring in some badly needed cash, but it might be worth even more if he waited a couple of years. He knew he didn't dare taste it personally, but that didn't mean he couldn't appreciate it as a good investment. One thing for sure, he wouldn't tell Karen he'd found it. She'd be worried sick if she knew there was any liquor in the house. She'd insist on selling it right away so it wouldn't be a temptation to him. No, he'd never mention it. It would be safe right here, hidden where it had been for years and years.

Mike licked his lips again and sighed. He wasn't getting any work done just kneeling here and staring at the brandy. He replaced the bottle with reverence and dropped the false bottom back into place. It was almost a sin to find brandy this fine and not even taste it.

He grinned again as he slipped the prints into their folders. It gave him a curious sense of well-being, having his own secret cache of great brandy. Karen was absolutely right about this house holding all sorts of antique treasures.

TWELVE

"Sure is hot enough for August. Weatherman says the heat won't break for another month." Hal Jenkins carried the heavy rolls of wallpaper upstairs and set them in the hall, where Karen had indicated. He was puffing a little from the steep climb, but he didn't really mind. After all, Mrs. Houston couldn't very well carry them in her condition, and Hal had been brought up to be polite. His mother always said there was man's work and there was woman's work, and carrying heavy rolls of wallpaper was definitely a job for a man.

"You folks sure do have this place fixed up nice. I'd never believe it was the same place. Bonnie and me were inside, back a couple of years ago, just taking a look around. Bonnie gets a kick out of these big old houses. Just one more load from the truck and I'll be through."

Hal took in all the details as he went down the stairs and out to his pickup again. Bonnie would ask a million questions when he got back to the store. The whole town was buzzing about these new folks.

Rumor had it they were weird, but he thought Mrs. Houston seemed nice enough. A little too quiet, maybe, but that didn't bother him. It was kind of nice to meet a quiet woman for a change. One thing for sure—if Bonnie could see this place now, she wouldn't call it a run-down, old claptrap. It must have cost a pretty penny to fix it up like this!

"Well, that's the last of them, ma'am." Hal knew the time had come and he dreaded what he had to do next. Mrs. Houston seemed all right, but she was an out-of-towner and you just couldn't tell about folks if you didn't know their families. He hated to ask for a payment right away, but Bonnie had good business sense and she was usually right.

The story around town was that these city folks had spent a bundle on decorating. Marilyn Comstock said they went through money like water. Before he'd left the store this morning, Bonnie insisted that he charge for the wallpaper on delivery instead of sending a bill as they usually did.

"Uh . . . ma'am?" Hal couldn't quite meet her eyes. "We have to ask for payment on delivery this time— a little problem with the billing. We've got too much outstanding on the books."

"That's quite all right, Mr. Jenkins." Karen smiled at the stoop-shouldered, nervous man. "Would you like a check now, or could you wait until my husband comes back from the Cities?"

"Well . . . I'd rather have it now, if it's not too much trouble." Hal reached into his pocket for a handkerchief to wipe his sweating face.

"Why don't I pour you a cup of coffee and then I'll

make out the check," Karen suggested. "We'll go over the bill in the kitchen and you can write a receipt."

"That sure would be kind of you, ma'am." Hal followed her back down the stairs. She hadn't acted the least bit insulted when he asked for the money right away. Bonnie said he didn't have any tact, but this time she was wrong. He had handled the whole money business just fine.

Karen hurried back up to the third floor after Mr. Jenkins was settled in the kitchen with his coffee. She was puffing with exertion as she reached the landing and opened the darkroom door. Mike's workroom was a mess, but she knew he kept the checkbook up here somewhere.

"It's got to be here!" Karen rummaged hastily through the drawers in Mike's desk. He handled all the money and took care of their checkbook. It had been a relief not to have to worry about payments and receipts, but now she wished she'd paid a little more attention to Mike's accounting system. Of course there was bound to be enough money to pay Mr. Jenkins's ninety-dollar bill. Mike had been paid the previous Friday.

"Aha!" She opened the checkbook and glanced at the balance in amazement. One hundred and fifty-three dollars? Perhaps Mike hadn't deposited his paycheck from the magazine yet. No . . . there it was, last Friday's deposit initialed by the bank teller. Where had their money gone?

She didn't take time to examine it closely until Mr. Jenkins left. Then she carefully added up the bills Mike had paid this week. Over nine hundred dollars had been paid out to various creditors, but that didn't explain why they were left with such a small balance. There should be at least a thousand dollars left.

Cash—$300: a small notation in printing on the side of the register . . . and a few days later, *Cash— $500.* Thoroughly puzzled, Karen began to skim the earlier entries. Last month Mike had drawn out over two thousand dollars in cash!

She looked up as she heard the truck in the driveway. Mike was back early. Now she could find out about those withdrawals.

"Hi, honey—I'm home." Mike came into the kitchen and poured himself a cup of coffee. "How's everything with my talented decorator today?"

"Fine, I guess," Karen responded automatically. "I don't understand these notations, dear. I had to pay Mr. Jenkins for the wallpaper and I noticed our balance is really low. How did we spend over two thousand dollars in cash last month?"

Mike glanced at Karen's bewildered face and almost groaned aloud. For a moment he was speechless. Why hadn't he taken the checkbook with him when he left this morning? She had no business going through his things!

"I told you I'd take care of the finances. We're in fine shape. . . . I just had a lot of overhead last month, that's all."

"But two thousand in cash?" Karen couldn't keep the note of anxiety from her voice. "I thought we paid all the bills by check so we'd have receipts."

"Well, sometimes businesses give discounts for cash." Mike knew he'd better change the subject in a hurry. Karen was asking too many questions he couldn't answer. "Let's see the wallpaper, honey. Did you get that flocked stuff you wanted?"

Karen nodded, but her mind wasn't on wallpaper. There was something about the cash withdrawals Mike wasn't telling her. Of course she could demand to know where the money had gone, but he'd think she didn't trust him. He'd been handling the finances for three years now and they hadn't run into any trouble yet. Maybe it would be wiser just to drop the whole thing. She didn't want to nag him or sound suspicious. A wife should have more faith in her husband.

She forced a cheerful smile. "The wallpaper's upstairs. Mr. Jenkins carried it up for me. You should have seen him, Mike—he said he'd seen the house a couple of years ago and he was really impressed by all the work we've done."

As Mike inspected the rolls of wallpaper, Karen decided to keep a closer eye on their finances in the future. She didn't need Mike's permission to check their expenditures once in a while. After all, they were in this together.

THIRTEEN

Leslie stood by her telescope, frowning. Sunlight streamed in through the high windows, and the breeze from the east was tantalizing. She could spend hours up here with her telescope, taking pictures, trying out new lenses. Or she could just gaze out of the windows, taking in the view in all its different aspects. But, of course, her mom would be much happier if she went outside to play. Leslie knew her mother was worried because she didn't play with the town kids.

Leslie sighed and made up her mind. She'd go out right now before she lost her nerve. She'd go down to the river and she'd try to be nice and friendly. Through the telescope she'd seen some kids jumping and swimming in the cool water and it looked like fun. Maybe they'd like to have their pictures taken if she promised them prints.

Leslie felt the key resting warmly against her chest. She kept it there still, and it gave her confidence. She had finally come to a decision about the ghost. If Christopher wanted to be her friend, she'd be his.

Ghosts had been real live people before they died and Christopher was a boy ghost. Once he'd been a kid, just like her. And just having the key there, if she ever needed it, made her feel a whole lot better, more sure of herself, somehow.

Karen was in one of the bedrooms on the second floor, hanging the new curtains. Leslie found her sitting on a stool, hooking drapery pins on a rod.

"Here, let me help you with that, Mom." Leslie started to lift the other end of the curtain. "You shouldn't be up on that stool, you might fall."

"I've got it. Don't bother, Leslie." Karen's tone was impatient, and she tried to soften it. "I'm really all set, honey. Why don't you run along?"

Mike was working away from home much more lately. This week he was shooting exteriors of highrises in St. Paul, commuting every day. He left early and didn't return until long after dark. And Leslie was usually off by herself. That was fine with Karen. Now she could do things her way. There was still so much to be done.

"Well, if you don't mind, then could I go down to the river and play?" Leslie asked hesitantly. "I saw a whole bunch of kids down there when I was looking through my telescope."

"Of *course* you can, kitten!" Karen was so surprised she almost dropped the box of drapery pins. Leslie had never asked to go to play before. Usually, she had to be coaxed even to go to the store, and now she was asking to join the other kids, all on her own. Things were definitely looking up.

There was a big smile on Leslie's face as she left the house. Mom was glad she was going out to play. Her smile stayed in place until she stepped outside the iron gate. Then all her old fears seemed to jump out at her at once and she wanted to run right back inside where she was safe. But she had her key to protect her, and at least one good friend—Christopher.

Drawing a deep breath, Leslie forced her feet to move. She took the dirt path leading to the river, her Nikes kicking up puffs of dust as she walked. She never would have volunteered to do this if it weren't for Mom, but now that she was outside in the fresh summer air, she couldn't help feeling good. The sun was warm on her back and she could feel the tender skin on her legs prickle with the heat.

There was a light breeze and Leslie's hair blew around her face in a shining cloud. It was a beautiful day, with high white clouds floating in a clear blue sky. Birds were singing in the trees along the path and there was a lazy hum from summer insects as they darted over her head. A fat gray squirrel scampered across the path in front of her and disappeared into the bushes, emerging several yards away to scurry up a tree. He circled around and around, ears perking up alertly to see if she would give chase.

"You're safe, squirrel. I just want to be your friend," Leslie said with a laugh. His eyes were bright and sparkling and he was so cute she almost wished she could take him home. There were probably squirrels in her own yard if she went out and looked for them. Maybe Mom would let her feed them if she asked.

The air was sweet and fresh and Leslie took big gulps of it as she walked along. It was wonderful to be outside. As she got closer to the river, there was a damp, exciting scent of cool water and lush green undergrowth. The sunbeams streaked through the tall trees, slanting on a granite rock to make it sparkle like a huge jewel.

As she got closer to the swimming hole, Leslie could hear the shouts of children as they played, laughter and catcalls, good-natured jeering and an occasional splash as someone jumped in. Everyone seemed to be having a great time and Leslie's spirits rose. This might be more fun than she had anticipated.

"Watch me stand on my head!" There was a splash and a loud burst of laughter. As Leslie pushed her way into the clearing, she saw kids on inner tubes floating in the lazy river, plump black rings bobbing on the sparkling water line, arms pumping and splashing furiously to change direction in the slight current. Smaller children played in the shallow water, splashing and screaming in excitement, sand pails and shovels abandoned in bright disarray on the bank. A young mother watched from the shade of a tree, idly turning pages in a magazine while her children played. Frequently one of them would dash up with a stone or a snail shell to add to the growing pile at her feet.

Leslie smiled. It was a lovely family scene and perfect for a picture. She moved nearer and snapped one of the children playing. She'd find out who they were and give their mother a print.

"Gary Wilson! Be careful!" the young mother called out, her voice sharp as water showered up around her children. Gary's head popped up from the water and Leslie heard him laugh as a small child squealed in fright.

"Sorry, Mrs. Jackson," he called out, not sounding sorry at all. He ran from the water, tanned legs flashing as he streaked for the shore and grabbed a rope dangling from a strong branch overhanging the river.

Leslie shivered as she watched him. Ever since her birthday party she'd been afraid of Gary Wilson, the big bully.

He was climbing up the riverbank now, heading for the huge granite rock with the rope in his hand. He gave a yell as he reached the top of the rock and grabbed the rope up high with both hands. Then he leaped up into the air and swung out, yelling all the while, and dropping off at the top of the arc to land in the deepest part of the river.

"Be careful, Gary!" the young mother called out again. "That's dangerous, and you're setting a bad example for the younger children."

This time Gary didn't even bother to reply, but Leslie could see why Mrs. Jackson was concerned. The tip of a large rock protruded from the water, directly in the path of the homemade swing. The arc of Gary's swing carried him right over the partially submerged granite slab. A young child, attempting the same trick, might jump short and land on that sharp rock.

"Time to go home now!" the young mother called out, glancing at her watch. She began gathering up sand pails and shovels. "Sally, you take Billy's pail. Billy, you can help Mother carry your rocks. Come on, Tina . . . you too. We have to go and meet Daddy."

Leslie had been so interested in watching the rope swing, she hadn't noticed that the kids in the inner tubes were gone. The young mother was herding her children toward the path, and now she was left alone at the river with Gary. It was time for her to go, too, while she could get away unnoticed. She didn't want to be alone with Gary Wilson.

"Hey, Leslie!" Gary hollered out, spotting her at the riverbank. "How come you got your fancy camera? Do you want to take a picture of me swinging?"

She didn't really want a picture of Gary Wilson. He'd been hateful at her birthday party. Leslie was about to refuse when she remembered how happy her mother had been when she went out to play. Maybe, if she took Gary's picture, he'd be a little nicer to her. Then he'd tell all the rest of the kids that she was all right.

"I'll take your picture if you want me to," Leslie agreed, giving Gary a timid smile. "Just let me focus on that rock out there and I'll shoot when you swing over it."

Gary chuckled as he climbed up on the bank and got ready to grab the rope. He didn't really care if she took his picture or not, but it was a good way to keep her here for a couple of minutes. They were completely alone, and it was a great opportunity to be even with her for those hornet stings. Now, what could he do to really get Leslie's goat? Maybe he could think of some way to ruin her picture . . . or her whole roll of film. He didn't dare grab her camera and throw it in the river or anything obvious like that. Then his mother would skin him alive. Just ruining her film would be enough.

"Hey, Leslie—do you develop your own pictures?" Gary forced a friendly note into his voice. Everything depended on whether she developed her own pictures or not.

"I can't do it by myself yet," Leslie confessed, giving Gary a shy smile. "Mike lets me print sometimes, but he does all my developing for me. He's teaching me how, but I can't use the darkroom alone."

"So he's right there to help you?" Gary asked quickly, double-checking. He gave a grin when Leslie nodded. "Then he looks at all your pictures and teaches you, right?"

"That's right." Leslie nodded happily. She hadn't known that Gary was so interested in photography. Perhaps she'd misjudged him. Gary might be nice if she got to know him.

"Holler when you start to swing, Gary." Leslie set her shutter speed on a thousandth of a second and checked the focus again. "I'll catch you when you let go of the rope and dive in. It's going to be a super picture—just wait and see."

Gary smirked as he climbed up on the rock. You bet it was going to be a super picture, but Leslie didn't know just how super. He could hardly believe how well his little plan was working. Leslie was holding her camera, looking through the viewfinder at the slab of granite. She couldn't see anything he was doing behind her back now, and that was exactly how he wanted it.

With a quick motion Gary unzipped his shorts and slipped them down. Ha! She was going to get more than she bargained for this time. She'd snap the picture and it would be a picture of his naked butt. She wouldn't dare let her stepfather develop it and she'd have to throw out her whole roll of film. He was a genius for thinking of it!

"Here I come!" Gary grasped the rope up high and kicked out of his cutoffs. He swung out with a yell and beamed expectantly as Leslie gave a startled scream. He just hoped that she had snapped the picture.

Gary hit the water with a splash that sent up a geyser of water. He resurfaced quickly and hooted with laughter when he saw Leslie's face. Her mouth was open and her fists were clenched by her side.

"How dare you?" she screamed. "You ruined everything, Gary Wilson! You ruined my whole roll of film!"

Gary saw the way her eyes snapped when he raced past her, wiggling his butt in a lewd display. He gave a huge laugh and rubbed it in even more.

"Come on, dummy. You can't be upset over a little thing like that!" Gary's voice was taunting and mean. "I bet it's the best picture you ever took!"

"You . . . you . . . !" Leslie was so angry she couldn't speak. The blood rushed to her face and she grabbed the key around her neck in desperation. Gary Wilson was awful! He was crude and nasty! Helpless tears of rage rolled down her cheeks and she stood there, trembling in anger.

"Hey, I'll give you another great picture!" Gary called out, laughing loudly. He stood on top of the big rock and did a mocking dance—white, untanned buttocks jiggling in the sun. "Take another one—take the whole roll!"

"I hate you!" Leslie's eyes narrowed to slits and she grabbed the key tightly in both hands. Her voice was a mere whisper, but the sound carried clearly to the rock where Gary was dancing.

The sun gleaming on the water made her eyes burn like fire. Leslie braced her feet against the dizzy feeling she knew would come and drew a shuddering breath. Christopher was coming. He'd make Gary stop.

That's all right, Leslie. I'll make it all better. We'll get even for this.

Gary glanced over his shoulder at Leslie and stopped dancing, noticing the funny expression on her face. Her eyes were huge and black. They were like pools of darkness, with a gleam deep inside that almost frightened him. He grabbed for his shorts and climbed into them as quickly as he could. His joke was over and he'd better get out of here. Leslie looked spooky. He wished there were others around; he didn't like being alone with that girl.

His bravado came back, though, as Leslie turned abruptly and stared at the water. Why should he have to run? It was his swimming hole before she ever moved in. She couldn't do anything to him. She was just a stuck-up kid and he had played a great trick on her.

Leslie was standing stiffly, both feet planted firmly on the ground, facing away from him. Gary didn't really want to quit yet. He wasn't quite satisfied. He wanted to rub it in a little more.

He grinned, realizing that he still held the rope in his hand. Leslie was standing close to the path of the swing and that gave him a great idea. He'd swing right past her and scare her half to death. Then she'd run home for sure.

He grasped the rope up high and swung out with a coarse laugh. He was headed right toward her, swinging widely so he could brush her with his feet. She was really going to scream this time! They'd hear her all the way to Main Street.

The tip of his foot grazed her arm. Gary gave a bloodcurdling yell and sailed by. He was almost over the rock now, preparing to jump. This was the best damn trick he'd ever played. Bud and Taffy would be in stitches when he told them about it.

Now. Christopher's voice was filled with urgency. *Watch, Leslie . . . now!*

There was an audible snap as the rope broke. She caught a picture of Gary framed by the tree branch. Terror was written on his face and he dropped like a stone, only a few feet away from safety.

His howl of fright hurt her ears, and Leslie winced as she clicked the shutter. He hit the rock with an ugly thud and there was a moment of terrible silence before the screams started. His arm was bent under him at a crazy angle, like a broken doll's, and now he wasn't dancing his lewd dance anymore. He was screaming, ashen-faced, on the rock, one scream after another, which finally trailed off into whimpers and then complete silence.

Now everything was still. The only sound was the lapping of the current against the sparkling granite slab, washing the blood from the edge of the rock.

Leslie stood there, unmoving, letting the sound of the water soothe her. She didn't have to worry about Gary Wilson anymore. He wouldn't tease her again.

Go home, Leslie. Christopher's voice was fading now and Leslie turned from the river obediently. She didn't want to stay here. Her place was at home.

As Leslie walked slowly, mechanically, up the path toward town, she passed a group of kids headed in the opposite direction. They were carrying towels and inflatable rafts. She stopped for a moment, disoriented. Why was she here, and why did she feel so strange? There was something she wanted to tell the children, but she couldn't remember what it was. Her eyes hurt dreadfully and she was shaking. It was sunny, but she was so cold, she shivered. Well, it didn't matter anyway. Why should she bother to stop and talk to them? There seemed to be something wrong with her head; it was spinning, and she couldn't think or see clearly.

It was too late now. They were gone. She had to hurry home and not worry about what she'd forgotten. It probably wasn't important, but getting home was. Away from this town and all the people in it. Home was where she belonged.

FOURTEEN

She was just sitting down at the table when Leslie came in. One glance at her daughter's face told Karen there was something horribly wrong.

"Leslie! What happened?"

Leslie blinked and opened her mouth, but no words came out. She looked dazed and helpless.

"Here . . . sit down, darling!" Karen pushed her into a chair. It was like trying to seat a large rag doll. Leslie's body slumped down into place, but there was no awareness in her eyes. She was clearly in shock, just as she had been at the birthday party.

"Are you hurt, honey?" Karen looked her over carefully; she had no visible signs of injury. Perhaps it was sunstroke. Leslie was shaking, and she was unnaturally pale.

Karen ran for a glass of water and held it to Leslie's lips. "Drink this, baby. . . . That's it, honey—just sip it slowly."

As Karen watched anxiously, a little color came back to Leslie's face. She looked better and Karen drew a deep breath. She should have known it was too hot for Leslie to play outside today. This was all her fault.

"Oh, no, Mom—I have to go back!" She looked wildly around her. "He's hurt! I have to go back and help him!"

"Who? What are you saying?" Karen demanded loudly, shaking Leslie's shoulders. "Who's hurt, Leslie? What happened?"

Just then they heard the sirens, going down the road to the river. Karen gazed out the window. Leslie's eyes widened and she shuddered convulsively. Now she remembered everything. Gary Wilson was hurt. He was hurt really bad!

"Gary's hurt and I did it!" Her voice was tortured. "I did it, Mom! Maybe I even killed him!"

"What do you mean?" Karen felt her heart pounding wildly in her chest. "Tell me what happened, Leslie! Was there an accident at the river?"

"It was no accident." Leslie's voice was small and scared. "Gary Wilson was down at the river, swinging on that rope. It's my fault he fell. The rope broke because I got mad at him. I wanted him to fall and he did!"

Karen put her arms around Leslie. She smoothed her hair and held the shaking girl as she tried to make some sense out of Leslie's words.

"Gary was swinging on that rope by the riverbank," Karen repeated carefully. "Is that right, honey?" She waited patiently until Leslie nodded. "Then he fell. Is that what happened?"

Leslie dipped her head in another small nod. "He fell on a rock, Mom! The rope broke and he fell! He's hurt really bad! We have to go down and help him!"

"The ambulance is there by now, honey. Don't worry, they'll know what to do." Karen tried to comfort her overwrought daughter. "I'm sure Gary will be all right. It couldn't be very serious."

"I did it." Leslie's voice was a whisper. "I did it, Mom. He fell on the rock because I wanted him to."

"Leslie, listen to me." Karen's voice was firm. "Wanting something doesn't make it happen. I know you were mad at Gary and maybe you wished that he'd fall, but that isn't why he did. It's just a coincidence, honey—an unhappy coincidence. Wishes don't come true, you know that."

"I guess not." She wanted to tell her mother how her birthday wish came true and all the kids got stung. And how she had wanted to stop the ladies from gossiping and the cans fell, but she couldn't find the words to explain. It was all so complicated— dreams, and voices, and Christopher, and the key. She had a friend, but whenever he was with her, scary things happened, and everything was out of her control. Her mother would never believe that a ghost came and talked to her and made things happen. She might think Leslie had done all those bad things to people. They'd all blame her. She couldn't tell anyone the truth.

"Sit right here and I'll make a call." Karen got to her feet. "I'll try to find out if Gary's all right."

"Oh . . . okay, Mom." Leslie put her head down on the table. She heard her mother talking on the phone in the next room and closed her eyes. She felt awful. She hadn't meant to hurt Gary. She'd just wanted him to stop teasing her—that was all.

Leslie shivered again. She knew everything was her fault even if Mom didn't think so. She had the power to hurt people whenever she wanted—whenever she got mad. She was going to stay in the house from now on, where it was safe. And she was never going to get mad at anyone again.

"No news yet." Marilyn Comstock sighed as she came back into the kitchen. "I've been on the phone all morning and no one's heard a word from the hospital. Janet said she'd call just as soon as she got the doctor's report, but there's no word. Old Dr. Simmons says it was a nasty break and they were almost afraid to move him. His elbow is shattered completely and he's positive they'll have to do reconstructive surgery."

"I just don't understand that rope snapping." Rob rubbed his forehead and pushed his half-eaten lunch to the center of the table. "The Rotary checked it just last week and I know that rope was sound. I guess we never should have allowed that swing in the first place, but no one's ever been hurt on it before."

Marilyn shook her head. "It's not your fault, Rob. Nobody can blame the Rotary. Who could guess that rope would break?"

The phone rang shrilly and Marilyn rushed to answer it. Rob sighed and lit a cigarette. Marilyn's phone was the nerve center for the entire town.

She came back to the kitchen, her lips set in a tight line. "That was Dorothy Jackson. She had her kids at the river this morning and she saw Gary swinging.

She said when she got ready to leave, there were only two children left—Gary Wilson and a blond girl with a camera. She thinks it was Leslie Houston, Rob. You know, it wouldn't surprise me at all if Leslie had something to do with Gary's accident."

"Leslie? How can you say that?" Rob's voice was incredulous. "What can you mean, Marilyn? The rope broke! How could a little girl have anything to do with that? What's gotten into you now?"

Marilyn sat down heavily. "I'm not sure," she faltered, "but there's some connection, Rob. Remember the hornets' nest? Everyone got stung, except Leslie. And those cans falling on Roberta and me in the store? Leslie was right there, waiting at the checkout stand. And now this. There's something wrong, Rob. I don't know how she's doing it, but Leslie Houston is at the bottom of these accidents. Nothing bad ever happened in Cold Spring before the Houstons moved in."

"That's ridiculous, Marilyn!" Rob couldn't believe his ears. "Think about what you just said. Do you realize how crazy you sound?"

There was a moment of silence as Marilyn dropped her eyes. She looked embarrassed and upset and Rob reached out to pat her arm.

"It's all right, Marilyn. You're just too upset about Gary to think straight. Why don't you get out of here for a while . . . go down to the store. Maybe you can help out a bit. I'm sure the Wilsons would appreciate that."

Marilyn nodded. That's just what she'd do. She could help mind the store and be right there when

Janet called. And she wouldn't say a word about Leslie Houston. Rob was right. The whole idea was crazy, blaming the little girl. It was a horrible accident, a broken rope, nothing more. Why, there couldn't be a connection between Leslie and the strange occurrences lately. That sort of thinking just didn't make any sense at all.

FIFTEEN

Doing the laundry was one of the most boring jobs in the world. Karen switched on the radio as she sorted the basket of clothes into piles: one for the whites, one for the colors, one for the delicates, one for the permanent press. It was humid and steamy hot today and she stopped to wipe her face. The weather report was just coming on.

"WCCO reports the weather on this Wednesday, the seventeenth of August, brought to you by Land O'Lakes, the best in dairy products. It's a scorcher today, folks—a hundred and one degrees, the hottest day for this date since 1943, when the temperature reached one hundred and four. The weatherman says that old mercury is going to keep right on climbing, with a high of one hundred and five predicted for the Twin Cities and surrounding areas. There's no relief in sight and it looks like we're in for a record-breaking heat wave."

Karen lifted the hair from the nape of her neck and sighed as the announcer's voice continued.

"If you're looking for a way to beat the heat,

WCCO suggests you good folks settle down in front of your radio with your air conditioner on high and pour yourself a frosty glass of Hamm's beer, bottled right here in the Land of Sky Blue Waters. Relax, kick off your shoes, and enjoy our own dynamic duo, Boone and Erickson."

Karen reached out and snapped off the radio. She didn't want to hear any more about the heat. The small laundry room was like a sauna already, and it was still early morning. By the end of the afternoon it would be miserable.

She filled the washer and started the first load, checking pockets carefully for forgotten change or ballpoint pens. The pants Mike had worn yesterday were on top of the pile and she sighed as she pulled out the checkbook. It was lucky she had checked. Karen looked at it again and swallowed hard. Her fingers shook as she opened the leather-covered folder. She was almost afraid to look. For the past week and a half, Mike had taken it with him wherever he went.

"What?" Karen's eyes widened. Their current balance was even lower than it had been before, despite two new deposits. The number of cash withdrawals was staggering. Mike couldn't have used all that money for supplies and overhead. Three thousand dollars in ten days! It couldn't be. If they kept on spending money this way, they'd be absolutely penniless in no time at all. This time she was going to be firm. She had to confront Mike and demand to know exactly what he was doing with all that cash.

"Oh, no!" Karen gasped as her suspicions began to coalesce. Mike had been edgy and nervous for the last month or so, and it all tied in with a pattern she knew only too well. He had acted this way before, when they'd first met, when he was gambling heavily and losing.

Karen shivered, remembering. The day after a big loss Mike would be sullen and crabby. He'd drink too much and sink into depression. There were times when she wouldn't see him for days. When he won, it was another story. Then he'd be on top of the world, confident and cocksure. He'd knock at her door and take them out for a big dinner, spending money lavishly on presents for Leslie and herself.

Lavish presents . . . Karen winced as another piece of the puzzle came together for her. Leslie's telescope was lavish and so was her birthday party. The more she thought about it, the more certain she was that Mike was gambling again. And if he was gambling, he was probably drinking again, too.

"Karen? Where are you?" It was Mike's voice, calling to her from the kitchen.

"Coming!" Karen hollered back, squaring her shoulders. It was about time they discussed this, and she wasn't going to take no for an answer. She'd demand to know why Mike was going back to his old habits. Now, with the feature and the importance of the new house, he could ruin everything.

"You left the checkbook in your pants pocket, and I want to know where all that money went." Karen stood with her hands on her hips. "You're gambling again, aren't you? You gave me your solemn word you'd quit for good when I married you!"

Mike was sitting at the kitchen table. He looked up at Karen in surprise and winced. One thing he didn't need was this kind of an assault first thing in the morning. He was worried enough as it was, and he didn't appreciate Karen's going at him like a prosecuting attorney.

"Now, wait a minute, honey." Mike tried to put on a sincere smile. "You've got it all wrong. I'm not really gambling. I just got into a couple of those office pools, that's all. It's just small stuff—not like real gambling at all."

"Three thousand dollars?" Karen was incredulous. "You're trying to say that's not really gambling? Come on, Mike—we don't even have enough money left to make the house payment and it's due next week. What's going to happen to us if we lose this place? We'll be out on the street!"

Her voice was grating on his nerves, as shrill and loud as fingernails on a blackboard. Mike winced again and shook his head.

"Please don't shout, Karen." He tried to be reasonable. "There's always a grace period, so stop worrying. You're being ridiculous."

"I'm being ridiculous?" Karen glared at him. "You're the one who's being ridiculous! You've been gambling for months now and you hid it from me! And you're probably drinking, too!"

"Shut up, Karen!" Mike had reached the end of his patience. He pushed his chair back so hard it clattered over on the floor. Her crack about his drinking was a low blow. If she only knew how hard it had been to stay away from it, how hard he'd been working to be a good husband, a good father to Leslie.

"I saved enough for your precious house payment, so stop screaming at me. And I'm *not* drinking! Maybe I should be. It'd make things a hell of a lot more pleasant around here, and you seem to expect it out of me. You've never trusted me completely, have you? You always thought I wasn't good enough, wasn't strong enough to quit."

The way Karen was glaring at him made Mike even angrier. And gambling wasn't all that bad. Businessmen gambled every day.

"You wouldn't say a word if it was the stock market," Mike accused. "Then you'd applaud if I made money. Be reasonable, Karen . . . I had to get the money for your fancy house from somewhere. A couple of thousand for a sofa! Nine hundred to get that old piano fixed! My gambling paid for the whole fancy birthday party and the telescope, too. Where would I get that kind of money if I didn't gamble? You know the magazine doesn't pay that much."

Karen stared at him for a long moment and then she dropped her eyes. She really shouldn't have yelled at him. She'd been making some pretty heavy demands for cash lately, and Mike was under a lot of pressure. At least he said he wasn't drinking and that was a positive sign. She had to calm down so they could discuss this reasonably. If he'd just agree to stop gambling, they could work this out somehow.

When Karen looked up, prepared to apologize for her outburst, Mike was headed up the stairs. His shoulders were set stiffly.

"Mike—wait! Let's talk about this. If you just stop gambling, we'll cut down somehow. I know I've been spending a lot of money, but we can cut back. We can make do with cheaper things, now that I know we have a problem and—"

But he didn't even look back. Karen gave a sigh

and hot, stinging tears filled her eyes. He wasn't going to stop. And he wouldn't even talk to her about it. Now it was too late for her to stop him and he'd keep right on gambling with their savings, risking their beautiful house.

She heard the door of his studio slam shut and a shiver went through her in spite of the heat. It was impossible to take back the words she'd hurtled at him in anger, and now there was a wall between them, a wall Karen didn't know how to tear down.

Karen's hands were shaking badly and she clutched her coffee cup as if it were a life raft. Even the heat of the scalding coffee failed to take the chill from her. He had broken his promise. How could she ever trust him again?

"Damn!" Mike flung the checkbook on his desk and kicked out at the wastebasket, scattering paper and ashes wildly. She had no right to poke her nose in his business. Everything would have been fine if she hadn't snooped around. What did she expect him to do? Create a miracle to pay the bills? Of course she was right that he shouldn't have started gambling in the first place, but it was too late for that now. Now he was in over his head and he had to get out.

Mike laughed bitterly. And she wanted him to stop when any day he was due for a big jackpot. She had no sense of timing; she didn't understand the rules of the game. It would be stupid to quit now, Mike knew that. He'd wait for that jackpot and then he'd quit. He'd been planning on quitting anyway, just as soon as he cashed in one more time.

There was film to develop and more prints to be made, but he didn't dare start working when he was so upset. He needed something to calm him down so he could stop shaking.

A drink. It would serve her right if he had one. She thought he was drinking again anyway, so what difference would it make? Of course he knew he shouldn't, but a man could only take so much, and he had to begin taking hold of his own life again. All he'd been thinking of lately was work, the house, Karen, and Leslie. He was smart enough to know when to stop now, even if she didn't think so. A little sip of the poor man's tranquilizer would settle his nerves and make him feel good again. It was about time to open a bottle of the Napoleon brandy and do exactly what he'd been wanting to do for days.

At first he just sipped and savored, rolling the brandy around on his tongue, not swallowing. It was superb, and the guilty feeling he was getting for yelling at Karen was melting away.

Mike found himself staring at the calendar over his desk and he groaned softly, thinking of the house payment and Karen's concern. He didn't have the money in savings as he'd told her, and he'd have to ask Rob for an extension. Maybe he could do Rob a favor, hand him a bottle of the Napoleon brandy before springing the request. Rob was bound to agree.

It would all work out. Mike took another sip of brandy. The little, niggling pangs of guilt were uncomfortable, but they would fade soon enough. Brandy was food for the soul.

There was a timid knock at the door, which Mike ignored. He sat down in his swivel chair and leaned back, resting his feet on his overturned wastebasket.

"Mike? Are you busy?" It was Leslie's tentative voice. Karen must have sent her up here to check on him. Well, he wasn't in the mood to be nice to Karen or her kid. They could knock as long as they wanted, but he'd stay right where he was, doing whatever the hell he liked. The money worries, the damn house—it could all wait until he felt like dealing with it.

Karen ignored the work to be done and climbed the stairs wearily to the master bedroom. She felt awful, and the green canopy bed looked so inviting. Mike was locked in the darkroom and she hoped he'd stay there for a good, long while. She couldn't bear to face any more problems today. Her white embroidered maternity top was sticking to her back and it was just too hot to live. She'd lie down for a little while until she felt better.

She folded back the satin coverlet and stretched out with a sigh. She felt forlorn and uncertain of him, of their ability to create a happy family together here in this wonderful old house. A tear rolled down her cheek and she brushed it away with an ironic smile, thinking that this bed had seen its share of tears. According to the diary, Dorthea had cried many times in this very spot, longing for her lover.

At first she had assumed this room to be Amelia

and William's, but to her surprise she discovered that the older Appletons had slept in separate bedrooms. This room and this bed had been Dorthea's, her place of refuge in this lovely house. The thought comforted Karen. Life didn't change so very much over the years. Dorthea had been just as unhappy as she was today, and perhaps life had worked out well for her. She'd know just as soon as she finished the journals.

"Mom? Are you all right?" Leslie stood in the doorway, watching her with concern.

Karen nodded. She knew she looked terrible. Her eyes felt scratchy, and they were probably red and swollen from crying. It wasn't surprising that Leslie looked worried.

"It's not time for the baby yet, is it, Mom?" Leslie's voice was small and scared. "Do you want me to call Mike?"

"No, it's not time for the baby, and you don't have to call Mike." Karen mustered up an ironic grin at the thought. Mike probably wouldn't come out of his darkroom even if she went into labor this minute.

"I'm just tired, honey." Karen reached out and squeezed Leslie's hand. "Why don't you go up and play with your telescope and let me nap for an hour or so."

"Sure, Mom." Leslie was relieved as she bent over to give her mother a kiss. She tiptoed out and closed the door softly behind her. Mom looked really tired and a nap would be good for her.

She stood in the hallway for a moment, wondering what to do. She didn't really feel like using her telescope right now. Maybe she should take a look at the bedrooms up here. There might be some way she could help Mom with the redecorating.

Leslie opened a door at random and peeked inside. This room was going to be nice. A brass bed stood against one wall and there was an oak washstand in the corner. A sampler with a Bible verse done in cross-stitch was propped up against the mirror, ready to be hung as soon as the wallpaper was done. The room was old-fashioned and pretty and it matched the miniature perfectly.

Leslie traveled the length of the hall, opening doors and peering at the partially completed rooms. Mom had done an awful lot of work up here. No wonder she was so tired.

She stopped at the end of the hall and looked out the window. Everything was quiet and peaceful in their big yard. Sunbeams streamed in through the lace curtains and fell on the floor in patterns. The only sound in the whole house was her own soft breathing.

Leslie sighed morosely. She felt very alone with Mom napping and Mike in the darkroom. Unconsciously, she lifted her hand to touch the key lightly. At least she had one friend, even though he scared her a little. If she got really lonely, she knew Christopher would come.

A slight dizzy feeling made her reach out and find the wall with her hand. She stood that way for a long moment with her eyes closed. Then she turned and walked to her room. There was something she had to do.

She went straight to the closet and opened it. All her clothes were here—the expensive, color-coordinated outfits her mother had given her. Looking at her pretty clothes usually made her happy, but Leslie frowned as she fingered the soft cashmeres and rich materials that filled hanger after hanger. For some reason these clothes weren't acceptable anymore.

She looked down at the blouse she was wearing. It was light pink polished cotton with a dainty lace trim. She had always loved it.

With a deliberate motion Leslie yanked it off over her head, ripping a seam. This blouse wasn't right for her anymore. It was too fussy and feminine.

She found an old white shirt in the back of her closet. Mike had given it to her to wear when they were unloading the trailer. She rolled up the sleeves and slipped it on. It felt just right. Now she had to do something about her designer jeans.

Leslie grabbed her favorite pair of designer jeans and ripped off the pockets with their fancy designs. Then she snipped off the legs in a ragged line. Now she had a pair of cutoffs. She stood in front of the mirror and smiled at her reflection. She looked perfect now, except for her shoes.

Quickly Leslie removed her Gucci loafers. She threw her socks under the bed and wiggled her bare toes happily. Now she was dressed just the way she should be, just the way she'd been in . . . ?

She stopped, confused. As she'd been . . . when? She couldn't remember. She had known for a second, but now the memory was gone.

It didn't matter. She felt much happier now and she wasn't lonely any longer. And now she knew exactly what she wanted to do. She wanted to go up to the cupola and take a little nap. When she woke up, her mind would be clear again. Then she might be able to remember whatever it was she had forgotten.

SIXTEEN

Karen sipped her orange juice and read, the leather-bound diary propped open against the sugar container. She was nearing the end of Dorthea's last diary now and she couldn't bear to put it down. Her heart went out to the poor girl. Just reading between the lines convinced her that Dorthea had been victimized by Kirby Shaw.

Leslie sat across from her, elbows propped on the table. Her bare feet were hooked around the legs of the chair and Karen grinned at the sight. She'd never seen Leslie in a more undignified position! All of her ladylike ways seemed to have disappeared overnight and Karen shook her head in amusement.

She had been shocked when Leslie appeared in this ridiculous outfit two days ago. "How do I look, Mom?" Leslie had grinned expectantly. "These clothes are perfect for here, don't you think?"

Karen was ready to scold her, but she thought better of it. If that's what Leslie wanted to wear around the house, she supposed it was all right with her. She wasn't exactly a fashion plate herself lately.

And the outfit, as unattractive as it seemed at first, was certainly practical. In a tomboyish sort of way, Leslie looked cute.

It took Karen some time before she figured it out. Then she was glad she hadn't said the wrong thing. She really hadn't considered it before, but Leslie's wardrobe was a direct contrast to the things the Cold Spring children wore. They seemed to dress exclusively in old shirts and cutoff jeans. It was kind of a reverse snobbery. With her makeshift outfit, Leslie was just trying to fit in.

Leslie looked up from her work as she felt her mother's gaze. She was braiding a new strap for her camera from long leather thongs. "Did you find out any more, Mom? Did Dorthea get married yet?"

Karen smiled at her daughter. They were both fascinated by Dorthea's story. The Appleton family was real to them, as real as friends they had always known.

"Dorthea's father caught them together in the rose garden." Karen pointed to the page. "He threw an absolute fit and threatened to kick Kirby out of town, but Amelia stepped in. The portrait wasn't finished yet, you know. She persuaded Mr. Appleton to let Kirby stay until the painting was completed. Amelia agreed to chaperone all Dorthea's sittings."

"Does her mother know Dorthea's in love with Kirby?" Leslie leaned closer.

"Oh, Amelia knows, but she's not happy about it, either." Karen sighed. "Amelia thinks Kirby's not good enough for Dorthea, but she's more sympathetic than Mr. Appleton. She's hoping that Dorthea will come to her senses eventually. Mr. Appleton hired a detective to investigate Kirby's background. He thinks Kirby is after the family money."

"Is he?" Leslie questioned eagerly.

"I think so," Karen went on. "Let me read a little more and I'll tell you. I think Dorthea's heading for big trouble."

A few moments later Karen gasped aloud. "Oh, no, this is terrible, Leslie! Dorthea's pregnant. Just listen to this."

Father still forbids our marriage and I am to be sent to my Aunt Jane's in Boston until the child is born. There is no time to waste. We will have to flee tonight. Kirby has convinced me to take my jewelry and sell it when we arrive in the West. I know Mother will understand what we've done even if Father is furious right now. I am sure she will manage to convince Father to take us back once Kirby has made a name for himself in artistic circles. Then we can return and take our rightful place in the family. I am convinced my course of action is guided by fate and I will return to you, dear Journal, before many months have passed.'

"That's the end!" Karen paged through the rest of the diary, but it was blank. Dorthea had indeed run off as she had written, leaving her locked diaries behind. No wonder her family had replaced her portrait with the pastoral scene! Dorthea had left Cold Spring in disgrace, disappearing into the night with her lover. It was romantic and terribly sad. Karen swallowed hard as she closed the diary.

"But did she come back?" Leslie sat on the very

edge of her chair. "Does it say what happened to Dorthea and her baby?"

"There's no more here." Karen looked wistful. "Maybe we'll find something else in the trunks upstairs, honey."

"I hope so! I want to know what else happened, Mom. I really like Dorthea!"

The ringing of the telephone interrupted their speculations, and Karen hurried from the room to answer it.

"Karen?" Mike's voice was thin and there was static on the line. "I'll be late tonight, so don't hold dinner for me. I won't be home until midnight or maybe later. We ran into some snags here and it's going to take a lot longer than I thought."

Karen heard a burst of laughter and loud conversation. There was a jukebox playing in the background and she drew in her breath sharply.

"Are you working now?" she asked, her voice skeptical. "It sounds like you're in a bar, Mike. You swore to me you weren't drinking again."

"I'm not drinking! Christ, Karen! You're really getting paranoid lately! I just ran across the street to use the phone in here."

"But, Mike—"

"Got to run now. I'll be home as soon as I can."

There was a click and the line went dead. Karen stood staring at the receiver for a long moment before she replaced it in the cradle. Mike didn't fool her for a second. He wasn't working late; he was drinking again! Damn him for being such a fool!

"Mike won't be home until late." Karen covered her feelings with a smile for Leslie's benefit. "I think

I'll get started refinishing the dining-room table. Is there anything special you'd like to do, kitten?"

"I'd really like to read these journals, if you don't mind, Mom. I could take them up to the tower room and learn all about Dorthea. I'll be careful with them, I promise."

"That's fine, honey." Karen smiled broadly. By reading the journals Leslie would learn about the history of this house. And maybe tonight, before Mike got home, they could go through some of the boxes and trunks in the ballroom. Leslie seemed just as interested as she was in finding out more about Dorthea.

The table was finally stripped and Karen stepped back to survey her work. The grain of the wood she'd uncovered was gorgeous. It was going to be lovely when she was through.

Karen stood up and rubbed the small of her back. The stripping was hard work and two hours had passed in a rush. Soon Leslie would be getting hungry. She really should go up and check on her daughter. There hadn't been a peep from the cupola.

"Leslie? Aren't you getting—oh!" Karen gave a soft smile as she opened the door of the cupola and saw her golden-haired daughter sleeping soundly, surrounded by pillows. Leslie's hair was tangled and Karen noticed she looked warm. She gently touched her forehead. While Leslie wasn't feverish, it was probably good for her to nap. She'd let her sleep now and stay up later tonight.

Karen saw the key on the floor as she turned to

leave. The string was frayed and broken. Idly Karen picked it up and turned it over in her fingers. She didn't have the faintest idea why Leslie was so attached to this rusty old key, but she had worn it around her neck ever since she'd found it. At least it would look nicer on a pretty ribbon or chain. She thought Leslie would like that. It would be a surprise for her when she woke up.

Karen slipped the key into her pocket and went back down the stairs. She paused as she passed the hall window. She could hear the mower outside, a high-pitched humming that made her head hurt. Red Fischer was working on the yard.

Red was a real gem. Karen smiled as she caught sight of him rounding the corner. He wore blue denim overalls and a straw fishing hat bobbing with lures. Red said he'd always itched to get his hands on this beautiful estate and get it into shape.

"Oh, dear!" Karen frowned in irritation. She had forgotten to tell Red about the rose garden. If she went outside right now, she could catch him before he left for the day.

She could still smell the fumes from the stripper and took a deep breath of the clean air outside. The yard smelled wonderful. A smile took the place of her frown as she walked across the lawn. Damp cut grass stuck to her shoes and she kicked up puffs of green as she walked.

Red was working at the side of the house now. Karen brushed her fingers against the trunk of an old elm tree as she passed it. Perhaps Dorthea had played under this very tree as a child. It looked very old. It was a joy to have huge old trees on their property, and Red said they were all healthy and thriving.

"Mr. Fischer?" Karen raised her voice, but she was no competition for the whine of the power mower. *"Mr. Fischer?"*

The elderly gardener stopped and turned, shutting off the machine as he saw her standing there. He grinned widely, showing the gaps in his tobacco-stained teeth.

"Found you a little surprise, Mrs. Houston. Your husband told me to cut real close to the house this time, so I mowed down these bushes and look what I found!"

Karen's eyes followed his pointing finger and she saw a weathered door, flush with the ground. Before Red had mowed here, it had been completely over-grown and hidden by shrubbery.

"Bet a city dweller like you don't know what that is." Red grinned as Karen shook her head. "That's a root cellar. People used them all the time to store things like potatoes and onions. Sometimes they even hid valuables down there. Do you want me to saw that lock off so you can look inside?"

"Not today, Mr. Fischer." She stared at the root cellar with interest. "It's getting late and I'd like you to stop at the store and pick up the supplies we need for the rose garden. Leslie and I want to help with that. We want to learn more about gardening if you'll teach us."

"My pleasure, Mrs. Houston. That little girl of yours looks like she's got a green thumb. It does folks good to work in the earth and make things grow. You want me to pick up some stakes for the arborvitae, too? The ones in the front are leaning some."

"Pick up whatever you need." Karen gave him a smile. "You're the expert, Mr. Fischer. You've certainly done a beautiful job so far."

Karen couldn't help walking closer to the root cellar and she knelt down to examine the lock. She heard the sound of Red's pickup truck as it started with a cough, and she sighed. Perhaps she should have asked him to saw off the lock. She'd really love to take a look at the root cellar right now. It was too bad the key wasn't hanging in the shed.

"The key!" Karen drew Leslie's key from her pocket. She *had* found it in the yard. It was certainly old enough and it was a padlock key. If she was really lucky, it might fit.

Karen felt uneasy as she reached for the lock. She wasn't sure if she felt up to exploring right now. Somehow she had the feeling that she should leave well enough alone and let the shrubbery grow back to hide it again.

She gave a short laugh and felt silly. She was a grown woman, and it was just an old root cellar. She'd never know what was down there if she didn't try to unlock it.

The lock was rusty and Karen jiggled the key, trying to turn it. She was almost ready to give up when something clicked inside the lock. It opened with a protesting squeak. What a stroke of luck. So Leslie's key had been valuable after all! She could hardly wait to tell her.

Karen lifted the door carefully, propping it open with a sturdy branch from Red's woodpile. Then she looked dubiously at the rotten wooden steps leading downward. She'd have to be very careful not to fall. It actually might be better to wait until Leslie woke up to climb down there, but she was anxious to make this discovery all by herself. She'd just take a quick peek around and then lock it up again. That way Leslie could have the same exciting discovery later.

Slowly and carefully Karen started down the steps, testing the wood first with one foot before she put her full weight on the step. An odor greeted her as she descended. It was the smell of damp darkness and musty wood. And it was cool, at least ten degrees cooler than the air outside.

She stopped halfway down and blinked. Now she wished she'd thought to bring a flashlight. It was dark down here and all she could see were dim shapes in the gloom. She'd go all the way to the bottom and then stop to let her eyes adjust. There should be enough light coming in through the opening to illuminate the shelves right in front of her.

She didn't hear the rustling until she was three quarters of the way down. There was something here! Karen gave a scream and tried to turn on the narrow steps, her heart pounding frantically. Her foot slipped and then she was falling clumsily, clutching with her hands for a railing that wasn't there.

She hit solidly, so solidly that her teeth bit into her lip. There was blinding pain and she gasped weakly, pressing both hands to her rounded stomach. *The baby!*

The pain was so intense it drove everything else from her mind. It hit her like a blow, rhythmic and searing, tearing her breath from her body. There was a sticky wetness between her legs and she called out weakly for help.

It was darker now and there was a high-pitched ringing in her ears. Karen knew she had to get out of here before she fainted. The scrabbling sound from the darkest corners of the root cellar was getting louder. It was coming for her!

She screamed once in terror and then she crawled, fingers clawing desperately in the earthen floor to pull herself forward. *Too slow . . . God!* It was coming closer and she couldn't get away!

The first step was in front of her now and she hoisted herself up, not caring about the pain, not caring that the wooden splinters dug into her hands. She had to get out of here.

Another step and then another. She fought to stay conscious, pulling herself forward on bleeding knees and painful hands. Something was waiting down there in the darkness, waiting for her to faint and fall back, waiting to trap her in the dead blackness. She couldn't fall; she had to keep climbing. There was the square of sky, growing larger with each step she mounted. The sky and the sunshine . . . she had to make it.

She could see the old elm tree in the square of bright daylight. Karen willed herself forward, fighting the weakness that was stealing over her body in waves. She was almost there . . . just another few seconds and she'd be at the top. Her fingers grasped the opening . . . up . . . up . . . the sky dull red as she dragged herself into fiery daylight. . . . She'd made it! She crawled forward until her fingers were buried in the freshly cut grass. Now the sky was fading to black, coming in a rush before she could even open her mouth to scream.

SEVENTEEN

Leslie awoke with a sense that the house was much too quiet. She blinked and rubbed her eyes, noticing it was getting dark outside. She wondered where her mom was and what she was working on now.

Leslie went down the stairs and stopped at the landing, listening. "Mom?" she yelled. "Where are you? Mom?" Had she gone out without even waking her to let her know?

There was no answer from the third floor or the second. She looked around the kitchen and out the back door. Where was she? Leslie felt very alone, and automatically reached for the key around her neck, thinking Christopher would calm her down and possibly help her out. It was gone! Panic rushed over her. She had to find her mother.

She ran outside, shouting for Karen. She tripped on the exposed root of a tree, but she kept right on running, unreasoning panic driving her on. She didn't see the open root-cellar door until she rounded the corner. Then she screamed wildly as she found her mother lying there motionless on the ground.

"*Mom!* Oh, Mom. . . . *Please!*" Leslie threw herself on the ground next to Karen, but was afraid to touch her. Her mother looked like a wax mannequin, she was so white. There was blood seeping under her, staining the newly cut grass deep red. For a moment she froze, breath caught in her throat. She was all alone and Mom was hurt, maybe dying.

Get help—she had to call for help. The moment she thought of it she was racing toward the house on shaking legs, running so fast she almost fell. She stopped at the phone, suddenly panic stricken. She didn't know who to call.

Rob Comstock. Now she was dialing, fingers shaking in fear. Rob would know what to do. He had to be at his office. He had to help her.

Leslie fairly shouted into the receiver when he answered. Mom was hurt and she told him to come right away. Then she ran back to her mother's side to wait, squeezing Karen's unresponsive fingers, tears streaming down her cheeks. There was blood all over and Mom was hurt . . . a trail of blood leading from that hole in the ground.

Then she saw it and reached out frantically . . . a rusty padlock in the grass with her key inside. She pulled out the key and sobbed in relief. She had her key back. Everything would be all right now.

"Good thinking, honey." Rob hugged Leslie hard. She was so scared, her whole body was trembling, and he kept his arms around her.

"Dr. Simmons will take care of your mother, honey. Don't worry. Everything's going to be fine. You were really brave, Leslie. You did exactly the right thing, calling me."

The poor kid. Rob could see how pale she was. Of course she was terrified, having found her mother that way.

"Can you tell me how to reach Mike, honey?" Rob made his voice warm and reassuring. "I think we should call him right away, don't you?"

Leslie nodded. She found the number of the magazine and stood right by the phone while he talked to Mike. She was so glad Mr. Comstock was staying until Mike got here. She got scared every time she thought of her mother's white face.

"Let's go upstairs and check on your mother." Rob gave her an encouraging smile. "I think Dr. Simmons is through with his examination by now. Don't worry, Leslie. I'm sure your mother is going to be fine."

The doctor stepped outside when they knocked softly on her mother's door. He nodded at Rob and leaned down to talk to the pretty, little blond girl.

"She's just fine, honey." Dr. Simmons patted Leslie on the head. "She needs a lot of rest, but I don't think we have to take her to the hospital. You look like a good nurse, young lady. Just make sure your mother gets lots of sleep and stays nice and quiet. Can you do that?"

Leslie nodded quickly. She'd do anything the doctor said.

"The new baby?" Leslie almost whispered the words. "Is the new baby all right, Doctor?"

Dr. Simmons winced. He didn't like to be the

bearer of bad news, but someone had to tell her. He supposed he ought to be used to the unpleasant after thirty years as a small-town physician.

"I'm afraid not, honey." He knelt down and held her small hands in his. "There is no new baby anymore, dear. Your mother had a very serious fall."

Leslie nodded solemnly. She'd read all her mother's books on pregnancy and she knew what had happened. Mom had had a miscarriage from the fall. She'd have to take very good care of her now. And just as soon as the doctor left, she'd find a very strong leather thong for her key. It seemed as though bad things could happen if she lost it. She decided she'd never let it out of her sight again.

He broke speed laws all the way home. An accident! Rob had said that Karen and Leslie were both all right, but wasn't that what they usually said? Mike screeched into the driveway, gravel scattering as he skidded to a stop and jumped out of the truck.

Rob was waiting for him in the kitchen. "Sit down, Mike. Everything's fine now." Rob pointed to a chair.

"Where's Karen? What kind of accident? What happened?"

"She's upstairs, resting comfortably," Rob assured him. "Leslie's with her. She took a bad fall, Mike. I guess she was exploring that old root cellar outside and she slipped on the steps. Leslie found her and called me. Dr. Simmons says she's going to be fine."

"Oh, my God!" Mike stared at Rob with a horrified expression. "The baby. Is the baby all right?"

"I'm afraid not." Rob swallowed hard. He wished

that Dr. Simmons had stayed for this part of it. "She lost the baby, Mike. . . . I'm really sorry. There was nothing the doctor could do. Karen's fine, though—thank God for that! She was lucky, Mike. It's incredible she wasn't hurt worse. I locked that old cellar up again. It's a menace."

He stopped talking and stared at Mike. Nothing he said seemed to be registering. Mike was just sitting there, hands clenched on the table in front of him, eyes vacant and fixed at a point on the opposite wall. Rob wished he knew what to do. He'd never seen a man look so miserable.

"How about a drink?" Rob suggested thoughtfully. "Do you have anything to drink in the house, Mike? You look like you could use one right now, and so could I. There's absolutely nothing you can do for Karen right now. Dr. Simmons gave her a shot and he said she'd sleep until morning. Leslie's going to stay with her, just in case she needs anything. You've got a fine daughter there, Mike. Most kids her age would have panicked, but she ran straight to the phone and called me. Dr. Simmons said it could have been much worse if Leslie hadn't acted so quickly."

"Yeah." Mike nodded, but he didn't really hear Rob's words. A drink, he'd said. Rob could use a drink. Mike's legs felt rubbery as he pulled himself upright by levering his elbows on the table.

"Come on up to the studio." He motioned toward the stairs. "I've got a bottle up there."

As Rob followed him up the stairs, Mike's mind began to work again. Christ, what a shock. Why on earth had Karen been climbing around in an old root cellar in the first place? He hadn't even known the cellar was there, but he'd lock it up for good. In her condition she should have been more careful.

Mike opened the darkroom door and switched on the lights. He needed a drink badly. He hadn't touched a drop yet today, even though he had joined the guys in the bar. He had wanted to prove himself to Karen. He needed something now, though—something strong to wipe out his grief. She'd lost the baby! He wanted to go to her and take her in his arms so they could cry together, but she wouldn't even know he was there if the doctor had given her a sedative. And he didn't want to face Leslie. She'd be terribly upset if he broke down and cried in front of her. He'd be better off staying up here with Rob.

It was late; two A.M. by the luminous dial on her mother's clock. She'd heard Rob leave hours ago, but Mike had stayed up in the darkroom. Now his heavy steps on the stairs awakened her.

Leslie got up quickly, wrapping her blanket around her like a sarong. She peeked out the door and saw Mike. He was weaving back and forth and she recognized that crablike walk instantly. He'd been like this a lot when they first met him. Mike was drunk. What if he came in here and upset Mom?

She held her breath and let it out again in a grateful sigh as he turned in the opposite direction. He was going downstairs. Leslie hoped he would stay there. Mom needed to rest. The doctor had said so.

"I love you, Mom, and I'll take care of you always." Leslie whispered the words as she settled back down again in the overstuffed chair by the bed. Her mother couldn't hear her, but it made Leslie feel better anyway. The key was warm and comforting around her neck and she snuggled up in her blanket. Everything would be all right again. She just had to believe that.

EIGHTEEN

"How do you feel, honey?" Mike opened the door and stepped inside. She looked so white! Karen had always been so healthy and now she looked so very sick.

Her eyes opened and she looked at him. Then they closed again and tears squeezed out to roll down her pale cheeks. "Oh, Mike!" she whispered. "I'm so sorry!"

"I know, honey." He sat carefully by the side of the bed. He reached out for her hand and held it gently. "It's all right, Karen—don't think about it now. Just concentrate on getting well. We'll have our baby, just as soon as you're up to it."

"We can't." Karen's voice was small and frightened. "We can't have another baby now. We can't afford it. The house, Mike. We're going to lose this beautiful house . . . and we don't have any money!"

"We're not going to lose the house, darling." Mike patted her hand. "I'll make sure we don't lose it. And we're going to have money, too. We can have as many children as you want. I've given up gambling for good, Karen. I swear it!"

Something in her expression made him stop and swallow hard. She really didn't trust him, he could see that.

"Oh, I don't expect you to believe me yet," Mike said, acknowledging the doubt in her eyes. "But I'll prove it to you. I've made some terrible mistakes, but everything's going to be all right now, honey, I promise."

Karen still didn't reply. It made him nervous and he went on in a rush.

"We'll speed everything up, and that'll bring in the money," he explained. "I'll talk to Red and see if he can work full-time. I know you can't do much right now, but in a couple of days you'll be on your feet. Then we can finish the house in record time."

Her eyes closed and Mike shifted uncomfortably on the spindly antique chair. He didn't know what else to say. Karen certainly wasn't being very responsive.

"Honey?" Mike waited until she opened her eyes. "What were you doing in that root cellar? I can't use that in my photographs."

"I just thought there might be some antiques down there." Karen's voice sounded weak and she sighed.

"You should have waited for me." He shook his head. "Really, honey! You took a terrible chance going down there alone."

"But you're never here." Karen looked aside, not meeting his eyes. "If I waited for you, nothing would get done."

"That's why I hired Red. Stop thinking like that,

Karen. You don't have to do everything by yourself. You should have asked Red to go down there and poke around. We've got enough antiques for the pictures anyway. We don't need any more."

"But I'm not just doing it for the pictures, Mike. This house is more than a series to me. It's our home! It's got to be authentic!"

"Authentic?" His patience snapped and he stood up, glaring. "You're going crazy with this authentic crap! Who cares if it's authentic? I just want it finished in time for the deadline!"

A tear ran down her cheek and it made him even angrier. He was sick of hearing about antiques and authenticity!

"You and your damn authenticity killed our child!" The words poured out before he could stop them. "If you cared more about being a good wife and mother, we wouldn't have lost the baby!"

Karen stared, horrified, as he stalked from the room. He was blaming her for everything and it wasn't fair. All he cared about was his series! She turned her face to the wall and sobbed.

Mike knew he had to get out of the house. He rushed past Leslie without a word and ran to the truck. He'd drive around until he calmed down a little. *Forget Karen and her precious antiques! She cared more about them than him!* He was still fuming.

"Morning!" Rob looked up with a smile as Mike came through the door. "How's Karen?"

"Oh . . . she'll be all right." Mike dropped into a chair and sighed. Now he felt terrible for having yelled at Karen. It must be this damn hangover. His head was killing him.

"You look like you could use a little Comstock remedy." Rob pushed the aspirin bottle Mike's way. "Shake out a couple of these and I'll fix you up."

Rob opened the small refrigerator under the counter and took out a pitcher of juice. "This'll do the trick. I mixed up some for myself this morning."

Mike sipped from the glass Rob gave him. "Not bad. What is it?"

"Tomato juice, Worcestershire sauce, and an egg." Rob laughed as Mike made a face. "It sounds terrible, but it works. We really tied one on last night, didn't we!"

"Yeah." Mike sighed. "I wish I'd had this sooner. I had a big fight with Karen, and I don't know how I'm ever going to make it up to her."

"Tell me about it and maybe I can think of something." Rob leaned forward and crossed his legs. "I'm a master at things like that. I've been pacifying Marilyn for years."

By the next morning Karen was much better. The doctor said she could sit up, but she still had to stay quiet. Leslie was determined to keep her mother cheerful. Mike was busy in the darkroom and it was her responsibility to make sure Mom didn't get bored or upset.

"It's beautiful, isn't it, Mom?" Leslie was dusting the huge carved oak coatrack, which stood at the foot of the bed. "Is it really the same one that used to be in the downstairs hallway?"

Karen nodded. "It's the original. When Rob's grandfather bought this house, he took it for his office. It's been in the Comstock family for eighty years. Just as soon as I can get out of bed, I'll put it back where it belongs."

She sighed slightly as she stared at the lovely antique. It was a peace offering from Mike—a bribe, really. It was intended to make her forget the fight yesterday. Of course she had accepted the gift and Mike's apologies. But she didn't believe for a minute that he hadn't meant the things he'd said. She'd never trust him again, and she'd never forget his awful accusations.

"Shall I bring a trunk down from the ballroom?" Leslie suggested, warming to the task of entertaining her mother. "I could ask Mike to help me."

"No, he's very busy, honey. We shouldn't bother him unless it's absolutely necessary."

"I could ask Mr. Fischer," Leslie offered, noticing how her mother had brightened when she'd mentioned the trunk. "I'm sure Mr. Fischer would be glad to help me."

"Yes . . . that would be fine." Karen spoke absently, her eyes on the miniature. Mike had carried it up here last night and placed it strategically where she could see it from the bed. She supposed it was his way of priming her for all the work that had to be done on the house. Mike didn't seem to realize that she needed no coercion to go back to work. She was eager to get on with the renovation. It was the only thing that made her happy lately.

She reached out to finger the glass case, her touch almost a caress. How she wished it were 1900 again.

She'd be dressed in rich silks and laces. She could walk around this house and see for herself exactly how it was arranged. Perhaps she'd have become friendly with Dorthea and they could have confided in each other. She identified more and more with Dorthea these days—her unhappy love for an unworthy man, her feelings of being cast off, abandoned. Still, she imagined life in this house must have been much easier then. Amelia Appleton had a full staff of household help, and her husband was rich. What she wouldn't give to turn back the clock for just a day.

Leslie pushed the trunk next to the bed so Karen could see. She propped pillows behind her mother's back and helped her sit upright. Then she opened the lid and both of them peered inside.

"Here's a bunch of old letters, Mom." Leslie picked up the bundle and handed it to Karen. "Maybe there's something in them about Dorthea and her baby."

"That's odd. These letters have never been opened. They're addressed to Amelia, see?"

"I bet Mr. Appleton put them away and never gave them to her," Leslie suggested. "This is his trunk; his name is on the lid. Maybe he hid them for some reason."

The letters were arranged by date. It gave Karen a strange feeling to tear open the old envelopes and read them for the first time.

"They're from Dorthea!" Karen gasped as she glanced at the signature. "Look, Leslie, this one's from San Francisco."

"Read it to me, Mom." Leslie clasped her hands together and sat on the edge of the bed. She listened attentively as Karen began to read.

"You were right, Mother. I should have heeded your warnings. Kirby is a gambler and a drunkard. I shudder to think what will happen when my resources run dry. Please take me back, Mother. Tell Father I beg for his forgiveness!"

"But her mother never got the letter!" Leslie twisted her hands nervously. "Oh, Mom! What happened to Dorthea?"

"This one's almost five months later." Karen read quickly.

"He ran off and left me, dear Mother. I am writing this from the lying-in-hospital and my time is near. I only wish that I could be with you. I am so desperately lonely! Please, Mother . . . if you still love me, tell me you have forgiven me."

Karen swallowed past the lump in her throat and blinked away a tear. Dorthea was frightened and alone. She knew what the girl was going through, pregnant and deserted. Karen was sure that Amelia would have forgiven her daughter, but these letters had never been opened. Dorthea's pleas for help were never heard. William Appleton was a hardhearted man to hide them from his wife.

"Here's the next one." Karen's voice was shaking as she opened it.

"I cannot lose faith, Mother, even though you have not answered my letters. You have a grandchild, a beautiful healthy boy. I miss you so, Mother. If you can find it in your heart to forgive me, please tell me so. As soon as my son is able to understand, I will tell him about his family and the heritage of the fine name he carries. I pray that someday you will welcome him into your home. Please do not blame him for the pain I have caused you, and try to think kindly of us."

"Poor Dorthea! She wants to come home so badly." Karen sighed. "I'm so glad the baby is all right."

"There's something heavy in this one." Leslie handed her mother the last envelope. "Hurry and open it, Mom."

Karen noticed there was a lapse of ten years between this letter and the last. She tore open the envelope and a tintype fell out. It was a picture of a somber-faced blond boy, approximately Leslie's age. He was standing stiffly by a chair, facing the camera directly. Dorthea was sitting in the chair, holding his hand, looking even more beautiful than in her portrait over the fireplace.

"He looks like me!" Leslie bent closer to look. "See, Mom? Dorthea's son looks just like me!"

Karen nodded. Leslie was right. The boy bore an uncanny resemblance to Leslie.

"Can I keep it, Mom?" Leslie's voice was eager. "It would look great on my dresser!"

Karen nodded again and handed her the tintype. She swallowed and sighed heavily. Reading Dorthea's letters made her feel like crying. The story was so real to her that Dorthea's pain was her own. They were alike in so many ways, and now Karen was living in her home. Every time she touched a piece of antique furniture or finished a room exactly as it had been in Dorthea's day, she wished that Dorthea were alive somewhere, so she could return to her home and find it hadn't changed, at all.

"I think I'll rest for a while, honey." Karen forced a smile. "We can go through the rest of the trunk later. Can you find something else to do for an hour or so?"

"Sure, Mom." Leslie closed the lid of the trunk and put the letters on her mother's night table. "I'll go up to the tower room. I haven't been up there in ages."

Leslie shut the door quietly and hurried down the hall. She bounded up the steps two at a time and arrived in her favorite room, panting. She flopped down on a pillow and looked at the tintype again. Yes, she looked like Dorthea's son.

Gently Leslie removed the picture from its paper folder. She turned it over and saw there were words on the back.

CHRISTOPHER APPLETON, MAY 1901.

"Christopher!" Leslie gasped and stared at the inscription for a long moment. Christopher Appleton was her friend, her ghost! And this was a picture of him when he was alive! Leslie was so stunned she could barely think. She looked just like her ghost. No wonder he had picked her for his special friend.

NINETEEN

"Here, honey. Let me help you with that." Mike came into the kitchen as Leslie was putting away the dishes. It was a week since Karen's accident and he'd finished one assignment and started on a second. Rose said she could use his features heavily in the next few issues and everything was looking up. His last bets, the ones he'd placed before he promised to quit gambling, had paid off. He was going to take the money he had won and spend every cent of it on Karen.

Leslie smiled up at Mike tentatively. He'd been around more after the big fight with Mom and she knew he wasn't drinking. She'd gone in the dark-room this morning and there weren't any bottles or glasses. Of course she knew it wasn't right to check up on Mike, but she'd had to make sure.

"I got paid for the third installment today." He reached up to put the mugs on the top shelf. "That's the section featuring this kitchen. They're printing the shots of the miniature opposite the actual pictures of our work so the reader can compare."

Leslie was excited. She could hardly wait to see it. There was one shot of Mom and her, sitting at the antique kitchen table.

"I need your opinion on something, Leslie." Mike looked down at her seriously. "We're going to have some money left over this month. Do you think we should use it to hire a housekeeper?"

Leslie thought hard. "I don't know." Taking care of the house was a lot of work and it would be nice if Mom didn't have to do it.

"You know school starts next week and you won't be here all day to help," Mike went on. "I'm taking a couple of assignments on the road and I don't like the idea of leaving your mother all alone here. I thought a housekeeper might be the answer. We could hire a lady to do the cleaning and the cooking and that would leave your mother free to work on the house. Does that sound like a good idea?"

"Yes . . . I think it does." Leslie nodded thoughtfully. Mom couldn't do all the housework and decorate besides. And she did have to go to school, even though she was dreading it. They really did need a housekeeper.

"I thought you'd agree. That's why I talked to Rob Comstock yesterday. He suggested Harry Wilson's older sister, Thelma. She's a widow and she lives all alone out in the country. Rob thought she might be willing to move in for a month or so, until your mother has the house all finished."

Leslie frowned. "Would she live right here? In the house with us?"

"I think that would be best. Thelma doesn't drive and transportation would be a problem for her.

We've certainly got plenty of room and it might be nice, having someone right here when we needed her. Rob could call her for us; and if we like her, we'll hire her right away."

"I guess I could live in." Thelma Schmidt settled her large bulk into a chair and faced the three of them. "Of course I just hate to close my house, but it could be arranged if you really need me."

"We certainly do!" Karen smiled at the older woman. "This house is too big for me to handle all by myself, and it would be nice to have company."

"When could you start, Mrs. Schmidt?" Mike gave Karen a quick smile. She had taken to the idea of a live-in housekeeper right away.

"Why, I can start later this afternoon, if you like." Mrs. Schmidt gave them all a big smile. "There's certainly plenty for me to do. I'll give this whole place a thorough turning out and have it spic and span in no time. You just leave everything to me.

"Of course you realize I have to bring Trixie with me." She looked at Karen anxiously. "I just couldn't put her in a kennel. Poor Trixie would pine away of loneliness. She won't be any trouble, Mrs. Houston. Trixie's very well behaved and your little girl will love to have a dog to play with."

"Rob didn't say anything about a dog." Karen looked slightly dubious. "How big a dog is Trixie, Mrs. Schmidt?"

"She's just a tiny little thing." Mrs. Schmidt laughed. "Why, you'll hardly know she's here. She's a Chihuahua, registered and purebred."

Leslie glanced at her mother and looked away quickly before she started giggling. All three of them hated small, yapping dogs. Mike said Chihuahuas looked like bug-eyed rats.

"Trixie sounds very nice, Mrs. Schmidt," Leslie said politely. She supposed she could put up with a Chihuahua for Mom's sake.

"Why don't you go out and get her right now," Mrs. Schmidt suggested. "That way we can all get acquainted. She's tied to the railing on the front steps."

"Oh, no!" Leslie untied the leash from the railing and groaned as she surveyed the damage Trixie had done. In the few minutes she'd been outside, the tiny Chihuahua had managed to dig under the new arborvitae shrub and uproot it. And she had messed all over the brick steps!

Leslie pushed the dog out of the way with one hand and gently replaced the small shrub. She patted the earth around its roots and made a face as she turned to the steps. She had a notion to just leave the evidence of Trixie's mischief right here where Mrs. Schmidt could see it, but the hose was handy and someone had to clean it up eventually.

"Bad dog!" Leslie hissed, squirting the steps clean with one hand and holding Trixie's leash with the other. She sighed as the dog started yapping sharply.

"Come on . . . let's go inside, Trixie." Leslie tried to be friendly, even though she already disliked the noisy little animal. "Let's go in and see Mrs. Schmidt."

Trixie dug her hind legs into the grass and wouldn't budge. Leslie pulled a little harder on the leash and the tiny dog was forced to move. As she pulled the yapping dog forward, Leslie saw something that made her giggle. Trixie's toenails, every one of them, were painted bright red! That, coupled with the fake diamond collar Trixie wore, made the dog look just plain ridiculous!

"Oh, well." Leslie scooped the squirming little dog up in her arms and carried her inside. Maybe it wouldn't be all that bad, having a dog in the house. She'd offer to walk Trixie so she wouldn't have accidents inside. Trixie might even be nice, once she got to know her.

TWENTY

"Leslie? Will you walk Trixie? I'm right in the middle of waxing the floor!"

Mrs. Schmidt's voice carried clearly through the whole house. Leslie groaned as she got to her feet. Their new housekeeper had been with them for three days now and the house had never been so clean. Mrs. Schmidt was a ball of energy, waxing and polishing and sweeping until the downstairs glistened. Leslie thought Mrs. Schmidt was working out fine, but Trixie was another matter. The little Chihuahua was a terror, destroying everything in her path.

She glanced at the two books on her dresser and frowned. There was a ragged hole in the corner of one of them and the cover of the other was chewed half off. With Trixie in the house, she had to close her door at night. And it didn't do a bit of good to complain to Mrs. Schmidt. She would never admit that her precious dog did anything wrong.

"I wish I had a lock!" Leslie sighed as she pulled her door tightly closed and hurried downstairs. The latch was worn and Trixie was a smart dog. She had already discovered how to push it open.

"There you are." Leslie found Trixie and snapped the leash on her rhinestone collar. "You'd better be a good little dog this morning or I'll—"

"Let Trixie lead you now," Mrs. Schmidt called out loudly, interrupting Leslie's threat. "She knows where she wants to go. She's a good girl, aren't you, sugar? Hurry and walk her before it rains. My arthritis tells me there's a storm brewing."

Leslie winced as the yapping Chihuahua led her around the flower beds and over the lawn. Any of these places would be fine, but Trixie had other ideas. She sniffed and yapped, but that was all. The little dog pulled Leslie on a merry chase all over the yard until finally they were forced to cross the crushed-granite driveway. There, defiantly, Trixie squatted in the exact center of the path.

"No! Oh, Trixie! You're a bad dog!" Leslie glared at her and the little dog glared right back, growling low in her throat. This was the third time in as many days that Trixie had gone in the driveway. The little scooper Mrs. Schmidt had given her didn't work on the crushed rocks, and Leslie had to remove the stones from that section and wash them with the hose before she replaced them. It seemed as if Trixie deliberately made things as difficult as possible. Leslie was sure the little monster did it on purpose.

Finally the odious chore was done and Leslie took Trixie back inside. She hung the leash on the nail by the kitchen door and tried to decide what to do. Mom was upstairs going over paint samples, and Mrs. Schmidt was scrubbing down the bathroom walls and floor. Mike had left for the Cities early that morning to shoot another series of buildings. There was no one to talk to.

Leslie slipped quietly out the kitchen door and wandered toward the greenhouse. The old building fascinated her. She knew that Amelia and Dorthea had raised exotic roses in here and someday they'd fill it up with flowers again. Thoughtfully Leslie opened the latched door and stepped inside.

The walls were filled with shelves and old earthen-ware pots. Leslie sat down on a potting bench and sighed. It was hot and muggy in the greenhouse and she knew Mrs. Schmidt's arthritis was right. A summer storm was approaching. Dark gray clouds were rolling in from the west and the air was charged with electricity. Above the amber glass roof the sky was an eerie sight, ominous and boiling.

The rumbling started as Leslie sat, looking up. She jumped as a bright flash of lightning cut across the sky. It was quickly followed by a second bolt and then a third. Usually she loved thunderstorms, but she felt a little frightened, out here all alone.

The air was still and heavy. Not a single leaf flut-tered outside. The whole sky seemed to be waiting and Leslie began to tremble. She didn't want to go outside now. The storm was too close.

There was a loud crash as lightning struck nearby and Leslie heard a tree branch fall in the yard. She reached up and grabbed her key, her heart pound-ing. She'd stay right here, where it was safe.

Perspiration dripped off Leslie's small body and made wet splashes on the redwood bench. The odor of old wood and wet heat made it hard for her to breathe. Leslie sucked the air into her lungs and swallowed nervously, her fingers squeezing tightly around the solid shape of the key. She was dizzy and the flashes of lightning made everything inside bright yellow. Her eyes hurt and she huddled up against the bench, terribly afraid.

I'm here, Leslie. Don't be afraid. Watch and I'll show you something.

She felt rather than heard his voice. Christopher was inside her. She held the key and gave a timid smile. Now she felt better. Her friend, Christopher, was here.

The next bolt of lightning was so brilliant it hurt her eyes and something shone like a star in the reflected light. Metal gardening shears lay on the far side of the bench, gleaming with each new bolt of lightning.

Use them, Leslie. . . . I'll show you how. If you cut off your hair, you'll be just like me.

Leslie stared at the shears as another flash of lightning set them shining brilliantly. Christopher wanted her to cut her hair—her pretty, long hair. He wanted her to cut it off as short as his.

She sat stunned for a moment and then she slid carefully along the bench. Her fingers reached out and grasped the shears. They were sharp and shiny, almost new-looking.

Cut, Leslie. I'll help you. Grab a handful of hair and snip it off.

Leslie raised the shears, holding them in her right hand. She pulled her long hair into a clump and held it above her head. As the lightning flashed, it sparkled along the blades of the shears. They squeaked and cut, severing the golden strands cleanly.

A laugh poured from Leslie's throat as she lifted more hair and cut again. The shears twirled and twinkled in her fingers. The pile of hair at her feet was growing deeper, floating down like strands of moonbeams.

It was finished. As the last clump of golden hair fell to her feet, Leslie smiled. She'd done exactly as Christopher wanted.

Perfect, Leslie. Go show Mother. She's going to love it.

Leslie turned and walked to the door. She felt strange and disoriented, as if she'd just awakened from a dream. A blast of heavy air hit her as she stepped out onto the lawn. The sky was dark and the lights were on in the house. She had to hurry and get inside before the rain started.

Lightly, her bare feet just brushing the grass, Leslie ran across the lawn. There was something she had to show Mom. Mrs. Schmidt gave a startled gasp as she pushed past her and up the stairs.

Karen was at her desk, samples of material and color charts spread out around her. Her eyes widened as Leslie burst into the room.

"Leslie! What—?" Karen's face turned white and she gave a gasp of shock as she saw Leslie's hair. "Your hair! Leslie! What happened to your hair?"

"I cut it." Leslie gave a smile as she remembered. "Don't you love it, Mother?" She fluffed out her short blond hair with her hand.

"I—I . . . yes." Karen spoke slowly, a little color coming back to her cheeks. "It's really a change . . . but . . . yes, I do. I really do like it, kitten! I never thought I'd like to see your hair short, but . . . well . . . it's just right for you."

Leslie gave her mother a hug and raced down the hallway to her room. She was so happy, she thought she'd burst. She picked up the tintype and held it close to her face, looking critically in the mirror. After a moment of careful consideration she smiled happily. She felt so much better now, now that she was just like her friend, Christopher.

TWENTY-ONE

It was a large room, with long, narrow windows, smelling faintly of sweeping compound and newly varnished wood. The erasers were lined up neatly on the chalk ledge, with the cursive alphabet on lettered green cards above. The desks were bolted to the floor in precise rows, stretching the length of the room. Each one was occupied, except the third-row front, Leslie's place.

Leslie stood in the front of the room by the teacher's desk, wearing the expensive dress her mother had insisted on for the first day of school. She felt terribly self-conscious up here all by herself.

"Class? Come to attention!" Mrs. Ogilvie clapped her hands sharply for order. "That's enough talking for now! Quiet down, please . . . quiet down!"

Mrs. Ogilvie blew a sharp blast on the whistle she wore around her neck. The sound made Leslie jump. None of her former teachers had been forced to blow a whistle for attention.

It seemed to take hours before the class finally stopped talking. At last the room was still and all eyes were turned toward the front of the room, fixed on her.

"This is Leslie Houston, our new student," Mrs. Ogilvie announced. "I think the rest of you know each other from last year. Of course we're missing a familiar face today, but hopefully Gary Wilson will be back with us soon."

Leslie shifted from one foot to the other. Talking about Gary made her uncomfortable, even though her mom kept telling her the accident wasn't her fault. She had a funny feeling about it all, and couldn't help feeling sorry for Gary, even though he was a troublemaker and a tease.

Mrs. Ogilvie cleared her throat and drew a lace handkerchief from her sleeve to wipe her face. "Leslie has a nice surprise for our first day of school," she went on. "She brought her camera to take our class picture. Won't that be wonderful?"

Taffy rolled her eyes heavenward, and Bud gave a little chuckle under his breath. Mrs. Ogilvie obviously didn't hear him because she went right on talking.

"Bud Allen and Taffy Comstock? I want you two to be Leslie's special friends today. Let's show her how nice and friendly we are at Cold Spring Elementary. I know we're all going to benefit from Leslie's contributions this year. She has a straight-A record from her school in Minneapolis."

There were several giggles from the back of the room, but again Mrs. Ogilvie didn't seem to hear. Leslie's face turned red and she stared very hard at the picture of George Washington hanging over the bookcase. It was humiliating standing up here this way, especially with Bud and Taffy whispering and making faces.

"Now, pick up your lunch boxes and form an orderly line at the door. Mary Ellen Ness? I want you to be Leslie's partner for the walk to the river."

Leslie took her place at the rear of the line with Mary Ellen. The rest of the kids were giggling and talking together and she felt like an outsider. Mary Ellen didn't say a word. She just fell into line without even glancing at Leslie.

The class moved forward with Mrs. Ogilvie in the lead. This seemed like a strange way to start the school year, but Mrs. Ogilvie said the Labor Day picnic was a tradition here. It was a celebration of the beginning of their year together and a reunion for all the kids who hadn't seen each other all summer.

"Now, class . . . we will march in orderly fashion to the river." Mrs. Ogilvie raised her voice as she stopped the line at the heavy wooden double doors that led to the sidewalk. "Let's all behave like responsible adults. Ready? Proceed!"

Bud Allen made a rude face behind Mrs. Ogilvie's back and Taffy rewarded his daring with a soft giggle. They had been in her class last year. Mrs. Ogilvie taught fifth and sixth grade combined.

"I think we've got a new teacher's pet this year." Taffy spoke in a low voice, which only Bud heard. "She sure made a hit with Mrs. Ogilvie."

"Well, she didn't make a hit with me!" Bud grinned at Taffy. "Did you get a good look at her hair? It looks like she cut it off with an axe! You've got the prettiest hair, Taffy."

"Maybe she got caught in a lawn mower." Taffy

grinned back and fluffed out her shining red hair. She knew she was the cutest girl in the class. Today was super, being paired with Bud, even if they did have to put up with Leslie.

Bud leaned over and whispered in Taffy's ear. "Let's ditch her. How about it, Taffy?"

"Sure." Taffy grinned back, pleased by Bud's attention. "It should be easy to ditch her once we get to the river. We'll give her the deep freeze. I'll pass the word to the girls, and you take care of the boys. We'll fix it so nobody even looks at her. If we're lucky, she'll start crying and have to go home."

Leslie sighed as she marched along behind her class. The fresh air was making her hungry, but there wasn't much to look forward to for lunch. The other kids probably had things like potato chips and bologna sandwiches, her favorites. Mrs. Schmidt thought bologna was contaminated and potato chips were too greasy. She said Leslie needed iron, and liverwurst on whole wheat bread was the best way to get it. Instead of Kool-Aid or soda pop, she had buttermilk in her Thermos. Leslie had asked for Twinkies or at least a cookie for dessert, but Mrs. Schmidt said white sugar was bad for the digestion. There were dried prunes and apricots in the bottom of her lunch sack.

As Leslie walked along, an occasional student would turn to stare at her. There would be giggles and whispering and then it would happen all over again; the stare, the whisper, and the giggle. It was obvious everyone was talking about her, and she couldn't understand why. She tried hard not to notice, but she felt like turning around and running back home. That was impossible, though. She'd just have to get through the day somehow. Perhaps she should try talking to Mary Ellen. At least she wasn't staring and whispering.

"Mrs. Ogilvie seems very nice. Was she your teacher last year?"

"Uh-huh." Mary Ellen kept her eyes straight ahead and her brown ponytail swung from side to side as she walked. Leslie waited a moment, but Mary Ellen didn't say anything else.

"Does this picnic last the whole day?"

"Uh-huh," Mary Ellen replied quickly, and clamped her lips shut without even glancing in Leslie's direction. Leslie felt her face flush with embarrassment. It was clear that Mary Ellen didn't want to talk to her.

"Do you think the picnic will be fun?" It was difficult trying to start a conversation when Mary Ellen just grunted out one-word answers.

"It'll be fun if you stay away from me!" This time Mary Ellen turned to look at her directly and Leslie read the coldness in her eyes. Why did these kids all hate her so much? She hadn't done a thing to them. Mike said it was just being the new kid in the neighborhood, but she'd been here for months now and nothing had changed. Maybe they were really as mean as she thought they were.

For the rest of the walk Leslie trudged along with her eyes fixed on the ground in front of her. She had tried her hardest to be friendly, but Mary Ellen had snubbed her. None of the kids so much as gave her a friendly glance.

An hour later Leslie was sure that she was the most unpopular girl in the history of Cold Spring Elementary. No one would talk to her at all unless Mrs. Ogilvie was right by her side. Her face felt stiff from trying to smile and she wished she were anywhere but here at the river with these horrible kids. She stood by herself on the riverbank, squinting through her viewfinder at a log in the water. They were all expecting her to cry, but she wouldn't. She'd smile even if it killed her.

"I don't think it's working." Bud nudged Taffy and pointed toward the shore where Leslie stood alone as they saw a smile on her face. "It doesn't seem to bother her at all that nobody's talked to her all day."

"If she'd just start crying, Mrs. Ogilvie would send her home." Taffy's voice mirrored her frustration. "What can we do, Bud?"

"Hey! That's easy!" Bud began to grin as he got an idea. "We'll scare her. She'll start crying if she's scared."

"Super!" Taffy looked up at him in admiration. Sometimes Bud had really great ideas. It would be fun to scare Leslie and show the rest of the kids what a baby she was. Taffy was still mad at Leslie for having had straight A's. She was used to being the smartest girl in the class.

"What are girls scared of, Taffy?" Bud was thinking out loud. "You ought to know."

Taffy thought for a moment and then her eyes began to sparkle. "Snakes!" She grinned triumphantly. "Chase her with a snake, Bud. She'll be scared to death. Are there any snakes around here?"

"Sure. Come on and help me look."

Taffy followed his lead gingerly, poking through the long grass with a stick. "Oh!" She jumped back quickly as a garter snake slithered across the toe of her sneakers. "Bud? I found one!"

"Great." He grabbed the snake, head in one hand and tail in the other. "Just look at that! It's a beauty!"

Taffy shuddered slightly, watching the snake writhe in Bud's hands. "Leslie's still over there by the bank," she said, pointing urgently. "Go on, Bud. I'll be right behind you. I'll keep an eye out for Mrs. Ogilvie, and you chase her."

Leslie was adjusting the focus on her camera when Bud came stealthily out of the bushes in back of her. He gave a loud laugh and she whirled around to face him. Then she stepped back in horror as she saw the wiggling, squirming reptile in his hands.

"Here's a little present from Taffy and me!" Seeing Leslie cringe, he laughed even harder. He moved closer and extended his arms, waving the snake and grinning. "Why don't you take a close-up of this beautiful snake with your fancy camera? This snake would just love to have its picture taken!"

For a timeless moment all Leslie could do was stare at the snake twining and slithering over Bud's arm. Then she gave a shrill scream and ran for the safety of the clearing. She could hear Bud's footsteps thudding behind her, but she didn't dare turn back and look. He was chasing her with that awful, slimy thing! It had looked straight at her with its beady black eyes!

Leslie was gasping by the time she reached the clearing. She was sure that Mrs. Ogilvie would save her, but the teacher was nowhere in sight. Leslie gave a cry of pure terror as she realized that she had run the wrong way. In her fright she had gotten her directions confused.

She caught her foot in a clump of roots and twisted her ankle. In a panic Leslie wrenched her foot free and kept on running. Her ankle was throbbing painfully, but Bud was right behind her. She could hear him laughing as he ran through the trees after her.

The ground was wet and Leslie felt her feet go out from under her. She fell heavily, stumbling on both knees, her camera swinging out to hit her painfully in the chest. It felt as if she couldn't breathe, she was so terrified. Then Bud was on top of her, waving that horrid, squirming snake in her face, laughing like a maniac!

Leslie opened her mouth to scream, but no sound came out. The snake's slick green body was next to her face now, its flickering tongue almost touching her cheek. Her eyes rolled up and then she was hurtling down a narrow tunnel into blackness with the sound of Bud and Taffy's laughter ringing in her ears.

Someone was whistling, sharp and strident. Voices were calling out her name. For a moment Leslie didn't know where she was. Then reality came rushing back. Mrs. Ogilvie was blowing her whistle and they were calling for her.

Leslie jumped to her feet and whirled around. The snake was nowhere in sight. Her ankle throbbed and she reached down to touch it. She didn't want to go back and face Bud and Taffy and the rest of the class. She wanted to go straight home and never see any of them again.

Tears stung her eyes and she reached up for the key. She needed Christopher. Christopher would stop Bud from being mean to her.

It was much brighter now. Her eyes were opening wide and she leaned against a tree as the pleasant dizziness came. Christopher was right there inside her.

I'll help you, Leslie. Just go back to your class now and pretend nothing happened. I'll fix Bud for you. I promise he won't ever chase you again.

Leslie took a deep breath and steadied herself. She waited until the dizzy feeling had passed, then shuddered slightly. It had been awful when Bud was chasing her with the snake, but it was all over now. She didn't have to be afraid any longer. Now Christopher was here to help her.

The whistle blew again, three sharp blasts. "Leslie? Leslie Houston! It's time to come back now!"

Leslie straightened her dress and squared her thin shoulders. She hoped that Mrs. Ogilvie wouldn't be angry with her for coming back late. She'd tell the teacher that she had fallen, taking some nature pictures. Then she'd do exactly as Christopher had said and act as if nothing had happened. There was a faint hint of a smile on Leslie's face as she started off through the trees to join her class.

TWENTY-TWO

She had been walking behind them all the way from school and Bud could tell that Taffy was getting nervous. It was strange the way she was keeping back a half a block and just following without saying a word. They were both sure she'd turn at the corner and go toward her house, but she didn't. She was going out of her way to follow them.

At first they turned around and shouted insults at her to make her go home, but she kept right on pacing them silently. The whole thing had Taffy really spooked.

"Bud, do something!" Taffy glanced back once more and moved closer to Bud. "Make her go home!"

Bud liked it when Taffy depended on him. It made him feel brave and strong, even though it was only skinny little Leslie Houston he had to chase away.

"Get out of here!" Bud called out, stopping in the center of the tree-flanked sidewalk to glare back at Leslie. "Don't you know when you're not wanted?"

Leslie stopped, too, and stood there staring back at him. There was a peculiar blank expression on her face and she looked straight into his eyes without blinking.

"She's weird!" Bud turned back to Taffy in disgust and grabbed her hand to pull her forward. "Don't let her bug you, Taffy. Just ignore her and she'll go away. Come on—I'll walk you all the way home."

Taffy let Bud hold her hand and did her best to ignore Leslie the rest of the way home. She sighed in relief as she reached her front steps at last.

"There's something strange about her, Bud." Taffy stood on her front porch, glancing back up the sidewalk nervously. "Be careful!"

"Aw, come on, Taffy. Leslie Houston doesn't bother me a bit. She's just got a couple of screws loose somewhere."

"I hope so." Taffy managed a small smile. "Thanks for walking me home, Bud."

Bud shook his head as Taffy opened the door and stood in the entryway. She really did look scared. He couldn't imagine being scared of Leslie, but girls were funny sometimes. He'd give Taffy a good laugh to cheer her up before he left.

"Come on, Leslie Doggy!" Bud snapped his fingers and whistled shrilly through his teeth. "Come on, boy . . . time to go! Follow your master now. . . . Be a good little mutt!"

Taffy giggled, but it was a pale imitation of her usual laugh. She slipped inside and closed the door behind her, snapping on the lock. She could see what was happening through the window and she shivered a bit. Leslie was following Bud, keeping half a block behind him as he swaggered up the street.

Bud glanced back as he rounded the corner. She

was still back there. He wished he knew why she was following him. Maybe he shouldn't have chased her with that snake. She'd been weird ever since.

They were really surprised when she hadn't squealed on them to Mrs. Ogilvie. Naturally, they were planning to deny it anyway, but she hadn't said a word to their teacher. Instead she had smiled quietly through the rest of the picnic as if she knew a secret. Taffy was right. Leslie Houston was really strange.

Even though he tried to keep his pace even, Bud was aware of walking faster as he headed toward his father's car dealership on the edge of town. Of course he wasn't afraid of a little girl like Leslie, but it was unnerving being followed like this. He didn't like to admit it, but Leslie had him a little spooked, too.

Bud crossed the used-car lot with its sign, PREVIOUSLY OWNED AUTOS, weaving his way in and out of the old clunkers his father sold and traded. He stopped in front of the huge plate-glass window of the showroom and looked back. Leslie was standing across the street, motionless, as if she were waiting for something. The way she was smiling made Bud shudder. He and Taffy would laugh about this whole thing tomorrow at school, but right now it was more than a little scary.

He turned and glanced in the showroom. It was deserted. Three brand-new Fords gleamed behind the glass, chrome sparkling in the sun, but there was no sign of his father. His dad must be in the office with a customer.

When he turned back, she was still there. There was something different about her now, and Bud took a couple of cautious steps closer. Her eyes were different . . . that's what it was! Earlier he would have sworn that she had blue eyes, but now they were as black as night, shining and cold like a snake's. He couldn't help but stare at her. He'd never seen anyone with eyes like that before.

Leslie squeezed the key tightly as her eyes locked with Bud's. She tingled all over, and there was a rushing in her ears. The sky seemed to lighten and everything was sharp and clear, the focus perfect and the colors so vivid they hurt. She squinted against the brightness, but she knew she couldn't shut her eyes. She had to see everything.

Bud frowned as Leslie raised her camera. She was taking a picture of him. That was a crazy thing to do. Surely, she couldn't have followed him here just to take his picture.

He raised his hand and gave her the finger. She could take a picture of that if she wanted. Taffy wasn't going to believe any of this when he told her. That dumb Leslie Houston had followed him here just to take his picture. Well—she had her picture, and now she could go. He had to get inside and help his dad.

Bud tried to turn to go in the door, but his feet wouldn't move. It felt as if his shoes were cemented to the sidewalk.

"Hey!" He let out a shout as he struggled to move. What was happening?

Watch, Leslie. It's going to happen right now.

Leslie watched through the viewfinder as the black car rolled smoothly forward toward the inside of the window. Its heavy chrome bumper pressed against the glass, making it bow out like a giant fish-eye.

There was a crack like a pistol shot as the window shattered and huge slivers of glass exploded into the street.

Leslie watched with unblinking eyes as a piece of glass shaped like a gleaming scythe hurtled forward, severing Bud's arm at the elbow. She saw his mouth open in a silent scream as his other arm was hit and then his legs. His leg flopped grotesquely like a dismembered scarecrow's as he fell to the sidewalk in a red, writhing heap.

Leslie walked quickly past the streetlight and rounded the corner. There was noise and shouting behind her, but she couldn't stop. It was late and school had been over for thirty minutes. Mom would be wondering what was keeping her. She would go straight home like a good girl and take a nap. She was tired from her first day at school.

Karen glanced around her and smiled. The dining room was definitely taking shape. She set the antique silver candlestick holders on the sideboard and stood back to admire them. She should run to the store and pick up some candles. The exercise would be good for her. She hadn't been outside the grounds for days.

It was only seven-thirty, but it was already dark outside. She could run to the store and back before anyone even missed her. Mike was in Duluth for three days, shooting a feature on a solar-energy housing unit, and Mrs. Schmidt had retired to her bedroom to watch TV. Leslie was in her room sleeping. She had come home from school completely exhausted and asked to take a nap. Karen supposed the first day of class was always difficult, especially in a new school.

Karen grabbed a sweater and stepped out the door, breathing in the night air. September was her favorite month. The night was cool and leaves crunched under her feet as she walked through the yard to the gate. The stars were brilliant tonight and she smiled in contentment. Her work on the house was coming along beautifully. The downstairs was practically finished. The parlor was exactly like the miniature and she had found the missing hand-hooked rug in a corner of the ballroom. Mrs. Schmidt had worked all day on it, removing old stains and years of dust from the fibers. Mike would be pleased when he came home. At last the parlor was ready for him to photograph.

Karen turned back to look at the house, huge and sedate against the night sky. The chandelier in the dining room gleamed softly and she was glad she'd found replacements for the broken cut-glass teardrops. The house was so close to being finished that she almost hated to leave it, even for a minute. The moment she got back, she'd try her hand at repairing the canework in the antique rocker she had found. The instruction book had arrived in today's mail, along with the supplies she'd ordered. When the chair was finished, it would go in William Appleton's library, along with all his old books and papers.

At the far end of the ground floor was the morning room, Karen's pride and joy. She had left the light burning, and even from the street it looked cozy and inviting. It had been Dorthea's favorite room. She had described it in detail in her journals. The room looked out over the side lawn and caught the bright morning sun. The refinished French doors opened directly onto the garden, and Red Fischer was trying to fix the old granite fountain, which had once provided the water for the surrounding flower beds. Now Dorthea's desk was there, as it had been long ago, and Karen loved to sit with her receipts and papers and look out into the garden. She felt old-fashioned and serene in that spot, much as Dorthea must have felt years ago. It was almost as if, when she placed herself in a completely renovated room, she were communing with the spirit of those days long past.

Resolutely Karen turned her back on the house and glanced at her watch. Eight o'clock! She'd have to hurry to get to the store before it closed. Time seemed to pass so quickly when she was thinking about the house.

The gate squeaked as she opened it, and Karen made a mental note to oil it the next time she went out. She stepped out briskly and started down the sidewalk, then slowed abruptly as a wave of dizziness came over her. She felt her heart pound frantically and the palms of her hands were wet. Her knees trembled and almost buckled as she took another faltering step forward.

"Oh, my head!" Karen leaned weakly against the wrought-iron fence. There was a searing pain at her temples and she felt as if her head were splitting in two. There was no way she could shop tonight. She'd go right back to the house and sit down.

As she slowly retraced her steps, she began to feel better. Her dizziness had all but disappeared by the time she reentered the yard, and her headache was but a dim throbbing memory. That was strange. She felt almost normal now, but she wasn't taking any chances. She hadn't really wanted to leave the house anyway. She'd much rather recane the chair and let Mrs. Schmidt pick up the candles tomorrow. If she was coming down with a virus, she had to be careful. She certainly couldn't afford to get sick when she had the whole second floor to finish.

Leslie was sleeping soundly, a small shape in the big brass bed. Karen bent down to kiss her lightly and smiled. It was nearly midnight and she had finished the chair. If Leslie hadn't awakened yet, she'd probably sleep through until morning.

As Karen turned to leave, the picture of Dorthea's son caught her eye. She glanced at her daughter and then back at the picture again. Leslie certainly did look like Dorthea's son, with her hair cut short this way. Karen picked up the tintype and turned it over, noticing the inscription on the back. Christopher Appleton. That was a nice name. Where had she heard it before?

Karen tried to remember. Leslie had asked about prophetic dreams, that day in the cupola. She had been dreaming about a boy named Christopher. What a strange coincidence.

Karen put the picture back and sighed. Now it would be even more difficult to convince Leslie that dreams didn't really come true.

TWENTY-THREE

"Are you sure you're feeling all right, Leslie?" Karen stared anxiously at her daughter over the breakfast table. "You look so pale this morning."

"She looks a bit peaked to me, too." Mrs. Schmidt poured a glass of freshly squeezed orange juice and set it down in front of Leslie. "I'm going to make sure she eats right, Mrs. Houston. There's nothing like a big bowl of hot cereal for a good start in the morning."

"I'm all right, Mom." Leslie smiled politely as Mrs. Schmidt dished up a steaming bowl of oatmeal. She didn't feel much like eating, but Mrs. Schmidt was trying to be nice. Leslie blew on her spoon to cool it and took a big mouthful so she wouldn't have to talk. She wasn't sick, but she almost wished she were. Then she could stay home and not go to school today.

Last night had been awful. She kept waking up, seeing the blood and hearing the screams in her head. She had just wanted Bud to stop teasing her— that was all. She'd never thought something so frightening could happen. It was all her fault for getting mad again. When she got mad, and Christopher came, accidents happened. People were hurt. She could never let herself get mad again.

"You'd better hurry, kitten, or you'll be late." Karen gave her daughter an encouraging smile. It was clear that Leslie didn't want to go to school. School here in Cold Spring was bound to be different and it was natural for Leslie to have adjustment problems at first. Karen decided she'd take time to help Leslie with her homework tonight. That would make her less nervous about her new school.

As soon as Leslie had left, Karen went up to the bedroom and put on her warm-up suit. She hadn't been taking care of herself lately and a nice run would do her good.

It was a gorgeous day. She ran around the inside perimeter of the fence, checking the grounds. The lawn was beautiful now, thanks to Red Fischer. She felt like just staying in the yard and jogging up and down between the huge old trees, but that was silly. She'd take a nice, long run down the path to the river and back. It would be lovely with the trees changing color.

She arrived at the gate, rosy-faced and smiling. Being out in the air was definitely good for her. She felt better than she had in weeks!

The gate squeaked again as she opened it. She had forgotten the oilcan. She'd take care of it right after she came back.

This time she didn't even get to the corner. The

headache hit with the force of a physical blow. Spots swirled in front of her eyes and she gasped in pain. It was the same way she'd felt the previous night.

She made her way back slowly, stooped over, stopping to lean against the fence, breathing deeply every few steps. She was trembling and could barely pry open the gate.

As soon as Karen reentered the yard, the throbbing eased. She stood upright. It was as if her strength had miraculously returned and now she felt fine again. She stood leaning against the gate, completely mystified. What on earth was wrong with her?

"This has got to stop!" Her voice was weak but determined. She swallowed hard and jogged off toward the side of the house, running at her usual pace. She must be drastically out of condition to feel this way. She'd just run around in the yard for a few minutes and see if it happened again. At least if she got sick, she'd be close to the house.

Karen jogged for ten minutes, back and forth on the side lawn. She felt just fine now. Perhaps it just took a few minutes for her body to get used to the exercise. It should be safe to try the path to the river again if she took it easy.

This time it happened even sooner. The slight dizziness started the moment she stepped out of the gate and got progressively worse as she moved down the sidewalk. Her temples throbbed with pain and Karen turned back in dismay, not quite believing what was happening to her. Every time she left the grounds, she got sick!

She walked around the side of the house and went in through the French doors. She didn't want to run into Mrs. Schmidt and answer any questions. She had to think this out before she did anything else.

She sat at her desk in the morning room with her head in her hands. She felt a rush of fear as she remembered the other times she had tried to leave the house.

The church bazaar . . . she had gotten sick then, too, without knowing why. And she had felt fine the moment she returned home.

Last night on her walk to the store . . . she hadn't gone half a block before the headache hit her.

And now, today, she'd been barely able to leave the gate. It was ridiculous—and utterly terrifying.

She drew a deep breath and tried to think. Of course she'd read about things like this in psychology books, but it was another matter to actually experience them. She must have some sort of mental block about leaving this house.

Most mental blocks were caused by guilt. Perhaps she felt guilty about leaving the house with so much work to be done. That had to be it. And if that were true, the solution was simple. She'd finish the house completely and then everything would be fine.

Karen sighed and shook her head. The whole thing made some sort of crazy sense, but she was still upset. It was frightening, being a prisoner of her own emotions. Mike would be convinced she was insane if she ever told him about this!

"I can't leave this house." Karen stared at the framed drawing of Dorthea she'd hung over the desk. It was one of the many sketches Kirby Shaw had drawn in preparation for the lovely oil portrait. "You should have had my problem. If you'd stayed here, everything would have been fine."

"What did you say, Mrs. Houston?" Thelma Schmidt stood in the doorway of the morning room, a cleaning rag in her hand.

"Oh!" Karen looked up, startled. "Nothing, Mrs. Schmidt. I was just talking to myself."

The housekeeper frowned slightly. "Do you want me to take the wooden cover off the microwave? Mr. Houston spilled coffee on the inside."

"Yes, the cover just slides to the left." Karen gave the housekeeper a troubled smile. "Be sure to replace it, though. I can just imagine the expression on Dorthea's face if she came home and found a microwave in her mother's kitchen!"

Mrs. Schmidt looked puzzled and Karen sighed. "It's just a little joke, Mrs. Schmidt. Dorthea is the girl who lived here before the turn of the century."

"Oh, the Appleton girl." Mrs. Schmidt nodded. "I remember my grandmother talking about her once. There was some kind of scandal, I think, but that's all forgotten now. The Appleton girl's long gone, Mrs. Houston. She probably died before I was even born."

Karen shivered a little. It upset her somehow to remember that Dorthea was dead. She seemed so close, so alive.

"It feels a bit odd to have the house done up just the way it was then," Mrs. Schmidt went on. "It makes me feel like I'm living in a time warp, like they used to show on *The Twilight Zone*. I tell you, it gives me a start every time I open that cabinet and see the dishwasher. It sure doesn't fit with the rest of the house."

Karen laughed. "That's why I had that cabinet

built," she explained. "But really, Mrs. Schmidt, don't you think that an old-fashioned decor is beautiful?"

"Some of it is." The housekeeper leaned against the door frame. "Take that table in the dining room . . . you don't find wood like that anymore. All the furniture is beautiful. It must have been wonderful to live in this mansion back then."

"Exactly!" Karen smiled. "Restoring this house makes me feel like I'm living back then. Sometimes I almost imagine Dorthea's here, just waiting for me to put the house back the way it was so she can come home again."

"Well . . . I don't know if I'd go that far." Mrs. Schmidt laughed nervously. "That's almost like wishing for the dead to come back to life." She paused, looking uncomfortable. "Well, standing here talking isn't going to get the work done. I'll go put up that roast now, Mrs. Houston."

Karen sighed as the housekeeper hurried away. Mrs. Schmidt was a nice woman, but she didn't really understand about this house. She wasn't trying to bring the dead back to life; that sounded so grim. Perhaps she was bringing a dead age back to life by restoring the house. She was reliving the times and experiencing the events that had belonged to her house in the past. Was there any harm in that? But sometimes she did feel that Dorthea was alive, watching her and approving the work she was doing. She guessed she was keeping Dorthea's memory alive, or her spirit, or something like that. In any event she didn't have time to think about all that now. She had to get to work on the second floor.

Mrs. Schmidt shook her head as she seasoned the roast and turned on the oven. All that talk about Dorthea Appleton was crazy. And Mrs. Houston was forever trying to make everything old-fashioned. There was nothing wrong with antiques, but she was going overboard. And she'd been talking to that picture. It was a good thing Leslie wasn't home. It wasn't good for a little girl to hear her mother talk to pictures just as if they could talk back.

"She's a strange woman," the housekeeper muttered under her breath. Mrs. Houston didn't seem to care what Leslie did as long as it didn't interfere with her decorating. If Leslie were hers, Mrs. Schmidt knew she would have tanned her bottom for cutting her hair, but Mrs. Houston hadn't even batted an eyelash. The child was running wild and it seemed no one cared but her. Mr. Houston was never home to take charge, and Mrs. Houston was too busy with her antiques and her silly notions. That poor child would be better off anywhere but here.

TWENTY-FOUR

Of course she'd heard all about it the night before. Her mother had been on the telephone for hours, getting the latest news from the hospital. But Taffy's eyes were still red and swollen from crying about what had happened to her friend. She had trouble believing it was true.

Poor Bud! Taffy glanced over at the empty desk on her right and blinked back tears. He was still alive, but he would never be the same. His left arm was gone from the elbow down, sliced off by the flying glass, and his legs were injured so badly the doctors said there was a chance he'd never walk again. And only yesterday he'd been running and playing games with her at the picnic!

"Class? Attention, please!" Mrs. Ogilvie stood in front of the class and immediately the room was quiet. Their teacher looked older than ever, and Taffy noticed that she had trouble looking directly at them as she faced the class.

"I know all of you have heard about Bud Allen's tragic accident." Mrs. Ogilvie cleared her throat. "I think it would be nice if we wrote letters to Bud for our English lesson today."

Several students nodded and Taffy heard Mary Ellen sniffle into a handkerchief behind her. A few of the children looked tearful, frightened. Bud had been the most popular boy in the class.

"Now let's try to write cheerful things that will lift Bud's spirits for his stay in the hospital," Mrs. Ogilvie went on. "I'll be glad to help anyone with spelling."

Taffy blinked back tears as she picked up her pen. *Dear Bud,* she wrote. Then she stopped, unsure what to say next. She wanted to ask him how it had happened, to tell him that she'd cried all night because she was so sorry for him, but she didn't have the words. She looked out the window and saw the baseball field in the distance. Bud would never play baseball again. How could any letter she wrote make up for that?

Tears were filling her eyes again and she blinked hard. This had been a summer of unhappy accidents. First Gary Wilson had been hurt at the swimming hole, and now Bud, too, had suffered a terrible injury.

Thinking about Bud's accident made Taffy feel sick inside. No one really knew how the car had started rolling. There weren't any witnesses. Mr. Allen had been in the office with a customer. Bud had been all alone on the sidewalk when it happened. *Poor, poor Bud!*

There was a sigh from the seat next to her, and Taffy glanced over at Leslie Houston. Leslie's blond head was bent over her paper and her pen was moving steadily. Taffy drew in her breath sharply as she stared at Leslie. A cold chill crept up her back as she remembered what had happened after school yesterday. Everyone said there were no witnesses, but what if Leslie had followed Bud to his father's car lot? What if she'd seen everything that had happened?

Taffy shuddered and her heart beat painfully in her chest as she had another, even more hideous thought. What if Leslie had somehow caused Bud's accident? Was it possible? Leslie had really been scared when Bud chased her with the snake. Could she have done this horrible thing to get even with him?

The thought was so frightening that Taffy felt weak. Her hand shook violently and her pen dropped from her fingers, clattering on the desktop. She had to go home right away and tell her mother.

"Yes, Taffy?" Mrs. Ogilvie saw her raised hand at last and called her up to the desk.

"Please, Mrs. Ogilvie, I don't feel good!" Taffy could feel the tears of fright run down her cheeks. "I want to go home!"

"My, my!" Mrs. Ogilvie felt Taffy's forehead and clicked her tongue. "You feel a little warm to me, Taffy. Go straight to the office and have Joyce call your mother to pick you up. You shouldn't be in school if you're coming down with something."

Taffy sat miserably in the office while her mother signed the release slip. She shivered as she walked out to the car. She'd never go to school again with Leslie Houston there. Leslie knew she had helped with the snake. Something awful might happen to her, too!

Twenty minutes later Taffy was home and in bed.

Her mother tucked the covers around her and took the thermometer out of her mouth.

"It's normal." Marilyn squinted at the thin silver line and held the thermometer close to her eyes to recheck the tiny numbers on the side. "It's 98.6, Rob. She's not running a fever."

"I told you she wasn't sick." Rob came in from the hallway, where he'd been waiting. "Now, what's all this about, Taffy? You know you should be in school if you're not sick."

"Tell us what's wrong, darling." Marilyn sat on the edge of her daughter's bed and stroked her forehead. "Are you in trouble at school?"

"No." Taffy glanced nervously at her father. She had hoped that he wouldn't be home. It seemed every time she said anything about Leslie Houston her dad got angry. Her mother understood, but her father always sided with the Houstons.

"Well . . . come on, Taffy." Rob frowned slightly as he stared at his daughter. Taffy seemed more frightened than ill. Something must have happened at school; and the sooner they knew what it was, the sooner they could clear it up. It was probably some silly girl's thing that Marilyn was perfectly capable of handling by herself, but he wanted to make sure. It just wasn't like Taffy to get upset over nothing.

"It—it all started at the picnic yesterday." Taffy drew a deep breath and shivered. "You know how stuck-up Leslie Houston is, Mom."

Taffy looked to her mother for encouragement and Marilyn nodded. She'd heard this before.

"Well . . . Leslie was even worse yesterday. She brought her camera and Mrs. Ogilvie thought it was wonderful. She got treated like the most important kid in the class, and the rest of us got mad. Leslie was acting all snotty and . . . well . . . some of us got together and decided to snub her."

Rob's lips tightened, but he didn't interrupt Taffy's explanation. He wanted the whole story before he said anything. As far as he was concerned, Leslie was a fine little girl. She'd had a real bad break when her mother lost the baby, and now Mike was gone most of the time, working. It was a pity the kids couldn't be more understanding. Leslie needed friends, but she had three strikes against her here in Cold Spring.

"Well, we . . . we were just playing around and having fun, and we—I mean, Bud—chased her with a snake!" Taffy blurted it out and her face turned red. It made her nervous that her dad wasn't saying anything.

"I know we shouldn't have done it, but we didn't hurt her or anything. Bud didn't even touch her with the snake. Then, when Bud was walking me home, she kept following us. We told her to go home, but she wouldn't. She just kept following, and it was spooky, Mom!"

"She kept following you?" Marilyn was curious. She didn't understand why Taffy was so upset over such an ordinary occurrence. "What did she say, darling? Did she want something?"

"She didn't say anything!" Tears were now rolling down her cheeks. "That's what scared me! She didn't say a single word. She just followed us all the way here, and she stood right outside until Bud left. Then she followed him. I think she stayed behind him all the way to Mr. Allen's car lot. I know she was mad at him for the snake, and I think she made that glass fall on him on purpose!"

Rob couldn't help it. He snorted and shook his head. He'd never heard anything so farfetched in his life.

"You think Leslie caused Bud's accident? Taffy . . . I just can't believe you said that! It's absurd! Leslie had a perfect right to be angry with Bud, but she couldn't possibly have caused the accident. Don't you know how it happened? One of the cars in the showroom wasn't blocked properly and it started rolling. The car hit the glass and Bud was standing right outside. Now, surely you don't think Leslie ran into the showroom and pushed that two-ton car through the window, do you?"

Taffy began to sob and Rob raised his voice.

"Now, Taffy, be reasonable! Even if Leslie wanted to get even with Bud, she couldn't push that car. You're just imagining things, honey. Leslie probably followed Bud partway and then went home. I'm sure she didn't even see the accident."

Rob stood up and patted Taffy lightly on the shoulder. "I know you're all upset over Bud, honey. It's perfectly normal to be afraid for your friend, but don't you see how silly you're being about Leslie?"

"I—I guess I was being silly." Taffy gave her dad a sheepish smile. "It just seemed like . . . well . . . I don't know, Dad. It just scared me, that's all."

"Bud's accident was enough to scare anyone." Rob's voice was kind. "It scared me, too, honey. Just remember that sometimes, when we're upset, we make mountains out of molehills. If you really would only try to get to know Leslie, you'll find she's a sweet, friendly girl. And she's got some family problems that are pretty tough for her to handle. I really think you should try to be nice to her. Leslie's probably just as upset over Bud's accident as you are."

"Well . . . maybe . . ." Taffy's voice trailed off and she gave a tired, little whimper. "I still don't like her, though, Dad. I just can't help it. I don't think she's as nice as you say she is."

"I'm not asking you to like her, Taffy," Rob explained patiently. "I'm just asking you to be polite to her. Do you think you can do that—just for me?"

"I guess so." Taffy closed her eyes and sighed. She really did feel a lot better now. Her dad was right. She'd been silly thinking that Leslie had hurt Bud. Of course that was impossible. She was just tired from crying all night.

"You get a little sleep, honey, and I'll see if I can get my work done early at the office." Rob smoothed back Taffy's hair and kissed the top of her head.

He was going through the door when Marilyn grabbed his arm, whispering, "Downstairs. I want to talk to you! I'll be right down."

"Taffy's not the only one who's upset." Marilyn sat on the edge of her favorite living-room chair and sighed. "Just listen to me for a minute, Rob. Doesn't it make you suspicious that Leslie was there at the scene of an accident again? Remember what I said? I told you that if there was another accident, Leslie would be right in the middle of it! Now I'm positive that there's some kind of connection."

"Oh, Marilyn—not again." Rob sighed deeply. "I thought we went through all this! You're just tired, dear. You've been up all night worrying about Bud and the Allens and you're letting your imagination run wild. You heard what I said to Taffy, and it made perfect sense. Now, think about it for a minute. Do you really believe that Leslie Houston is running around making accidents happen?"

"I guess not." Marilyn shook her head slightly. "But there was Gary Wilson's arm, and now Bud Allen. You don't know how terrible I feel, not being able to do anything for Roberta. I just wish there were some way I could help."

"There is." Rob patted his wife's shoulder. "You *can* help, dear! I think it would be wonderful if you started a community fund to help pay for some of the hospital bills. You'd be just the person to organize that, Marilyn. No one else could do it as well. Why don't you start on it right away this morning?"

"Why . . . yes, dear." Marilyn looked thoughtful and then she beamed at her husband. "That *is* a good idea! I'm sure I could get some of the other women to help with the telephone canvassing. There's no reason why we can't make it two funds—one for Gary Wilson and one for Bud. I could even get Taffy to help organize the elementary students. There's a lot they could do: bake sales . . . paper drives. . . . I don't know why I didn't think of it before."

When Rob left the house, Marilyn was already on the telephone, a list of hastily penned names spread out on the table in front of her. Rob gave her a wave and escaped through the door. After fifteen years he'd finally learned how to handle Marilyn when she got on one of her stubborn, irrational streaks. All he had to do was suggest something useful to be done and she was off and running. And Marilyn was a wonder when it came to raising money for community affairs. She loved to be in the limelight and she was good at it. At least organizing the fund would keep her mind off her crazy suspicions. Imagine blaming little Leslie Houston for those accidents!

TWENTY-FIVE

It was Friday night, his first night home after his boring trip to Duluth. Mike was amazed at everything Karen had done during his three-day absence. The parlor was fantastic, and she was ready with the dining room, too. She must have worked day and night to get all this finished.

"Leslie?" Mike turned to his stepdaughter and smiled. "Rob told me about a ballet teacher in St. Cloud. I think we could take you in on Saturdays if you still want to take lessons."

"Ballet?" Leslie looked shocked. "Oh, Mike! That's really nice but . . . well . . . I think I'm going to give up on ballet. It just doesn't seem very important anymore."

Mike shrugged, smiling at her across the table. She had certainly changed in the past couple of weeks. She'd eaten second helpings of everything tonight and now she was sitting with her elbows propped on the table, looking like a little tomboy with that short haircut. She was turning into a regular kid right before his eyes. The dainty, ladylike manners she'd always shown had all but disappeared. That was good. It meant that Leslie was adjusting to country living.

Mike's eyes turned to Karen and he frowned slightly. She worried him a little. She was changing, too, but he wasn't sure he liked it. It could be the shock of losing the baby, but she was so distant lately. The only thing she wanted to talk about was the house. Of course he was glad the work was going so well. Still, when he mentioned putting in a tennis court, something she'd wanted desperately when they first moved in, she hadn't even wanted to consider it. They couldn't destroy a section of the grounds, she said. The Appletons hadn't needed a tennis court and she didn't, either. She didn't want to change anything from the way it had been in the past. Karen was making this house into a living museum, some sort of a shrine to the Appletons.

"Seconds, Mrs. Houston?" Thelma Schmidt held the platter filled with her delicious fried chicken.

"No, thank you." Mike gave her a big smile. Hiring Mrs. Schmidt was the smartest thing he'd ever done. She was a great cook and she'd taken charge of the house beautifully. It was a relief not having to worry about Karen and Leslie when he was gone overnight.

He should take them all out for some fun tonight, Mike decided, sipping the last of his coffee. They hadn't done anything together in ages. They could go into St. Cloud and take in a movie. Leslie could stay up late. It was the weekend and there was no school tomorrow. Karen and Leslie needed a break from the redecorating.

"Will you help me with my school project, Mom?" Leslie spoke up as Mrs. Schmidt served the dessert.

"My teacher wants me to write a paper on the history of this house for class."

"Oh, that sounds like fun!" Karen smiled. "We could go through Dorthea's journals tonight and copy out the important events. You'd let her take some prints of the miniature to show her class, wouldn't you, Mike?"

"Sure," Mike replied shortly. He speared his Dutch apple pie savagely with his fork. He might have known it. Leslie and Karen were going to go over old books again tonight. All they ever did was talk about this damn house!

"I thought maybe you two would like to see a movie tonight. We could go to the drive-in in St. Cloud and I'll spring for a tub of buttered popcorn."

"No!" Karen reacted immediately and drew a deep breath as Mike stared at her curiously. She hadn't meant to be so vehement, but going to a movie was out of the question. There was no way she could leave the house.

"I just think it would be a better idea to stay here tonight," she added, trying to soften her tone somewhat. "Leslie and I should start working on her project right away. Schoolwork comes first, you know."

Mike was still staring at her and Karen blushed guiltily. She didn't dare explain her real reason for not wanting to leave the house. He'd know something was wrong and ask questions. Mike must never find out about her paranoia against leaving the house.

"Well, I guess I might as well work, then." Mike pushed back his chair with a sigh. "You two are going to be busy and there's nothing else for me to do.

Do you want me to come down and check in a couple of hours? Maybe all three of us can do something after Leslie's homework is done."

Karen stared down at her plate. She didn't really want to do anything tonight, except help Leslie with her project. After Leslie went to bed, she wanted to be alone to think and plan. She needed to be by herself to wrestle with some of the problems that were confronting her. And she certainly couldn't discuss them with Mike.

"I'll come up if it isn't too late." Karen looked up at last. "You have a lot of work to do, don't you, Mike? If it gets too late, I won't disturb you."

Karen saw the disappointment in his eyes. He looked hurt by her dismissal, but that simply couldn't be helped. Actually, she was almost sorry Mike had come home this weekend. He just made more problems for her. Things were much better when Mike wasn't here.

TWENTY-SIX

Leslie woke up happy. They'd finished half the project last night and it was going to be wonderful. She hummed a little tune as she pulled on her cutoff jeans and buttoned her favorite white shirt. It was Saturday and she had the whole day free. Just as soon as she had breakfast, she'd go and offer to help Mom on the house.

Leslie pulled her door shut behind her, but the wood was warped from the humidity and it was impossible to latch. She didn't think Trixie could get it open, but she'd have to be careful. Mike had promised to put on a new lock, but he was gone all the time. She'd just have to keep her eye on Trixie. That little dog was a menace.

Leslie found their housekeeper in the kitchen, chopping up vegetables for Sunday's stew. She said she always had beef stew on Sundays so everyone could eat whenever they wanted. Mrs. Schmidt smiled when she saw Leslie.

"My goodness, you're up with the birds this morning! I guess we're the only early risers today. They're still sleeping. Why don't you run up and take your bath and we'll all have breakfast together when they wake up. And make sure you soak those fingernails. Cleanliness is next to godliness, you know."

Leslie shook her head as she ran the water in the bathtub. Mrs. Schmidt really had a thing for cleanliness. She looked down at her hands and shrugged. Her fingernails were awfully dirty and she hadn't even noticed. She used to give herself manicures and put polish on them, but that didn't seem very important anymore.

Leslie draped her clothes over a stool and tested the water with her bare toe. It was just right. It might be nice to relax in a hot tub.

"Oh!" She remembered just in time and reached up to remove her key. The leather thong was very dirty and she decided to find a new one right after her bath. She dropped it by the side of the tub and stretched out in the warm water until only her head was visible. Then she shut her eyes and leaned back, totally relaxed.

The water was cold and she sat up, blinking. She must have fallen asleep. She stepped out and dried herself on a fluffy towel, thinking that she should have stayed in bed longer this morning.

She didn't see the open door until she was dressed. It was open only a little way and Leslie frowned. Mrs. Schmidt wouldn't have come in while she was in the tub. She was always talking about modesty. It must have been Trixie. That dog could push any door open.

"My key!" Leslie gave a cry as she discovered it was gone. Trixie must have dragged it off somewhere. She had to find it right away. Terrible things happened when she lost her key!

She ran from the room in a panic. As she rushed to the top of the stairs, looking for the annoying little Chihuahua, she heard Mrs. Schmidt on the phone in the parlor. Maybe Mrs. Schmidt had taken her key away from Trixie.

"That's right, Harriet." Mrs. Schmidt's voice was low, but Leslie could hear her perfectly. "She spends money like it's going out of style. I don't know how that poor man puts up with it. Every time he comes home, there's something else she wants to buy, and it's always expensive. No wonder he has to work his fingers to the bone. I tell you, I just don't know what's holding that marriage together. . . . Heavens, no!" Mrs. Schmidt gave a loud snort. "I told you they don't even sleep together. She's got a big bedroom on the second floor and he sleeps in his studio when he's here. It's just not right, Harriet. They certainly don't behave like normal people."

Leslie drew in her breath sharply. There was a short silence and Mrs. Schmidt spoke again.

"Yes, I'm sure of it now. There's definitely something wrong with her mind. You should hear her go on about the people that built this place—the Appletons. She acts like she knew them personally, and that's not all. . . ."

Mrs. Schmidt dropped her voice to a conspiratorial level.

"She talks to that big picture of the Appleton girl just like it's alive! I caught her doing it just the other day. She's headed for a breakdown; I recognize the signs. I don't know, Harriet. . . . I just hate to think about what's going to happen to Leslie when her mother finally goes over the edge. I know it's not my responsibility, but I can't help but worry. Leslie's only ten and he can't take care of her. His work takes him away most of the time and she's not even his child, you know."

There was a pause and Mrs. Schmidt sighed loudly. Leslie could hear the chair creak as she rose to her feet.

"Well . . . he'll just have to put her in a hospital if she gets much worse. I don't see what other choice he's got. Then I suppose they'll put little Leslie in a foster home. It might be better for her in the long run. It can't be good for her to see her mother going crazy right before her very eyes. I certainly won't hesitate to call the authorities if I have to. That child shouldn't be exposed to this sort of thing. Sheriff Olson can take care of it if something happens while Mr. Houston's gone. I think I'll give him a call on Monday and alert him. One has to think of the child, you know."

Leslie began to shake as Mrs. Schmidt hung up and walked back into the kitchen. Could the sheriff take her away from her mother and send her to a foster home? The thought made her weak with fear. She had to stop Mrs. Schmidt from calling him.

She reached up for her key with trembling fingers. Then she remembered. That hateful Trixie had taken her key. Now even Christopher couldn't help her.

Leslie rushed to her room and flung herself on the bed in despair. She was all alone and she was scared to death!

Sharp teeth bit into her toe. She pulled her foot back quickly and her whole body shook with the unexpected assault. There was something under her bed!

As Leslie peered fearfully over the edge of the mattress, there was a low growl. Trixie poked her head out into the light. The little Chihuahua looked pleased with herself and she stared up at Leslie with glittering eyes.

"What are you doing under there? Get out of there! Get out of my room! You know you're not supposed to be in here!"

Trixie made a dash for the open door, painted toe-nails sliding around the corner as she ran into the hallway. *That horrid creature!* Where was her key?

Leslie's heart pounded hard as she lifted the blanket and got down on her hands and knees to peer under the bed. There was something in the very corner and Leslie's heart beat wildly in her chest. She crawled on her stomach under the mattress and reached out to grab it. Her key! She had it back and now Christopher could protect her from Mrs. Schmidt and those cruel foster-home people.

Leslie's fingers curled around the key in desperation. It was dark under the bed and her eyes didn't hurt this time. He was coming. . . . Christopher was coming and he wouldn't let Mrs. Schmidt call the sheriff. Christopher would stop her.

Don't worry, Leslie. I'll take care of everything tonight.

You don't have to be afraid. No one can take your mother away from us.

The house was completely still and it was time. Everyone was sleeping—everyone but Christopher and her. The bright moonlight streamed through her window and it was easy to see without turning on the light. Christopher knew it was the perfect time.

Leslie reached out for the tin of corned beef and opened it quietly. She knew exactly what to do. She set the can just inside her open door and stood there waiting. Trixie couldn't resist the smell of corned beef. It was her favorite treat.

Her heart pounded with anticipation as she heard the clicking of Trixie's toenails coming down the hallway. A second later she had the small dog in her arms and was tiptoeing down the stairs.

The greenhouse, Leslie. Take Trixie to the greenhouse.

It was no problem to make her way through the silent kitchen. Trixie was so intent on munching her unexpected treat that she didn't even struggle as Leslie hoisted her under one arm in order to open the kitchen door.

Now they were out on the lawn, the wet grass brushing cold against her feet. Her white nightgown flapped around her legs with each step and Leslie broke into an awkward run, carrying Trixie with one arm and holding her key in her other hand. Then they were inside the greenhouse and Trixie looked up with a slightly startled expression on her pointed face. The little dog had never been outside in the dead of night before.

Put her down, Leslie. We'll leave Trixie here until morning. Then it will be time. Go back to bed now. We have to get up early, before Mrs. Schmidt starts breakfast.

Leslie put Trixie down on the wooden bench and gave her the rest of the corned beef. Then she left, closing the greenhouse door tightly behind her, and ran across the lawn to the house.

It was early and the sun had just risen over the horizon. Leslie stood motionless, her hand on the latch of the gate. Her pretty blue eyes turned huge and dark and she listened to Christopher.

Go ahead, Leslie. Open the gate. I'll help you.

Leslie stared down into the Trixie's eyes for a moment and her face remained white and expressionless. Then she felt Chrisopher's hand cover hers and she lifted the latch.

Push it open. That's all you have to do. Everything will happen the way I planned it.

Leslie's hands trembled as she pushed on the gate. The sunlight glittering off the polished metal latch hurt her eyes. She wanted to shut them, but she couldn't. She had to watch.

Now! Push harder. We have to let Trixie out.

Leslie felt Christopher's hand cover hers again and she pushed. The gate opened and Trixie dashed out, her little legs churning as she headed straight for the road.

Leslie laughed as Trixie barreled down the ditch

and up the embankment. There was mud at the bottom of the ditch and Mrs. Schmidt would be livid if she knew that Trixie had dirty feet. Her laughter took on an edge of hysteria as Trixie neared the edge of the road. What if a car hit Trixie? It would be all her fault!

Don't worry, Leslie. You have to trust me. What we're doing is right.

Leslie felt her worries disappear. Of course Christopher was right. She had to trust him. And then she was calm again, numb to reality. There was a haze in front of her eyes and everything shimmered in the early morning sun as she watched Trixie reach the edge of the road. And then she heard the car coming, brakes squealing as the driver skidded to a stop and a little girl opened the passenger door and climbed out. It was like watching a movie through a fogged mirror and Leslie stood motionless, staring as the girl picked Trixie up and took her back to the car.

"Can we keep her, Mommy?" The little girl cuddled Trixie in her arms. "I'll take care of her, I promise. You said I could have a dog when I was five and it's almost my birthday. She's so sweet! She licked my face when I picked her up!"

Leslie couldn't believe her ears. Trixie had never licked her face, and she hadn't seen the little dog lick Mrs. Schmidt's face either. Trixie obviously liked the little girl more than she liked either one of them.

The mother smiled. "Yes, you can keep her. But you have to check with that girl standing over there at the gate to see if this is her dog. If she says yes, you have to give her back. It's not fair to keep someone else's dog."

The little girl didn't look happy, but she trudged toward the gate obediently. Leslie could tell that she really wanted to keep Trixie. What should she say when the little girl asked if Trixie was her dog?

I'll speak for you, Leslie. I know exactly what to say. You just watch and listen.

Leslie sighed with relief as the familiar cocoon of dizziness washed over her. Christopher would take care of everything. He always did.

"Is this your dog?" the little girtl asked when she'd made her way to the gate.

Leslie felt her head shake from side to side, and then her mouth opened and words came out. "No. That dog doesn't belong to me."

"Do you know if she lives around here?"

"I don't think so," Leslie's voice spoke again. "Nobody's said anything about losing a dog."

"Do you think I could keep her?"

Leslie felt her lips turn up in a smile. "I think that's a very good idea."

"Oh, goodie!" The girl bent down to nuzzle Trixie and the little dog looked up at her adoringly. "I just love her already and Mom said it was okay."

Go back to the house, Leslie. You have to go upstairs before Mrs. Schmidt gets up.

Leslie's hand gave a little wave to the girl and then she turned and went back to the house. It was over. Trixie was gone. Now all they had to do was figure out how to get rid of Mrs. Schmidt before she called Sheriff Olson on Monday.

* * *

"Have you seen Trixie?" Mrs. Schmidt took off her hat and hung it in the closet. "She always meets me at the door when I come home from church."

Leslie shook her head solemnly. "I haven't seen her, Mrs. Schmidt. Maybe she's sleeping somewhere."

"I suppose so." Mrs. Schmidt walked into the kitchen, with Leslie following closely. "Goodness, Leslie! What do you want? You've been stepping on my heels ever since I came in the door."

"I'm just hungry, I guess." Leslie smiled up at the housekeeper. "Could I eat a little early, Mrs. Schmidt? Your stew smells so good I can hardly wait."

Mrs. Schmidt nodded and Leslie seated herself at the kitchen table. The stew had been simmering all night and it was ready. She could hardly wait for Mrs. Schmidt to dish it up.

"Your mother doesn't want any lunch and Mr. Houston's working in the darkroom again, so I guess it doesn't matter if you eat early." Mrs. Schmidt beamed as she headed toward the stove. Children appreciated good nutrition if their systems weren't polluted by fast foods and preservatives. Leslie was beginning to show good taste in her choice of foods now that she was doing the cooking.

"Did you wash your hands, Leslie?" Mrs. Schmidt set a soup bowl on the counter. "You know how I feel about clean hands at the table."

"Yes, Mrs. Schmidt. I washed my face, too. And I'm really starving!"

"Patience is a virtue." Mrs. Schmidt smiled at Leslie

as she took the cover off the soup pot. It smelled different today, a little spicier, perhaps.

Mrs. Schmidt smiled as she stirred the stew port. She had gotten special stewing beef, cut it up into cubes, and braised it on the stove. Then she'd put it in the stew pot, added water, and let it simmer overnight. This morning, right after breakfast, she'd added plenty of good, nutritious vegetables, even the ones that Leslie didn't like. The beef flavor would be so delicious that she wouldn't even notice the fact that the stew contained cauliflower and turnips.

"You'll have some with me, won't you Mrs. Schmidt?"

The housekeeper turned to look at Leslie in surprise. This was the first time that Leslie had ever asked her to sit down at the kitchen table and eat with her. When she'd first started to work for the Houstons, Leslie had been a loner. The child had no friends and she didn't seem interested in making any. Perhaps Leslie was becoming more social under her tutelage.

"Of course I'll keep you company, Leslie," Mrs. Schmidt said with a smile. "I'll dish up two bowls now, but we'll have to wait at least five minutes before we can eat. The stew pot's boiling and it has to cool."

"That's fine, Mrs. Schmidt." Leslie watched her place the bowls on the table. "Let's go look for Trixie while it's cooling. I know she's got to be around her somewhere."

The housekeeper nodded. "That's a very good idea. Where would you like to start?"

"I'll go up to the cupola. Trixie goes up there sometimes. And after that, I'll check the ballroom. Why don't you start on the second floor and check the bedrooms? Then we can meet down here and have our stew."

Leslie climbed up the stairs with Mrs. Schmidt until they parted company at the second floor. The moment Mrs. Schmidt had gone into one of the extra bedrooms, Leslie ran back down the stairs to the kitchen and opened the housekeeper's purse. That's where Mrs. Schmidt kept her heart medicine and Christopher had told mer just what to do with it.

They were back at the kitchen table again, after a fruitless search. Of course they hadn't found Trixie and Leslie knew they wouldn't. Trixie had a new home now.

"Do you like the stew, Leslie?" Mrs. Schmidt asked.

"Oh, yes. It's delicious." Leslie took another spoonful and tried not to grimace as she bit into a piece of turnip.

"Mine has a slightly bitter taste. I think I'll add a touch of sugar."

"I'll get it, Mrs. Schmidt," Leslie offered, jumping up to get the sugar bowl.

"Thank you, Leslie." Mrs. Schmidt added a generous teaspoon of sugar to her stew and stirred it in. "Do you want some sugar?"

"No, thanks." Leslie took another spoonful of stew and forced herself to eat it. It might have been good without the turnips, but with them it was horrible. She avoided the turnip pieces and settled for meat and a piece of cauliflower, swallowing quickly so she wouldn't have to taste it.

"This is good, even if I do say so myself." Mrs.

Schmidt got up from the table and carried her empty bowl to the stew pot for another helping. "Would you like more, Leslie?"

"I still have some left, Mrs. Schmidt," Leslie replied, watching the kitchen clock carefully as the housekeeper refilled her bowl. Christopher had said that the medicine would take from fifteen to twenty minutes to work, although he hadn't been sure if the temperature of the stew would speed things up. Leslie hoped it would be over soon.

"I've been meaning to talk to you about your mother," Mrs. Smith said as she sat down at the table again and picked up her spoon. "Do you think she's become a little too . . . uh . . . involved with restoring the house exactly as the Appleton's had it?"

Leslie shook her head. "No, I don't, Mrs. Schmidt. She's very interested in the history of the Appleton family. And so am I."

"But you sit upstairs with your mother for hours, listening as she reads you those old letters. Wouldn't you rather be outside with your schoolmates? Or playing in the yard with Trixie?"

Leslie almost laughed, but she caught herself just in time. She didn't like any of the kids in her class, and she couldn't play in the yard with Trixie. Trixie was gone. And very soon now, Mrs. Schmidt would be gone, too.

That was when it happened. Mrs. Schmidt gave a strangled gasp she pressed both hands to her chest. Her face turned a pasty white color that reminded Leslie of the old snow that remained on the ground right before the spring thaw.

"Call . . . call . . . the doctor!" Mrs. Schmidt gasped

out. And when Leslie simply stared at her quizzically, she pushed back the chair, stood up on legs that were visibly trembling, and took two steps toward the phone on the kitchen wall.

Leslie was silent as Mrs. Schmidt faltered and fell heavily to the floor. She knew it wasn't polite to laugh, but she couldn't seem to stop. Mrs. Schmidt looked ridiculous with her arms and legs twitching and pounding on the black and white squares of the linoleum floor.

Now Mrs. Schmidt's face was turning gray and saliva dripped out of the corner of her mouth. Her fingers clutched at her chest, scrabbling just the way Trixie's toenails used to do. Then she was very still.

Leslie stood up in a daze. Mrs. Schmidt looked very pale and she wasn't moving at all anymore. Leslie stepped around her and walked up the stairs to get Mike.

TWENTY-SEVEN

One week had passed since the funeral and Karen still shuddered when she thought of their housekeeper's death. Poor Mrs. Schmidt! They hadn't known she had a weak heart. Dr. Simmons said he'd warned her to keep her weight down, but she had ignored his advice. Karen just hoped that the strain of taking care of their house hadn't contributed to her death.

It had been hard on Leslie, being the one to find Mrs. Schmidt. For a few days she had been silent and withdrawn, but she seemed better now. They had talked about it and decided not to hire another housekeeper. Actually, the housework wasn't that much of a problem, now that the house was nearly finished. Karen found that she loved taking care of the house again by herself. She had forgotten how much fun it was to polish the antique furniture and care for Amelia's possessions.

* * *

Karen glanced at her watch and hurried a little faster up the stairs. Leslie had just left for school and it was time to get to work. She'd found an old apron upstairs that was perfect for dusting and cleaning and she was determined to do the darkroom today while Mike was at the magazine. Mike didn't seem to notice that his workroom was a mess, but it bothered her every time she went in. Certainly, that corner of the third floor had never looked like this when the Appletons lived here!

It was a simple matter to mop the floor and empty the trash. She dusted his equipment and cleaned the long, troughlike sink. It looked better in here already and she'd barely started.

Karen tied her hair back with a piece of string and tackled the windows. Soon she had them sparkling. She looked around for something else to clean and she smiled as she saw the old cupboard in the corner. Dorthea's father had used it for his ledgers and accounts. She'd dust the shelves and straighten everything inside.

She gave a sigh as she opened the doors. No wonder Mike had trouble finding things! The closet was jammed full of old files and papers. It was a shame to treat a fine antique cupboard this way.

The rag caught on something as she dusted the bottom shelf and Karen reached in to pull it free. Her fingers found a latch and she gasped as the bottom slid back to reveal a secret compartment filled with bottles.

"'Napoleon brandy?'" Karen frowned as she read the label. There were ten bottles of old brandy in here. William Appleton must have hidden them here years ago.

Karen's hands shook as she pulled them out. It was a good thing Mike hadn't discovered them. She had to take care of them right away.

She didn't even stop to think as she carried the bottles to the sink and poured them out, one by one. The smell of brandy was strong and her eyes watered as she reached for the last bottle. It was open!

"Oh, no!" Her anger grew as she examined the tenth bottle. It was almost half gone. Mike was drinking again, and it looked as if it was becoming a habit. This bottle was wiped clean and the others had been covered with dust.

She brushed her hair back with an angry gesture and threw the dust rag into a corner. Now she knew why Mike was spending so much time alone in here. No wonder he'd told her not to clean his studio.

Karen was fuming as she slammed the studio door behind her. She remembered all the times she'd felt sorry for Mike because he was working all night. She'd even told Leslie not to disturb him because he was slaving away in the darkroom. And the whole time he'd been up here drinking. He'd told her when they were married that he'd lay off the drinking and the gambling, and here they were married only a few years and he was back to his old habits. After what she'd been through with the miscarriage, you'd think Mike would make an effort to be a good husband and provider. She did all the work on the house, and all he cared about was using it for his magazine feature. He didn't understand about Dorthea or about the past. He was insensitive, and a liar to boot.

* * *

Leslie was well prepared for geography today. She had worked with Mom last night and now she was glad she'd studied so hard. Mrs. Ogilvie beamed every time she gave a correct answer.

"And what is the principal export of Bolivia?" Mrs. Ogilvie's whistle bounced on her chest as the pointer whacked against the bright yellow continent of South America. "Yes, Leslie—I'm sure you know the correct answer. I want to see if anyone else does."

Taffy looked down at her book and slouched in her seat. It was clear that she hadn't studied. Several of the other students were also avoiding Mrs. Ogilvie's eyes, hoping their names wouldn't be called.

Mrs. Ogilvie looked up and down the rows of desks and stopped as she came to Taffy. "You had the highest grades in geography last year, Taffy. You should know this one. What is the principal product of Bolivia?"

The color rose in Taffy's cheeks until her face was bright red. She had been hoping Mrs. Ogilvie would leave her alone this morning. She'd watched television last night instead of doing her homework.

"I don't remember." Taffy swallowed nervously as she looked up into the teacher's stern face. "I—I didn't get time to study much last night, Mrs. Ogilvie."

The teacher clicked her tongue against the roof of her mouth. "Well, now, Taffy, it's perfectly clear that you spent no time at all studying. Leslie! Please give Taffy the correct answer."

Leslie spoke up hesitantly. "Tin. I think it's tin, Mrs. Ogilvie."

"Correct again!" Mrs. Ogilvie rapped sharply on the edge of her desk with her pointer. "Thank goodness for you, Leslie! Now, I want every student in this class to review the homework assignment immediately. There will be a ten-question test right after recess. And for homework tonight, you will outline chapters three through five in your text. Leslie is excused, of course. I know she did her homework."

Leslie blushed as she felt the cold stares of the class. Taffy turned and made a face at her as Mrs. Ogilvie wrote the assignment on the blackboard. The pleasure she had felt at her teacher's praise quickly disappeared under Taffy's angry glare. She hadn't meant to do anything wrong and it seemed she had goofed again. Now all the kids hated her for doing her homework. She just couldn't win.

It was late afternoon when he got home. They were in the yard with Red Fischer, working on the garden. Mike carried his black camera bag upstairs and kicked the studio door open with his foot.

He stopped in the doorway and blinked. His darkroom was immaculate. Karen must have cleaned up in here while he was gone. Of course it was nice to have it clean, but he wished she wouldn't poke around in here. This was his room.

He opened the door to the cupboard and frowned. She'd even cleaned up in here! He hoped she hadn't found the brandy!

"Oh, no!" Mike gave a loud groan. It was gone and

he knew exactly what she had done with it. He could still smell the scent of brandy in the air. Karen had poured it all down the sink.

"How *could* she?" Mike slammed his fist on the counter. Just when he was ready to sell it, she had poured it out! He had finally come to a decision on the trip home today. He was going to sell the brandy and use the money for their house payment. Now he was short and he had to ask Rob to carry them again.

Karen saw him stomping across the lawn, a scowl on his face. She knew what was coming and she was ready for it. Turning to Leslie urgently, she said, "Go into the greenhouse and help Mr. Fischer, kitten. And stay there until I come and get you. Mike and I have something to discuss."

Leslie took one look at Mike's face and hurried off. He was mad, and so was Mom. They were going to have another fight. They were like strangers with each other these days. Leslie remembered how happy they had been back in the Cities. Now all Mike did was work up in his darkroom. And to be honest, Leslie was glad he was out of the way. She loved having her mom all to herself, just the two of them like before. They talked about the Appletons and the house, and got along fine.

"What the hell are you trying to prove?" Mike stepped up to Karen and drew a deep breath. "Jesus, Karen! I told you never to go in my studio!"

"You also told me you weren't drinking again!" She stood there trembling, facing him squarely. "What's the matter, Mike? Did I spoil your evening?"

"You're spoiling my whole life!" He wanted to draw back his hand and hit her, but somehow he controlled himself. Her eyes were mocking him, daring him to say more. She thought she was clever, discovering the brandy and getting rid of it.

"I did you a favor by dumping out that booze!" Karen's face took on a righteous expression, and that made him even angrier.

"A favor? That was one stupid move, Karen. I could have sold that brandy for three hundred dollars a bottle. Add it up. Twenty-seven hundred dollars! You poured the next four house payments right down the drain!"

There was a long silence. Karen had reeled back in shock. Her face turned even whiter as she stared at him. It made him feel good to see her speechless for once.

"That's right, Karen. Stand there with your mouth open. We're going to lose this house and it's your fault. At least you can't blame this one on me!"

He turned on his heel and stalked off. Of course they weren't going to lose the house, but let her worry a little. She deserved to worry for pulling a dumb stunt like that.

Taffy was still fuming as she walked down the sidewalk after school. Mrs. Ogilvie thought Leslie was the smartest kid in the class and it made Taffy mad. Things had been just fine before the Houstons moved here. Then she was the smartest. Now Leslie was getting all the attention just because she studied and took class pictures with that stupid camera of hers.

She was almost home before she remembered that her mother was at bridge club. She didn't feel like going home to an empty house. Maybe she could drop in on her dad at the office. He was always glad to see her. He might even take her to the drugstore for a root beer if he wasn't busy.

Taffy pushed open the door and smiled when she saw Evelyn's bare desk. Her dad's part-time secretary was gone for the day. She could do her homework right here and her mother would never know that Mrs. Ogilvie had given her an extra assignment for punishment.

Her dad was in his private office and the door was closed. Taffy knew that meant he had a client. She'd just sit out here and wait for him to come out. She could even have a little fun while she sat here and did her homework.

Taffy reached out and pushed the intercom button. She'd done this before, but she had to be careful. Dad had told her never to play with that switch, but he wouldn't find out if she stayed quiet. It was fun to listen when he was closing a deal.

"I really hate to bring it up, but I'm a little strapped again this month." It was Mr. Houston's voice. "I could scrape together the house payment, but it would really make things rough at home. Do you think you could carry us one more month, Rob? I'll make three payments then, on the fifteenth of October."

"Let me see. . . ." Taffy could hear her dad shuffling papers on his desk. "Sure. No problem, Mike. Just don't mention it to anyone. Marilyn's the legal owner of the house and she'd start action in a minute if she knew. As long as you keep it under your hat, I'll carry you."

Taffy began to smile as she doodled on her notebook with her pencil. This was really interesting. Leslie's stepfather was late on their house payment and it wasn't the first time. Maybe they'd have to move!

The more she thought about it, the better she felt. Taffy's smile grew wider. Her mother didn't like the Houstons. Taffy was positive that she'd kick them out of the house if she could. Maybe she should tell her mother and see what happened.

No, she couldn't do that. Taffy let out a disappointed sigh. If she told, she'd have to admit that she had listened in on the intercom and then Dad would skin her alive. As tempting as it was, she didn't dare say a word.

All the lights were off as Mike pulled into the driveway. They were in bed already. He had a little trouble unlocking the door, but he managed. The whiskey sours they mixed at the Municipal Liquor Store were heavy drinks. The bartender was a regular guy and he'd mixed them doubles and charged for singles. Rob said he was a hometown boy. Everyone he met in the bar tonight had been friendly. These Cold Spring people were nice. He just didn't understand why Karen and Leslie didn't like them.

Mike chuckled ruefully as he faced the closed bedroom door. Some of the guys had had their wives in the bar tonight. It was a crying shame Karen didn't loosen up a little and have a few drinks with him. It might make her more human. They used to have fun. Hell—they used to have lots of fun before they moved here.

He had turned to climb the stairs to his studio when he remembered. All gone—the brandy was all gone. He was feeling good and there wasn't a damn thing to do. Karen was asleep and she wasn't any fun anyway. He really ought to go in and wake her up and show her how to have a good time.

"Why not?" Mike chuckled again. He opened the bedroom door and stepped inside, shutting it quietly behind him. He'd just get out of his clothes and hop into bed with Karen. It was about time she started acting like a wife again.

"Mike! What—?" Karen gasped as she turned on the light and saw him leaning over her. The sour smell of whiskey made her head spin. He was staring at her, leering drunkenly. Then his hand shot forward and fastened on the neck of her silk nightgown.

"No!" She gave a cry and jerked back in fear. The material pulled away in his hand and she cried out again as she covered herself with her arms. "Get away from me! You're drunk!"

"Yeah!" Mike laughed and grabbed her arms. He twisted them behind her back and pinned her to the bed. "I'm going to show you how to have a good time. Don't you remember? You used to like it!"

She pushed against him with all her strength, but she was no match for his drunken determination. He was grabbing her now, fingers digging painfully into the tender flesh.

"Mike! Please! Leave me alone!" She twisted from side to side, but he was too strong. She heard his laughter as he loomed over her, and pure panic made her struggle desperately. He was an animal, a drunken animal. She had to get away.

His hand snapped back to slap her viciously. She reeled in shock; and before she could react, he was on her, lunging forward brutally.

One cry was all she gave. Then she shut her eyes tightly, welcoming the blackness. She willed her mind away, leaving her body uncaring, unfeeling, unmoving. It was a nightmare and she would awaken soon. She had fallen asleep in the yard, tired from taking care of the rose garden, weeding and planting in the late-summer sun. Any moment now she would wake up and it would be over. None of this was real.

The taste of ashes was in his mouth. Mike opened his eyes to see the early-morning sky outside the window. He'd tied one on last night. Gradually the memory was coming back.

He rolled over to look at her, ashamed at his passion of the night before. She lay there, still and straight, the covers barely lifting with her shallow breathing. She was asleep.

He felt tears come to his eyes and he blinked them away angrily. He'd never done anything like this before. He felt as if something inside him had died last night and there was no way to bring it back to life. She was gone—the beautiful, passionate woman he'd married. And in her place was this shell, this doll-like stranger who had only one thought in her mind, an old house.

He slipped out of bed and dressed quickly in the

gray morning light. He had to go to Rochester for five days and it was time to hit the road. He couldn't wake Karen to say good-bye; he didn't have the guts for that. He'd write her a note before he left and tell her he was sorry. They could talk it all out when he called home tonight.

Mike started the truck and backed out of the driveway. He lit a cigarette and buckled his seat belt. There was no use in putting it off any longer. He had to do something. There had to be some way to patch up their marriage, to bring their life back to normal. Karen was obsessed with this damn house. But what could he do about that?

Mike felt a quickening of hope as the thought occurred to him. Maybe he could sell the house! He'd talk to some of the guys at the magazine and see what they thought. If he could move Karen back to the Cities, she might grow to love him again and maybe they'd even try to have another child. They'd all be a lot better off away from Cold Spring, and especially away from this house.

TWENTY-EIGHT

Marilyn gave one last glance in the mirror and nodded at her reflection. She thought she looked fine for her door-to-door canvassing. Now she was glad she'd let Bertha put that rinse in her hair. The slight blue covered up all traces of gray. In her green polyester suit, with the matching flowered blouse, she looked very smart and businesslike. She picked up her purse and her notepad and stepped briskly out of the house. She was determined to collect at least two hundred dollars for the hospital fund this morning.

Two hours later she had her quota. Mr. Jenkins had pledged fifty dollars, and Marilyn smiled as she marched down the street. Only two stores to go and then she'd start on the residential streets.

It was past four when she knocked on the door at the Appleton Mansion. Marilyn wasn't looking forward to this, but it wouldn't be fair if she left the Houstons off her list. She had to treat everyone the same, no matter how she felt about them personally. It was only right that the Houstons should be asked to contribute.

Marilyn frowned as Leslie opened the door. She couldn't believe that this was the same child she'd seen only a few weeks ago in the grocery store. Leslie's hair was clipped in a ragged pixie and she wore cutoff jeans and an old, dirty white shirt. What on earth had gotten into her mother to let her dress like this?

"Oh, hello, Mrs. Comstock." Leslie smiled politely. She stood with the door open only a few inches and there was a questioning look on her face.

Marilyn cleared her throat. "I came to see your mother or your . . . uh . . . Mr. Houston." Marilyn felt herself blushing. "It's about the community fund for Gary Wilson and Bud Allen."

"Sure . . . come in, Mrs. Comstock." Leslie opened the door all the way and led her to the parlor. "Just wait for a second and I'll get Mom. Mike isn't home. He's working in Rochester this week."

Marilyn's eyes widened as she took in the details of the room. It certainly looked grand. The parquet floor was polished until it looked like glass and the French love seat was gorgeous. It was clear to see that a lot of money had gone into making this room so beautiful. She just couldn't believe that it was the same run-down house Rob had sold only a few months ago.

"Hello, dear." Marilyn put on her best public-relations smile as Karen came into the room. "I came about the community fund for Bud and Gary. We're asking for contributions and I thought you might like to sign a pledge."

"Oh, yes . . . of course." Karen smiled slowly. "How much do you want, Mrs. Comstock?"

"Well, the usual pledge is ten dollars." Marilyn cleared her throat. Karen looked a little dazed. She hoped she hadn't come at a bad time.

"That's fine, Mrs. Comstock," Karen replied slowly. She blinked once or twice and leaned against the door frame.

"Just drop the money off at the bank sometime in the next few days." Marilyn handed her a pledge card and watched as Karen signed. "They're taking charge of the fund for us."

There was an awkward silence for a moment, and then Marilyn cleared her throat. "Well." she smiled nervously. "How are you doing, Karen? Are you managing all right without poor Thelma?"

"Oh, yes . . . just fine." Karen blinked again. Then she smiled fully for the first time. "Would you like to see the rest of the house? I'm almost finished with the renovation."

Marilyn smiled back. "That would be wonderful." She certainly did want to see the house. If it was anything like this room, it would be gorgeous.

Karen must have been napping when she came, Marilyn decided. She had seemed so disoriented at first, but now she was fine. Her face was animated and she talked nonstop as she led Marilyn from room to room, explaining the furnishings and showing the work she'd done.

"Oh, this is just wonderful!" Marilyn stood in front of the fireplace and looked up at the lovely portrait hanging there. "Wherever did you find it, Karen?"

"Oh, that's Dorthea Appleton." Karen smiled happily. "This portrait was in a trunk in the ballroom until I found it. Isn't she just lovely? She's Amelia and William's daughter, you know, and she's an artist in her own right. I have some drawings she's done upstairs. It's really too bad she ran off with the man who painted this portrait. He was a terrible scoundrel and he left her, pregnant and unmarried, in San Francisco. She wants to come home now with her son, Christopher, but her father's never forgiven her. Poor Dorthea!"

Marilyn swallowed nervously as Karen stood looking up at the portrait. She could hardly believe what she had heard. Karen acted as if this Appleton girl were still alive!

"Well!" Marilyn cleared her throat. "I'd really better be going, Karen. I have to get home and fix Rob's supper. Thank you for showing me the house. You've certainly done a lot of work on it."

"There's still a lot to be done before it's completely finished," Karen said as she walked her to the door. "I have to fix up Amelia's flower beds and carry on Dorthea's work in the greenhouse. Then there's the rose garden. That simply has to be done before winter sets in. I think, if we work very hard, it'll be the same showplace it was the year Dorthea left home. Can you imagine how wonderful she'll feel when she comes home and finds it just the same?"

"Uh . . . yes." Marilyn opened the door and stepped out quickly. "Well . . . thank you for the pledge, Karen. I'll call again soon."

Marilyn hurried to her car and got in. Then she reached out and locked the door. Karen Houston was completely out of touch with reality. "Just wait until I tell the girls about this!" she exclaimed as she drove away.

TWENTY-NINE

They spent the rest of the week making plans for the puppet show. It would be held in Taffy's backyard this Saturday, the last weekend in September. All the proceeds from the bake sale and puppet show would go toward the hospital fund for Gary Wilson and Bud Allen. Taffy's mother had volunteered their guesthouse for the puppet show, and all the kids in the class were doing something to help. Leslie was the class photographer. Her pictures would be in the school yearbook.

Karen spread out newspaper on the kitchen table and Leslie brought the big chest with the silver from the dining room. They were going to clean the silver tonight and she could hardly wait. It was a Queen Anne pattern with an *A* engraved on every piece. Leslie thought it was beautiful and she could hardly wait to see it gleaming on the lace tablecloth they had found.

"This is going to take a while, kitten." Karen dipped the first piece in the silver polish and started rubbing with a soft cloth. "Make sure you clean between the tines of the forks."

"Remember how Dorthea complained about cleaning the silverware?" Leslie grinned. "They used to do it every week when she was a girl."

For long minutes they worked in companionable silence, dipping the pieces and polishing them. Then Karen laughed.

"It almost makes me want to change my name to something starting with an *A*," she confessed. "Doesn't it look lovely when it's all clean?"

"Yes, it does." Leslie smiled up at her mother. Working on the house with Mom was fun and it was almost done. All they had left were the finishing touches. Yesterday the men from the roofing company had come to repair the shingles and they'd promised to have them done by Tuesday. And the new storm windows would be installed by the end of the month. All they really had to do was finish the rose garden, and the whole house would be completely restored.

The silver was almost done now and Leslie worked at the last piece. She wished that Mike would hurry and come home. She needed to ask him some questions about the puppet show tomorrow. She wanted to be sure to use exactly the right kind of film so her pictures would be perfect. And he might even lend her a strobe. That would solve a big lighting problem for her.

"That's all, honey." Karen replaced the last spoon and closed the chest. "You'd better get up to bed now. Tomorrow's a big day."

"All right, Mom." Leslie kissed her mother on the

cheek. She was disappointed that Mike hadn't come home yet, but there was nothing she could do about it. When she got up to her room, she took out her film and checked the ASA herself. She'd use Tri-X film and ask Mike to push it when they did the developing.

The first thing Leslie saw when she woke up in the morning was her camera propped up against the lamp. She smiled and hopped out of bed. She could hardly wait to take pictures today. Mrs. Ogilvie would be very proud of her.

Leslie dressed quickly and slipped her camera into its case. Then she hung the strap around her neck and stepped out into the hallway quietly. No one was stirring in the house. Her mother's door was still closed and Leslie hurried down the stairs. She'd skip breakfast and get right to Taffy's house.

Leslie left a note for her mother on the kitchen table and slipped out of the house. The driveway was empty. That meant Mike had stayed the night in Rochester. He'd be home sometime this morning, but she couldn't wait around to ask him for the strobe. They could fix it up later, if she made any mistakes. Mike was a wizard in the darkroom.

The air was clean and crisp. Leslie buttoned her light jacket and ran through the leaves to the gate. Even though it was only the end of September, the cold weather would be here soon. They'd have to hurry with the rose garden if they wanted it done in time.

She opened the gate and let it clang shut behind

her. If she hurried, she'd be the first one at the Comstocks'. She could help with the decorations, and all the kids would see she was trying to be helpful. That might make them like her more. And they were bound to be impressed when they saw her pictures.

Taffy's house sat on the corner, shaded by giant elms. It was a large green wooden house, with white aluminum awnings. The shades were pulled on the upstairs windows and the awnings glinted like snow in the early-morning light. Leslie pressed the bell and waited. She could see through the beveled glass in the door, and the grandfather clock in the entryway read ten minutes to eight. Was she too early? It would be awful if Taffy and Mrs. Comstock were still asleep.

Leslie rang the bell a second time, but there was no movement inside the house. She was about to sit down on the steps to wait when she thought of the backyard. If Taffy and her mother were up, they might be working in the guesthouse already.

Leslie left the front porch and went around the side of the house, stepping over the rhubarb bushes that grew out from the fence. The guesthouse was at the very back of the lot and she could hear the sound of a hammer as she cut across the lawn and ran toward the green-and-white building. She wasn't too early after all. Taffy and Mrs. Comstock must be putting up the decorations already.

"Taffy?" Leslie stepped into the small building and waved at Taffy. She was on top of a ladder, hanging streamers. She looked very different today. In school she was always impeccably dressed, but this morning she wore overalls and an old faded sweatshirt. Her hair was a tangle of uncombed curls. Taffy looked a mess.

"It's going to be super!" Leslie smiled as she looked around. Some of the decorations were already in place and it looked good already. They had chosen the school colors, red and gold, to decorate the inside. Folding chairs on loan from the Lutheran church stood in even rows. The stage was raised slightly on a platform Rob had constructed and some-one had rigged a curtain out of a white bedspread. It was a wonderful setting for their puppet show.

"Oh . . . Leslie!" Taffy put the hammer down and made a face. "You're much too early! You weren't supposed to get here until ten o'clock."

Taffy couldn't hide her irritation as she stared down at Leslie. She might have known it. The first one to show up was Leslie Houston! Why hadn't it been one of her real friends, like Mary Ellen or Susie? Now she'd be stuck with Leslie until her mother came back from St. Cloud. She should have gone along in-stead of backing out at the last minute.

"Let me take a picture of it now, before it's fin-ished." Leslie squinted through her viewfinder. "I can get one of you on top of the ladder, Taffy."

"No! I don't want to be in your stupid picture!" Taffy climbed down fast and stood to the side while Leslie snapped the shutter. She certainly didn't want to be in any pictures until she was dressed up, with her hair combed. She'd simply die if her picture went in the yearbook looking like this!

"That's a great braid, Taffy." Leslie stared up at the red-and-gold crepe paper that stretched across the top of the stage. "It's a little crooked, though. I'm sure it's down too low on the left."

"Well, fix it, then!" Taffy snapped. Leave it to Leslie to criticize. She'd spent hours last night making that braid and now Leslie had to criticize it. It was hard to be polite with people like that.

"Sure. I can do it." Leslie climbed to the top of the ladder and reached out to straighten the braid. Taffy wasn't being very nice, but she could take it. Just as soon as Mrs. Ogilvie got here, everything would be fine.

"Oh!" Leslie gasped as the ladder began to wiggle. "Catch it, Taffy—I'm going to fall!"

Taffy stood back and grinned as the ladder wobbled. She didn't really care if Leslie fell or not. The ladder swayed precariously and Leslie managed to step down two rungs. Then it toppled and she jumped clear.

Taffy let out a howl as the ladder crashed into her braid. The streamers sagged and snapped under the heavy weight.

"Oh, no! Now, look what you did!" Taffy turned to glare at Leslie with hate in her eyes. Her beautiful braid was wrecked and there wasn't time to make another. It was all stupid Leslie's fault!

"Get out of here!" Taffy stamped her foot on the floor, and two bright spots of color appeared in her cheeks. "You ruin everything you touch, Leslie! Go home and don't come back!"

"I'm sorry, Taffy." Leslie really felt bad about destroying Taffy's braid. "I think we can fix it, though. I'll help you, and there's more streamers right over there."

"Don't touch them!" Taffy's voice was loud. "I told you to go home and I meant it! Get out of here before you wreck something else!"

"Come on, Taffy. I said I was sorry." Leslie tried to be reasonable. "I know you're mad right now, but I didn't do that on purpose. It was an accident."

"An accident?" Taffy's voice was scornful. "Everything's an accident when you're around! Well, there won't be any accidents pretty soon, because you'll be gone. My mother's going to kick you and your family right out of your old house!"

Leslie's mouth dropped open. The house belonged to them. Mrs. Comstock couldn't kick them out of their own house.

"I know you're late on your house payment." Taffy was pleased, watching the stunned expression on Leslie's face. "I heard Mike talking to my dad at the office. Dad said he'd cover for you, but my mother doesn't know about it. I'm going to tell her you missed a payment and she'll kick you out on the street."

"She can't!" Leslie's voice was desperate. "You're lying, Taffy. Your mother can't kick us out!"

"Oh, yes, she can." Taffy grinned widely. "My mother owns your house. She can kick you out and I'm going to tell her to do it. You just wait and see if I don't!"

For a moment Leslie was frozen there, staring up into Taffy's jeering face. Then she whirled and ran out of the guesthouse and through the yard. She was panting by the time she reached the vacant lot behind Taffy's house. There, hidden by trees, she stopped, gulping noisily. She had to stop Taffy from telling her mother about the late payment. They couldn't lose Christopher's house.

Desperately, Leslie reached up for her key. She leaned against a tree trunk for support and sobbed fearfully. The leaves began to move, blurring and swimming in front of her eyes and the sun grew brighter. She blinked and squinted against the brilliant morning light, clutching her key even tighter. Christopher had to help her!

As she stood there, shivering, a current of pure rage swept through her mind. There was a moment of dizziness and then a small serene smile replaced the frightened expression on her face. He would help her. Christopher was right here inside her. He would stop Taffy.

Leslie's tears dried in the fall breeze and her eyes shone with purpose. She bent down to pick up the matches someone had dropped and walked silently back to the guesthouse. She had to be careful that no one saw her.

Hurry, Leslie. His voice was loud and she obeyed. *Quickly, before anyone comes.*

Taffy was still alone in the guesthouse when Leslie opened the door. There were more streamers hanging from the ceiling now, and Taffy had just finished tacking up one end of the banner with the name of the play on it. She was shocked when Leslie came in.

"I thought I told you to go home!" Taffy stamped her foot on the rung of the ladder. "How many times do I have to tell you, dummy? Nobody wants you here. Go home and start packing! I'm going to tell my mother just as soon as she comes back!"

Leslie stood there solidly, staring. She didn't say

anything and this time there were no tears in her eyes. She just stared without blinking, and Taffy felt the beginnings of fear flutter in her stomach as she looked into Leslie's cold, dead eyes. There was a strange absence of expression on Leslie's face, and there was something very different about her eyes, something that made Taffy start to tremble. Instead of being blue, as they always were, Leslie's eyes were coal black and they looked flat and menacing.

Taffy gulped. Maybe she'd been too hard on Leslie. Of course she wasn't really going to tell her mother. She had just said that because she was mad. She hated to apologize, but the strange way Leslie was staring at her made her blurt out the words.

"Leslie, I—I didn't mean it, honest!" Taffy's voice was high and desperate as Leslie started to move toward her. "I won't tell my mother, really! It'll be our secret, just yours and mine. I promise I won't say a word! I like you, Leslie—honestly, I do! I don't really want you to move away! I was just kidding around before—honest!"

Now, Leslie. Christopher's voice was firm. Leslie watched as he pulled her hand with the matches out from behind her back.

Taffy gave a cry of fright as Leslie moved. There was a rasp in the small room as she struck a match and Taffy knew she had to get away. She had to run for the safety of the big house, but something was very wrong. She couldn't move. Something was holding her here and she couldn't move!

The flame sputtered and then burned brightly.

See the streamers? Watch the flames, Leslie. It's going to happen now.

The tongue of fire touched the streamers, and bright fingers of flame licked across the red-and-gold ceiling. The curtain on the stage blazed and flames spiraled upward, catching and crackling on the dry wooden beams.

Now the fire was flickering at the hem of Taffy's denim overalls. The flames danced upward in bright ribbons and Taffy screamed with horror as her hair blazed in a halo around her shoulders.

Very carefully Leslie raised her camera and snapped a picture. Her eyes were huge and dazed as she opened the door and shut it firmly behind her, latching it securely from the outside. Taffy's ghastly scream echoed in the early-morning air as Leslie walked away, out of the yard and through the vacant lot toward home. She was tired and it was time to go back to bed.

She let herself in the kitchen door and picked up the note, slipping it into her pocket. The house was quiet. Her mother was still sleeping. She tiptoed down the hall to her room and crawled under the blankets, shutting her eyes wearily. The key fell from her tightly curled fingers and rested warm against her neck as she dropped into a deep, exhausted sleep.

THIRTY

Just home from Rochester, Mike was shouting for them from downstairs. Leslie awoke with a start and ran down to the kitchen. Mom was right behind her.

"Didn't you hear the sirens?" He was panting. "There's a big fire at the Comstocks' and they had to call in the fire trucks from St. Cloud. I was scared to death you might be over there, Leslie. Wasn't that puppet show supposed to be today?"

"Yes." Leslie nodded. "Mrs. Ogilvie told us all to be there at ten." She stopped and gasped. Suddenly she remembered. She had been there earlier this morning, and Christopher had started the fire! This time he had hurt Taffy!

"It's all right, honey." Mike put his arms around her. "No one was hurt. The fire broke out in the guesthouse. Faulty wiring, probably. Rob said Marilyn and Taffy went into St. Cloud this morning to buy more decorations. He's waiting for them to come back now."

Leslie breathed a sigh of relief. Nothing had happened. She must have dreamed the whole thing.

Taffy was in St. Cloud with Mrs. Comstock, and nothing bad had happened at all.

"That's terrible, Mike!" Karen shuddered slightly. "It really is a lucky thing no one was there. I'd want to die if we had a fire here. If this house burned down, I'd have nothing left to live for."

Mike sat down at the kitchen table and stared hard at Karen. He couldn't believe she'd said that.

"Come on, Karen. Don't be silly. It would be terrible, but we've got insurance. There's enough insurance on this old mausoleum to buy us a gorgeous modern house in the Cities. You'd forget all about this place in no time at all. It might even be a blessing in disguise. I hate to think of what our heating bill's going to be this winter!"

"Stop it!" Karen glared at him, clearly outraged. "If I ever lost this place, I'd kill myself! This house is my whole life!"

"Jesus!" Mike stood up and stared at Karen in amazement. She was really serious! Her hands were trembling and she looked ready to burst into tears.

"Now, don't get all upset, honey." Mike put his arms around her. "There won't be a fire here. This house is brick, with a granite foundation. Rocks don't burn. This place will last forever."

Karen let him lead her to a chair. Her face was still deathly pale. She stared at him malevolently.

"Why don't you and Leslie look over the layout for the series," he suggested. "It just came back from the printer yesterday. They really love it at the magazine. The whole thing's there, from the first installment to the last."

"Do you mean it's all finished?" Karen's mood shifted instantly. "That's wonderful, Mike! The Appletons would be so proud!"

"Well, I'd better get back to work." Mike patted Karen's shoulder awkwardly. "You call me if you need me."

Mike sighed as he hurried up the stairs. Thank God he'd gotten a chance to talk to Rose! Her brother was a psychiatrist and they'd called him from her office. After hearing Karen's symptoms, he'd suggested a change of environment. He'd said she was obsessed with the house, and the best thing was to bring her back to the Cities to familiar surroundings. She could get better care in the Cities, too. He had set up an appointment for the beginning of next week. With time, maybe they could pick up the pieces of their relationship, their marriage, and live as a normal family again.

At last he was taking some positive action. Mike felt relieved. He'd gone straight to Rob when he pulled into town this morning. Rob thought he was right in wanting to move. They'd been working out the details when they'd heard the fire sirens.

Mike lit a cigarette. They were getting out of this house the second the deal was firm. All it had taken was one call and Rob had a buyer lined up. Now that the house was renovated and decorated, it was prime real estate. Buying this house was the biggest mistake he'd ever made, but at least they'd come out ahead, financially.

He noticed the two rolls of film as he went into the small room he used as an office. They were sitting in the center of his desk with a note tucked under them. *IF YOU GET TIME?* The note was scrawled in Leslie's childish hand.

Mike grinned as he picked up her film. He'd make the time right after he finished his work for the magazine. Nothing would please Leslie more than developing her film, and she deserved it. He hadn't been paying nearly enough attention to her lately, poor kid.

The prints for the magazine went slowly. Mike's eyes were bloodshot from lack of sleep and he had to concentrate hard on the familiar process. The smell of the chemicals made his headache worse and the dark really bothered his eyes. It seemed to take forever, but at last he was through. He put the prints on the drum dryer and watched until the slow revolution of the cylinder made him dizzy. A few deep breaths helped.

He stacked the prints and examined the pile with satisfaction. They were fine—not as perfect as he'd like them, but they'd be pleased at the magazine. It was a good thing he'd told Rose about his problem with Karen. He might have to take some time off, and she had promised to cover for him if things got rough. Rose was a great friend in a pinch.

"Oh, God!" Mike groaned as he remembered the yellow film canisters in his pocket. He was supposed to develop Leslie's film and his chemicals were almost exhausted. He certainly didn't want to mix a fresh batch for just two rolls. Maybe he could get by with the old stuff. Leslie wouldn't mind if her film was a little muddy.

He slipped his prints into an envelope and went back into the darkroom. He had a little trouble winding Leslie's film on the reels, but after a couple of botched attempts, he finally made it. He took extra pains as he set the timer. His head was spinning and he didn't want to ruin Leslie's pictures.

Her film looked all right as he took it off the reels. Leslie was turning into a good photographer. He wouldn't bother to make a contact sheet. Of course he didn't want to bother with enlarging, either, but Leslie would be disappointed if she didn't have at least a couple of prints. Tomorrow he'd mix up a fresh batch of chemicals and print them all, but right now he'd just do a token few. His old hypo should be good enough for two or three more prints.

Mike watched as the first print came up. It was a picture of a kid jumping in the river, framed by a tree branch. It wasn't a bad picture at all. The kid was yelling as he jumped, and there was another boy up in the tree, watching. Leslie must have taken it at the swimming hole.

He turned to the second print and sighed. There was a boy outside a window. Was it Bud Allen, the boy who'd been hurt in that strange accident?

Mike pulled the print out of the soup to look at it more closely. Sure, it was Bud Allen and he was standing right outside his father's Ford dealership. And there, leaning against the back of the car inside, was another kid—a skinny blond boy who looked a lot like Leslie!

The veins at Mike's temples began to throb painfully as a thought occurred to him. The first one—the boy jumping in the river—could it be a picture of Gary Wilson's accident? The boy up in the tree might have done something to the rope!

With shaking fingers Mike turned to the picture of Bud Allen again. That blond kid was pushing the car—he was sure of it.

"Jesus!" Mike stared down at the print and shuddered. Was that how the car had started rolling? Leslie must have taken this picture right before the car crashed through the glass! Why the hell hadn't she told him? And who was that skinny blond boy?

When the third print came up, Mike laughed out loud in relief. Of course these weren't pictures of the accidents! He was so tired, he was imagining things. Leslie was experimenting with her camera. She was doing silly double exposures, the same thing he'd done when he was a kid. This picture proved it without a doubt. The subject was Taffy Comstock. Her face was a little blurred, but he recognized her. Her mouth was open and she was clowning around, yelling because she didn't want her picture taken. And over Taffy's image, Leslie had exposed a picture of a bonfire. There was another kid standing behind Taffy with a lit match. The second kid looked a lot like . . . Sure! It was Leslie! A friend of hers must have snapped the picture. The way that Taffy's sweatshirt showed right through Leslie's arm was the dead giveaway.

These were probably all double exposures. Mike nodded as he studied the other two prints again. Now that he knew what Leslie was trying to do, it was clear. The picture of Bud was a double exposure. Leslie must have propped the camera on a tripod across the street and taken Bud's picture. Then he had snapped the one of her as she stood behind the car in the showroom, leaning on it. The river picture

was the same. The kid in the tree was Leslie. She'd
had someone take her picture up there. Then she
had taken a picture of Gary jumping in the river and
double-exposed it. One of these days, when they got
back to the Cities, he'd have to teach her all about
trick photography. They could work out some multiple exposures with all sorts of subjects.

Mike scooped up the prints and threw them in
the wash. He was tired and his head was killing him.
He knew he hadn't left Leslie's pictures in the fixer
long enough, but he'd print them again tomorrow.
They'd spend the weekend here and then they'd see
about moving back to the Cities on Monday. He'd
hire someone to do all the packing. Two more nights
in this monstrous old house and they'd be free of
it forever.

"Mother's in bed, resting." Leslie looked up as
Mike came into the room. "This series is wonderful,
Mike! Mom thinks so, too. It's the best thing you've
ever done!"

Mike smiled down at her. "I like your pictures, too,
honey. I developed your film, but I only made three
prints tonight. I've got a book on trick photography
somewhere and we can go over it together. I'll teach
you all about multiple exposures."

Leslie looked puzzled. She was about to ask
Mike what he meant when he put his hand on her
shoulder.

"I'm really worried about your mother, Leslie.
She's just too wrapped up in this house. I talked to a
psychiatrist yesterday and he thinks your mother

needs some professional help. He recommended that we sell this house and move back to the Cities. We'd buy a really nice house there and you could go back to your old school. You'd like that, wouldn't you?"

A *psychiatrist*? Leslie's mouth dropped open in shock. Psychiatrists were for crazy people. Everything Mrs. Schmidt had said came back to her in a rush. A psychiatrist would lock Mother up and then they'd take her to a foster home. Mike had never formally adopted her. It was just easier for Mom if she used his last name. She couldn't let Mike do anything to take them away from Christopher's house. It was the only place they were safe!

Leslie was so quiet; it made him nervous. She was fingering that old key around her neck, staring down at the floor. After a long moment she looked up at him again.

"Did you tell Mother yet?"

Mike winced. "No. It's going to be hard, Leslie. I know your mother's going to be terribly upset, but we have to get her away from this house. I guess I'd better go up and tell her right now. The longer I wait, the worse it's going to be."

"No, you can't do that." Leslie's voice was strong and Mike looked at her, puzzled.

"Let me talk to her first, Mike. She'll understand it better if I prepare her for it. Then you can tell her. You just rest here on the sofa and I'll take care of it. I'll tell her we're just thinking about making a change. Then you can fill her in on the details."

"Well, maybe, if you think that's best." Mike gave her a smile. "You and your mom can talk to each other easily these days. And you understand it'll all be much better this way, right, kid? Call me if you need any help, honey, and I'll come up right away."

"I won't need any help." Leslie gave him a composed smile. Then she turned and walked up the stairs.

Mike stretched out on the couch and sighed. She had taken the news like a little trooper. If anyone could convince Karen to move, it would be Leslie. The poor kid had been through a real ordeal since they'd moved here, but he'd make it up to her the minute they got settled in the Cities. Everything would be fine, once they left this house.

"You know we can't leave here!" Karen was panic-stricken and Leslie patted her hand gently. Of course they couldn't leave. She knew that. Christopher would just have to stop Mike.

Leslie gripped the key tightly. She wasn't afraid with Christopher as her friend. Now she had to convince Mother to do everything just as Christopher said.

"It's all right, Mother." Leslie smiled serenely. "I know what to do, but you'll have to help me. If you don't help, we'll lose this house. You don't want that to happen, do you?"

"No!" Karen's voice was anguished. "I can't leave this house! I won't!"

"That's right, Mother." Leslie nodded. "Then you'll do what I say so we can stay here?" She watched her mother's face carefully.

"Yes," Karen agreed quickly. "Anything you say! Just don't let Mike take my house away!"

Leslie leaned down and kissed her mother gently.

She was sure now. Mother would do her part. She'd do anything to stay here, where they belonged.

"Just rest now, Mother," Leslie told her firmly. "I'll come and get you when it's time."

Leslie stopped at the head of the stairs and clutched her key. Everything was very clear as the pleasant dizzy feeling came. She blinked several times and drew in her breath. Christopher was here and he would take care of Mike. And this time Christopher would stay with her. Very soon now they would be together forever.

She held the key as she moved across the parlor to the sofa. Mike was sleeping and she shook him gently. She knew exactly what to do now.

"Mike? I need you. Mother is very upset about moving."

"Huh?" He sat up and blinked. "What is it, Leslie? What can I do?"

"She's upset about moving," Leslie repeated carefully. "I think she needs something to calm her down. Do we have anything to drink? I thought maybe some brandy would help."

"Oh, God!" Mike groaned and blinked groggily. "I don't have a thing, Leslie. You know I swore off drinking, and there isn't a drop in the house. What time is it?" He glanced at his watch. "The liquor store's closed. Do you think I should call Rob to bring something over?"

"No. Don't call anyone. That would make everything worse."

She stepped closer and took Mike's hand. "I know

where there's some homemade wine, Mike. Maybe that would do. I found it when we first moved here, but I kept it a secret."

"Where?" Mike got to his feet. "Get it, Leslie. Hurry up. Your mother shouldn't be left alone."

"It's down in the root cellar, but it's too heavy for me to lift." She made her face frown. "It's in a big jug, Mike, and I'm scared to go down there in the dark. Maybe it's not such a good idea, after all."

"I'll get it." Mike stood up. Poor Leslie was really upset. Her eyes were huge and black in her white face. "Just show me where it is and I'll carry it up. You don't have to go down there, honey. I'll take care of it."

It was light out, a nearly full moon shining in cold blue as they picked their way across the dewy lawn. Mike stopped short when he saw the root cellar.

"Are you sure it's down there?" His voice was unsteady. "I don't know, honey. . . . Do you think the steps will hold me?"

"Sure, Mike." Leslie gave him her most sincere smile as she unlocked the rusty padlock and put it carefully in her pocket. "Can you lift the door?"

Mike bent down and hefted the door with a grunt. It slipped out of his hands and banged open, clattering like thunder against the cement slab.

"It's really dark down there." His voice was low and he shuddered as he looked down into the pitch-black cellar. "You're sure there's wine? You're positive, Leslie?"

"I saw it myself. The steps look bad, but they're really very sturdy. I've been down there lots of times, Mike. Just climb in and feel around. You'll

find it. It's over there in the far corner, on the right.
I'll run back inside and get you a flashlight."

Mike watched Leslie run back toward the lights of
the house, her white shirt shimmering in the moonlight. He swallowed hard and turned back to the root
cellar. He didn't want to go down. He'd never liked
the dark when he was a boy and he hated cellars. This
one smelled damp and musty, and it reminded him
of an open grave.

He forced himself down the first step. It did seem
sturdy. He took a deep breath and went down another, then continued making his way down into the
inky depths, one step after another, his heart pounding hard in his chest.

Down at last! Mike took a deep lungful of stale air
as his feet touched the earthen floor. His hand
brushed against a cobweb and he flinched. He was
acting like a coward and it was inexcusable. There
wasn't anything down in this old cellar but a jug of
wine; and the sooner he found it, the quicker he'd
be out of here.

His foot brushed against something hard and he
reached down without thinking. His fingers curled
around it—dry, dusty, cold. Mike gave a shudder of
revulsion and dropped it quickly. It was a bone. Jesus.
There was a skeleton down here!

Not human, he told himself, shrinking up against
the shelves. It couldn't be human. Someone had
probably thrown a dead animal down here. He had
to get hold of himself and find that wine.

He made himself put out his hand and touch the
shelves. His fingers brushed against dusty shapes.
Where was Leslie with that damn flashlight?

Thank God! Mike gave a relieved sigh as he heard footsteps. Leslie was coming. He thought about what would happen if the door fell closed and he was trapped down here.

"Hurry, Leslie!" He yelled at the top of his lungs.

"Coming!" Her voice floated down to him. "Just a minute, Mike . . . just stay there."

He heard voices from above and he turned toward the steps, startled. Someone was with Leslie.

The crash was as loud as a thunderclap.

"It's done, Mother! Now he's locked up forever and no one can take our beautiful house away!"

They could still hear the pounding from the root cellar. Mother looked lovely tonight in the long silk gown with ruffled sleeves.

"I think I'll close the window, if you've no objections. The noise hurts my ears."

At Mother's nod, she got up and crossed the room to the window, shutting it firmly. The pounding was still audible but muted by the heavy panes of glass. It reminded her of something vaguely unpleasant, but it would stop soon.

"Play for me, Mother." She smiled happily. "I love to hear you play. I think it's wonderful that Grandmother provided lessons."

"The Chopin, darling?" Mother's voice was happy. "I know it's one of your favorites. And then we can try a little Mozart . . . the Piano Concerto in C Minor, perhaps. Wouldn't that be nice?"

"Very nice." Her voice was respectful and proper. She hurried to the piano bench and sat close to

Mother, watching her fingers fly expertly over the keys. Her spirits rose and soared with the lovely music.

Mother understood everything perfectly now. Christopher had explained it all to her very patiently. In a few days they would go to the store, dressed up in the funny modern clothes hanging in their closets. They would buy cases of canned and dried food. Food was packaged so conveniently now. They no longer needed to store anything in the root cellar.

"I'm so happy, darling." Mother turned to look at her and smiled. "Isn't it wonderful, being here in our very own house?"

"Yes . . . wonderful." Christopher smiled back and nestled a little closer to Mother's side. It was perfect being with Mother again. They were a family now, just the way they were always meant to be.

EPILOGUE

"I might as well tell you the gossip about this house before you hear it from someone else." Rob Comstock wiped his perspiring face with a damp handkerchief and cleared his throat. They were good prospects. You could tell that by just looking at them. He was from a wealthy family and she was wearing a Cartier watch, with twelve diamonds on the face. They could afford to keep up a place like this and they were definitely interested. This was the second time they'd come back to take a look. Rob had always found it best to be honest with his clients, but he hoped that what he had to tell them wouldn't ruin the sale. He needed this commission. Dr. Simmons said that Marilyn had to get away for a good, long rest so she wouldn't keep dwelling on the Houstons, the accidents, and this house. All Marilyn could think about was Taffy's horrid death, and not even the expensive psychiatrist could convince her that the Houstons were innocent.

"Yes?" the man inquired, raising his eyebrows a Rob shifted uneasily from foot to foot. "What is it Comstock?"

Rob cleared his throat and plunged in. "It's abou the previous owners." He took a deep breath "They—the Houstons—moved in here last year about this time. A mother, father, and a little gir about your son's age. They were expecting anothe little one before Christmas. He was a photographer— a good one, too, from what I hear. Anyway, I guess the pressures of renovating this big house were just too much for them and he got in over his head finan cially. He was working day and night to try to mee the bills. You can see what a good job they did."

The wife spoke up. "Is he the photographer whe did that series in *Homes*?" She smiled when Rob nodded. "That's what brought us here in the firs place, you know. I saw the series and I said I just had to see this lovely mansion, didn't I, dear?"

The man nodded. "So they defaulted on the pay ment? Is that what happened?"

"Eventually, yes." Rob cleared his throat again "This is unpleasant, but I think you should know. She lost the baby and she was never right in the head after that. He disappeared one night and never came back, and that drove her completely over the edge She holed up in the house with the little girl, dressed up in old clothes that she'd found in a trunk up stairs. She kept insisting that she was all right and threatened to have the servants put out anyone who came near them. Of course there weren't any ser vants. There haven't been any servants in this house for years."

The woman leaned forward, caught up in the drama. "Yes?" Her voice was breathless. "Please go on, Mr. Comstock."

"Well . . . we probably wouldn't have found them for months, but the school called me to go check when the little girl was absent for a week. People around town think the house is to blame for everything that happened. They . . . well . . . some of them say it's haunted."

Rob snapped his mouth shut tightly. There! He had said his piece and he wasn't going to say much more than that. He still got into a cold sweat when he remembered the photographs.

The first one had shown Gary Wilson at the swimming hole. It had caught the terrified expression on poor Gary's face when the rope snapped. There was another kid in the picture, a sort of fuzzy half-image of a blond kid up in the tree who looked enough like Leslie Houston to be her twin. That kid was laughing and holding the cut end of the rope.

The second photograph was worse. The same blond kid was inside Del Allen's showroom the day Bud got hurt. The kid was leaning against the back of a car, pushing it toward the window. Bud was right outside. Rob felt sick to his stomach when he thought about it.

The third picture was the real cause of his nightmares. It was a picture of his own daughter, Taffy, surrounded by a wall of flames. The same blond kid was striking a match, and Taffy's mouth was open in a horrified scream.

The pictures were on the parlor table when they found Karen and Leslie. Rob had stuffed them into his briefcase, and no one else had seen them. He didn't understand how they could have been taken in the first place and they haunted him. He had taken them home and hidden them in a folder, trying to figure out what to do. Then, when he'd finally decided to take them to Sheriff Olson, he had an even bigger shock. They were gone! There was nothing inside the folder but black glossy paper. He hadn't mentioned it to a soul. It just went to prove that he needed a vacation every bit as badly as Marilyn.

"A haunted house?" The man gazed up at the three-story brick mansion and chuckled. "That's supposed to be the 'in' thing right now, isn't it, dear? We'll be the envy of all our friends if we buy this place!"

"Really, Sam!" The woman shook her head, and her expression sobered as she turned back to Rob. "That certainly is a sad story, Mr. Comstock. What happened to the wife and the little girl?"

"Oh . . . they sent the wife to the state hospital. I imagine she's still there. The little girl was shipped off to a foster home. It was a sad day, I tell you."

"And him?" the woman questioned. "Did they ever find the photographer?"

"Nope." Rob shook his head and sighed. "He just disappeared and no one's seen him since. I think he was in some kind of trouble. I know for a fact that he was gambling pretty heavy. Anyway, no one's heard a peep from him. That's why you're getting the house at such a steal. He vanished into thin air and the house went back to us."

"That's all very interesting," the man said in a

bored voice. "It's a lucky break for us, though. I guess things like that just happen sometimes, but someone's got to pick up the pieces. You can't be that upset about making two commissions on the same house in a year, can you, Comstock?"

Rob's mouth tightened. He wanted to smack that rich bastard right in the face, but he forced himself to smile politely. He had to think of Marilyn. They needed this sale.

"It certainly doesn't change our decision to buy the house." The man nodded quickly. "You'll never catch me turning down a bargain. Personally, I'm glad that other family lost it. They did a bang-up job of renovating it for us."

"All right, then." Rob drew a deep breath and controlled himself with an effort. "I just wanted to play square with you nice folks. Let's take a final look around and I'll answer any questions you might have. Then we'll go down to the office and sign the papers."

The boy was bored by the adult conversation. He wandered away and tossed rocks at the trees in the yard for a while. It was a nice, big yard. There was room enough for a baseball diamond if they mowed down that dippy rose garden. This was going to be a pretty good place to live. His dad was rich and he'd be the most important kid in town as soon as the rest of the kids found out how much money his dad had. It was a lot better than their high-rise in Dallas. Here there was room for all sorts of things.

He was turning to go back to his parents when he saw something glittering in the overgrown rose garden. Curiosity aroused, he ran over to take a look. It might be a silver dollar or maybe even something better.

"Aww . . . it's just an old key!" He was about to toss it back when he reconsidered. Maybe it was a lucky find at that. You never knew when a key might come in handy. He'd find the lock it fit right after they moved in.

THE PERFECT CURE

On the surface they are beautiful and talented.
But few know of the harrowing darkness inside
each of them, how close they are to losing their
tenuous grip on sanity. Dr. Elias is their only hope.
But he's dying. And he's made his cold,
final judgment: Those he can't cure, he *must* kill.

FOR THE PERFECT CRIME

In order for Dr. Elias's deadly prescription
to succeed, none of the eight patients must
know someone is stalking them, murdering them
one by one. Even if they were to suspect that their
lives are in danger, no one would believe them.
But if there's any chance they can stay alive,
they must face the madness within . . .

**Please turn the page for an exciting sneak peek of
Joanne Fluke's next suspense thriller**

COLD JUDGMENT

coming in November 2014!

PROLOGUE

He did not look like a dying man. Dr. Theodore
Elias made a dispassionate examination. Excellent
muscle tone for a male, age fifty-three. Normal pulse,
blood pressure in the low–normal range. Hands
steady, no sign of tremor. Eyes clear, intelligent, pen-
etrating. A near-perfect specimen of the middle-aged
adult male. There was no evidence of physical imper-
fection, no outward sign of terminal disease. Yet there
was no cause to doubt the diagnosis. He had seen
the results of the ultrasound and the CAT scan. And
the exploratory surgery had been conclusive. Within
six to eight weeks, this body would die of carcinoma
of the pancreas. First the jaundice would appear, then
increasing pain and physical weakness. There were
drugs to control the pain, but death was inevitable.
And when the body was wasted and useless, the mind
would continue to function, the fine analytical mind
that was the source of his pride. Dr. Theodore Elias

would be fully capable of monitoring and cataloguing his own demise until the very end.

His steps did not falter as he crossed the tasteful gray carpet and took his customary place behind his large polished desk. He could not afford the luxury of self-pity, not when there were decisions to be made. He had to think of his profession, of his duties to his patients. Something would have to be done with his group immediately.

Dr. Elias's eyebrows met in an impatient frown. This cancer could not have come at a worse time. Progress in his only current group was exasperatingly slow and it was the holiday season, a time when depression deepened and suicidal tendencies became severe. It was a time ripe for crisis. His eight patients, the last of his toughest cases, brought together over the years, were presently under control, but they would need help to get through the holidays.

The files were right where he had placed them after yesterday's session. Dr. Elias lifted the bulky stack and weighed it in his hands. So much paperwork, so much effort, and his patients were still far from the cure he had promised and been willing to spend his remaining career trying to achieve. His colleagues called him a miracle worker. A cure rate of eighty-three percent was more than impressive. But it was no comfort when he knew he'd run out of time with his last eight dangerous patients.

It was possible these patients could maintain their equilibrium for a while, even in this perilous season. Dr. Elias forced himself to look on the bright side. His patients might take months to break down, even longer if he could refer them to the best therapists.

But eventually they would crumple. It was only a matter of time. And without the proper help, each of them was capable of violence that could destroy innocent people.

Dr. Elias remembered the late-night discussions of his college days. They were held in cluttered, smoke-filled student apartments, fueled with jugs of cheap red wine, and accompanied by loud idealistic arguments. One, in particular, came back to him in vivid detail. An animal trainer had spent his whole life training a brilliant but vicious dog that only he could control. When the trainer was told he was dying, he was faced with a decision. He could destroy the animal and annihilate his life's work or he could let the beast live and hope that another trainer could carry on with his project. No profound resolution had been reached that night. Undoubtedly a new group of students was debating the same question with no better results. Theoretical discussions were diverting in college, but real-life decisions were painful to reach. The guidelines set down by his profession were clear. He was obligated to refer his patients to other therapists and hope for the best.

ONE

Snow swirled past the window. The white, glittering particles seemed to have a life of their own, whirling gracefully fifty-seven stories above the city. The beauty of a snowflake was brief. Soon it would spiral inevitably downward to the street below, to turn to muddy slush under the wheels of traffic.

Dr. Elias opened his desk drawer and pulled out the list of alternate therapists he had prepared. These were the best psychiatrists in Minneapolis. He had to trust that they were competent to handle his patients. It would be inconceivable for one therapist to take over his entire group. That was a job only he could handle. His patients would be upset but the group would have to be disbanded. He was forced to refer them individually to eight different therapists.

He would tell them tomorrow and give them the names of their new therapists. Out with the old and in with the new. It was appropriate for the season, but Dr. Elias doubted his patients would appreciate the irony. There would be tears and panic, but he would be firm. Tomorrow would be their last group meeting. And the last time they would see him alive.

He opened the first folder and read the synopsis he had stapled inside. *Kay Atchinson, age 42, wife of Charles Atchinson, Mayor of Minneapolis. Diagnosis: Paranoid Schizophrenia.*

A photo was clipped to the sheet of medical background. Kay was a pretty black woman dressed in an expensive, well-cut suit, hair carefully styled. Everything about Kay was careful, from her fashionable but not pretentious home on Lake Harriet to her studious, well-mannered children. In the fall of 1980 Kay had been under a lot of pressure, caught between a conservative political party and the radical black caucus. Charles had made public his plans to run for the Senate, and both Kay and Charles had anticipated the governor's endorsement. It had been a shock when the governor had backed out at the last minute. The time wasn't right, he'd stated. It would split the party. The governor was sorry but he felt obligated to endorse a white candidate.

The night of the announcement Kay had put a gun in her purse. She'd planned to assassinate the governor. He was a racist, just as the black caucus claimed. Luckily Kay had been intercepted by Charles, who'd managed to keep the news from the press. After two months of unsuccessful therapy in another state, Charles had called in Dr. Elias. Now, after over four years of therapy, Kay was functioning well as the mayor's wife. Dr. Elias had successfully sublimated her hostility, but if the defense mechanism failed, Kay could be dangerous.

Dr. Elias selected a therapist for Kay and wrote a

referral. The new psychiatrist might help Kay maintain a cloak of normalcy. Of course, no one but Dr. Elias could cure her.

The next folder was thicker. It contained years of notes. *Greg Davenport, age 23, single. Diagnosis: Pyromania.*

Greg had not smiled for the camera. His elbow was propped on a table and his chin rested on his hand. A handsome young man with dark intense eyes, Greg had the world by the tail, as far as anyone knew. His inheritance was considerable, and now Greg was making a name for himself as a songwriter. No one knew much about Greg's childhood, no one but Dr. Elias. And certainly no one but Dr. Elias knew that Greg had set the fire that had killed his father.

Dr. Elias remembered the day, eleven years ago, when the trustees of the Davenport estate had called him in to examine Greg. The boy had been twelve years old, his slight frame making a barely discernible bulge under the maroon hospital blankets. His face had been pale, eyes turned inward, seeming not to notice Dr. Elias at all as he'd conducted the examination. Greg had been catatonic, unable to move or speak. He'd been like that since the night his father had died.

After long months of treatment, Greg had finally broken his silence with a tortured confession. He had set the fire in a desperate bid for attention. He'd been lonely after his mother's death, and his father had been more interested in women and wild parties than he'd been in Greg. The boy hadn't realized the small fire would spread so quickly, and he'd been horrified at what he had done.

As Greg's therapy had progressed, Dr. Elias had

discovered he was dealing with a classic pyromaniac.
Fire excited Greg. It made him feel powerful and
compensated for his low self-esteem. Now, after
eleven years of therapy, Greg's pyromania was under
control. Dr. Elias had taught him socially acceptable
ways to satisfy his need for power. But Greg was not
cured. Under stress Greg could revert to setting fires
that could kill anyone caught in their path.

Greg needed good maintenance therapy. Dr. Elias
consulted his list and finally settled on a compassionate young doctor with the University Medical Facility.
Now two of his patients were referred. Dr. Elias
picked up the third folder and massaged the back of
his neck as he read his notes.

*Debra Fields, age 30, widow of Steve Fields, newspaper
correspondent. Diagnosis: Postpartum Depression, Complicated by Severe Melancholia leading to a Psychotic Episode
of Kidnapping.*

Debra faced the camera squarely, her classic features perfectly balanced. She was a beautiful woman
who took pains to appear ordinary. Her short brown
hair was cut in a no-nonsense style, large green eyes
hidden behind tortoiseshell glasses. Her blouse was
severely tailored, without lace or frills. Debra's femi-
ninity was masked by an aloof professional exterior,
but Dr. Elias knew it was fear that made her appear
cold and unapproachable.

Four years ago when he had first met her, Debra
had been in restraints, screaming for her baby. She
had totally lost contact with reality. The shock of her
husband's death on assignment in El Salvador had
sent Debra into premature labor. The baby had
survived for a month but then died suddenly in

the night. Driven frantic by her grief, Debra had kidnapped another baby from the hospital nursery and fled in a cab to the airport. When the authorities had found her, she'd insisted she was taking her baby to her husband in El Salvador. The infant Debra had abducted was unharmed and the parents did not press charges. After several weeks of unsuccessful therapy at the hospital, Dr. Elias had been called in by Debra's employer, the *Minneapolis Tribune*. Since Debra's husband had been on assignment for the *Tribune* when he was killed, and because of her own employment by the *Tribune*, the newspaper had assumed the responsibility for her medical bills.

It had taken six months of intensive therapy to bring Debra back to her empty reality. After a year she'd been able to return to her work as a photojournalist. Dr. Elias used a process of substitution in Debra's therapy. A doll took the place of her baby; whenever Debra felt anxious, she rocked and cuddled her placebo. Even though Debra was performing well at work, her personal life was a void. She was afraid of social contact, afraid to get involved with anyone on a personal level. Unless she continued her therapy, Debra's depression could deepen and trigger another psychotic episode.

The list of therapists that had seemed so inexhaustible held only one option for Debra. The Psychiatric Institute had a pilot program for parents who had lost their children. Dr. Elias wrote the referral and moved to the next file.

The next case was critical. Dr. Elias read over his notes and frowned. *Doug Sandall, age 36, wife and children deceased. Diagnosis: Suicidal Depression.*

Doug's sandy hair and clear blue eyes gave him a boyish appearance. To his coworkers at MilStar, he appeared to be a conscientious pilot, never complaining about long back-to-back flights. Only Dr. Elias knew the fear and the compulsion that rode with Doug, thousands of feet above the ground. Six years ago Doug had flown his wife and small daughter to Detroit, to visit relatives. The plane had crashed in a sudden storm, killing Doug's family. Doug's friends said it was a miracle he wasn't injured, but Doug thought it was a curse. He still relived the accident in his dreams, agonizing over whether there was some way he could have avoided the tragedy. He had killed his family and he should have died with them.

Flying was Doug's life, and after a month of intensive therapy, Dr. Elias decided it was safe to let him return to work. Now Doug had five years seniority at MilStar Corporation and a reputation as a dependable, dedicated pilot. Only Dr. Elias knew that Doug needed continual therapy to keep his suicidal tendencies under control.

The Swiss clock on the bookshelf chimed the hour softly as Dr. Elias completed Doug's file. He pushed back his leather chair and got stiffly to his feet. There was a dull pain in his abdomen, which he decided to ignore. If he took the powerful analgesic now, he would not be alert enough to finish his referrals.

With slow, careful steps, Dr. Elias crossed to the window. The pain diminished a bit as he stood looking out at the city. From his penthouse apartment in the IDS Center he had a view of the entire downtown area. Lights gleamed from the offices in the Foshay Tower and the surrounding buildings. The copper dome of St. Mary's Basilica stood stark and solid against the darkening sky. A plane flew high above the skyline in the wide flight pattern that would take it to Wold Chamberlain Airport, midway between Minneapolis and St. Paul. And far off in the distance he could see the strings of headlights on the freeways that encircled the Twin Cities. It was the Wednesday before Thanksgiving and traffic was heavy. People were leaving work early, to avoid the rush. The grocery stores would be packed tonight. Turkeys and cranberries would be in short supply. Tomorrow was the traditional day of celebration and feasting and on Friday the downtown area would be crowded with Christmas shoppers. The Friday after Thanksgiving was the heaviest shopping day of the year.

Softly falling snow covered the grimy streets with a frozen blanket of white and the traffic slowed on Marquette Avenue below. The double glass window was cold to the touch as Dr. Elias watched in the gathering gloom. The temperature would be in the low twenties tonight. In a few weeks the mercury would drop to the below-zero figures hardy Minnesotans had learned to endure. This was the last winter he would see. Suddenly the icy streets with their early Christmas decorations seemed oddly dear to him.

This year Christmas fell on a Tuesday. A bitter smile crossed Dr. Elias's face. Celebrating a holiday on a weekday had always made him feel vaguely guilty. The week was for working, and Christmas was an excuse for a lot of commercial nonsense. This year he was spared his guilt. His work was nearly over. By Christmas his patients would be resigned to life without him.

Two men in parkas and moon boots were putting the finishing touches on the strings of lights that decorated the roof of the Northwestern Bank Building. Cables of bulbs were anchored to a huge circle on the roof and met at the top of a pole, thirty feet high. Dr. Elias saw the workmen step back and signal to someone below. A moment later there was a blaze of multicolor brilliance as the switch was thrown and a mammoth Christmas tree appeared against the night sky.

This would be his last Christmas, if he lived long enough to see it. The holiday was less than five weeks away. Chef Leon Lossing of the Orion Room was preparing a special holiday dinner for him, and Dr. Elias had been looking forward to it. Wild Rice Soup, Lobster and Sweetbreads with Raspberry Sauce, and Black Velvet Torte for dessert. Dr. Elias smiled in anticipation.

It was convenient to have a fine restaurant only seven floors below him. Every evening, at precisely five thirty, Jacques delivered and served his meal. Wednesday's menu was Rack of Lamb Boulanglere. Dr. Elias reminded himself to open a bottle of Château Margaux 1974 to complement the lamb.

Jacques had the perfect blend of deference and efficiency that Dr. Elias expected in a waiter. He would prepare Jacques's envelope with his yearly gratuity in advance this year, just in case.

On his way back to the desk, Dr. Elias turned on his favorite music. Gustav Mahler's *Ninth Symphony* would help him to concentrate. Mahler understood his anguish. He was a kindred soul. Mahler, too, knew torture and disappointment in his search for excellence.

There were four folders left. Dr. Elias flipped open the top file and stared at the photograph. The man's face was tanned and healthy, brown eyes, hair thinning slightly on top. His most striking characteristic was a wide smile that displayed a full set of perfect white teeth.

Jerry Feldman, age 44, married, no children. Diagnosis: Sexual Aberration—Child Molester.

Jerry was a successful dentist, specializing in cosmetic reconstruction. He claimed that he had fashioned caps for every one of the city's leading newscasters. It was an in-joke. All the dentists in town knew they could switch to any channel to see Jerry's handiwork.

His wife, Dotty, was a typical midwestern woman, warmhearted and eager for a house full of children. Jerry hadn't told her about his vasectomy. And Dotty knew nothing about Jerry's darker secret.

Jerry's trouble had started early in his marriage. In 1979, he'd come to Dr. Elias after he'd nearly raped a ten-year-old girl. After six years of therapy, Jerry still was not cured but he had learned to avoid situations that put him into contact with young girls.

In two weeks, Jerry would face a crisis. His ten-year-old niece, Betsy, was coming to stay with him over the Christmas holidays. Dr. Elias knew he had to find a good therapist to help Jerry deal with his niece. Without help, Betsy could be in real danger from her uncle.

The light in the room was fading rapidly. Dr. Elias switched on the Tiffany desk lamp and wrote a short letter of referral for Jerry. The golden circle of light illuminated the next file as he opened it, hitting the photograph like a spotlight. It was appropriate. Nora Stanford was an actress.

Nora Stanford, age 36 (actual 46), single. Diagnosis: Thanatophobia leading to Episodes of Psychotic Aggression.

Nora was a classic beauty with high cheekbones and a mass of shining blond hair swept back from her marvelously mobile face. She had refused to pose for a snapshot and had insisted that Dr. Elias use one of her publicity pictures, heavily retouched to make her appear younger.

Ten years ago Nora had viciously attacked the young ingenue who'd replaced her in *The Debutante*. The young actress had been hospitalized and Nora had been referred to Dr. Elias by the court. She was a brilliant actress, driven by her talent, desperately afraid of growing old and not being able to perform. Dr. Elias had discovered Nora had other problems in addition to her fear of dying. She was terrified of her attraction to other women. Once Nora had accepted her lesbian tendencies, her therapy had progressed. She'd found a compassionate lover and opened a theater workshop within walking distance of the Guthrie. There were no more aggressive incidents, but Dr. Elias knew that Nora's jealous rages were barely under control. She needed constant therapy to keep from becoming violent again.

After he had chosen a therapist for Nora, Dr. Elias reached for his eelskin tobacco pouch. He selected his favorite pipe from the rack, a handmade natural briar crafted by Ed Kolpin, founder of the Tinderbox. Every month he received a package of his personal blend of tobacco from the original store in Santa Monica. Several years ago Dr. Elias had voluntarily cut

down on his smoking. Now that precaution seeme
ridiculous. His smile was bitter as he lit the pipe an
tamped it with the gold tool a former patient ha
given him. There was no reason to deny himself an
of life's pleasures now. There was little enough tim
to enjoy them.

There were only two more patients to refer and h
would be finished. Dr. Elias opened the next file
*Father Vincent Marx, age 51, single. Diagnosis: Violen
Schizophrenia.*

Father Marx prided himself on being a moder
priest. In the photograph he was dressed in a blue
striped O.P. shirt and chinos. Only the small gol
cross that he wore around his neck was an indicatio
of his profession. Father Marx was streetwise. H
knew all the current street slang and used it in ever
day conversation. That made him especially effe
tive in his church on lower Hennepin, relating t
broken families and rebellious teenagers.

There was only one area in which Father Marx wa
not a regular guy. He hated prostitution and ever
thing it represented. When he was forced to confror
blatant sex, he turned into a religious zealot.

Father Marx had found Dr. Elias on his own, fiv
years ago. No one, including the Church, knew abou
his problem. A prostitute had propositioned him o
the street, and Father Marx had assaulted and near
killed her because she'd reminded him of his mothe

Father Vincent Marx was the illegitimate son of
prostitute. When he'd been barely old enough t
walk, he'd been punished for trying to climb into h
mother's bed. After that incident he'd been locked i
a closet every night so he could not interfere with h

mother's business. As soon as he'd been old enough to rebel, Vincent had run away. A kindly priest had found him and persuaded his mother to sign relinquishment papers. Vincent had grown up in a Catholic orphanage and had entered the priesthood out of gratitude.

The hatred was still there, but with Dr. Elias's help, the violent emotion was kept under control. Father Marx was now able to counsel his parishioners regarding sexual matters even though, in his heart, he still felt sex was dirty and wrong. If he suffered a setback, his hatred could erupt into violence again. Under the right circumstances, Father Marx was perfectly capable of cold-blooded murder.

Dr. Elias wrote a referral for Father Marx and turned to the file of his remaining patient. *Richard "Mac" Macklin, age 34, divorced. Diagnosis: Severe Guilt Complex resulting in Impotence.*

Kind blue eyes looked out from the photograph. Mac had an engaging face, one that inspired immediate trust. Laugh lines crinkled the corners of his mouth, and his curly red hair was charmingly unruly. The only evidence of the deep problems that plagued him was the permanent dark circles under his eyes.

Mac had been a detective on the Minneapolis Police Force when the incident had occurred, five years ago. Several attacks had been made on police officers in the preceding week and Mac had been wary when he'd answered the call to a tenement on Lake Street. Two armed suspects had been spotted there. Mac's partner had gone up the fire escape. Mac had taken the door. The apartment had been dark and the hall light out. Mac had overreacted when he'd seen the shadow of the gun. He'd fired, killing a twelve-year-old boy. The gun had been a toy. The boy had been playing a very real game of cops and robbers.

Naturally the press had had a field day, even though Mac was cleared by the department. There had been hate letters and anonymous phone calls in the middle of the night. Somehow Mac had managed to ignore the people who'd called him a kid killer, but the pressure had taken its toll. After the shooting, Mac had found he was impotent. At first Mac's wife had been understanding, but as time passed she'd become dissatisfied with the marriage. Six months later she'd filed for divorce. Mac had suffered a breakdown and been hospitalized.

The police department carried excellent insurance and Dr. Elias had been called in. After a year's leave of absence, Mac had returned to the force. His crisis was over but, even with Dr. Elias's encouragement, Mac refused to put his potency to the test. He was terribly lonely but he felt it was better to avoid women than to risk failure.

After several months at work, Mac's impotence had taken on a new complication, one that affected his career. His service revolver, an obvious phallic symbol, became the source of his anxiety. Dr. Elias knew the risks involved with a cop who could not use his gun. At any time a situation could occur where Mac would have to shoot to save a fellow officer's life. It would be a murder by omission if he could not fire.

There was only one practical way to deal with the problem. Mac studied nights and received his promotion to detective. Now the probability of his having to use his gun was greatly diminished. Both Mac and Dr. Elias were relieved.

Dr. Elias finished Mac's referral and stretched wearily. Technically, these eight patients were no longer his responsibility, but he was unable to relinquish the final thread that bound him to his group. He would ask for progress reports from the new therapists. It was only right that he follow his patients as long as he could.

Fifteen minutes remained before his dinner arrived. Dr. Elias uncorked the wine and poured a glass to let it breathe. Then he unlocked the door that led to his art gallery.

The long, narrow hallway was filled with portraits he had painted, one for every patient he had cured. Dr. Elias walked slowly to the very end, glorying in his successes. The portraits were the work of a talented amateur. Once he had wanted to be an artist but he'd felt compelled to continue his father's work in medicine. His therapy work was his art. He took disorganized psychic material and transformed it into human masterpieces. These portraits were glorious testimonies to his talent as a psychiatrist.

His studio was at the end of the corridor. The outside walls were of glass, to maximize the daylight exposure. An easel was placed in the center of the large room. Resting on it was his only unfinished canvas.

It was a portrait of his group: Kay, Greg, Debra, Doug, Jerry, Nora, Father Marx, and Mac. They were seated in a half circle around the conference table in his office. The portrait was precise, correct to the smallest detail. Only the faces were unfinished, startling white ovals of blank canvas.

His fingers itched to take up the brush and finish the painting, but it was impossible. He could complete a canvas only when the case was resolved. Dr. Elias felt a stab of remorse as he gazed at his painting. It violated his sense of order to leave a project unfinished. If only he could find a way to close these cases.